Advance Praise

Touch of Death

"HOLY MEDUSA AND HADES! … Come along for the greatest ride of a lifetime. You will love the mythology retelling and the cast of characters who will become family to Jodi… I am sure this series will be one people will talk about for years to come."

— Diary Of A Book Addict

"I Hereby Award This Book 5 Wings, but I would gladly award it a thousand times that… It is a MUST read. If you like zombies, necromancers, mythology, gorgeous men and fantastic writing, then you need to add this to your own TBR pile. NOW!"

— Gothic Angel Book Reviews

"I adored this book. Right from the start I found this positively one of the coolest books I've ever read… *Touch of Death* is phenomenal and it completely and utterly took my breath away. I am dying to read more and I cannot wait to find out what happens next. Kelly Hashaway is an author to look out for in the future. She is amazing and *Touch of Death* is one book that is not to be missed."

— K-Books

"*Touch of Death* was everything I expected it to be and so much more. It had a gripping story line, young romance, a fierce heroine, evil villains, and a swoon worthy hero. To put it simply, I really loved this book… *Touch of Death* is deadly addictive and I dare you to put it down."

— Readers Live A Thousand Lives

"Devastating truths, compelling characters and a brilliantly unique storyline, *Touch of Death* was unlike anything I've read before and I enjoyed it so, so much. It's going to be Hades waiting to read *Stalked by Death*… I rate *Touch of Death* Five out of Five!!!"

— BookSavvy

Spencer Hill Press

Please visit our website at www.spencerhillpress.com

First Edition: January 2013.

Kelly Hashway 1978
Touch of Death : a novel / by Kelly Hashway – 1st ed.
p. cm.
Summary:
Teenage girl discovers that her touch can kill—or worse—and that she must leave everything she's ever known and fulfill her destiny, or the gods may take drastic action.

The author acknowledges the copyrighted or trademarked status and trademark owners of the following wordmarks mentioned in this fiction: Band-Aid, Carhartt, Wal-Mart, Boy Scouts, Hallmark, Honda Civic, Ford Mustang, Sleeping Beauty

Cover design by K. Kaynak with artwork by Conrado
Interior layout by Marie Romero

ISBN 978-1-937053-30-7 (paperback)
ISBN 978-1-937053-31-4 (e-book)

Printed in the United States of America

Touch of Death

Kelly Hashway

SPENCER HILL PRESS

To Ayla,
the best daughter and inspiration I could ask for.
I love you!

Also By Kelly Hashway

Stalked by Death (July 2013)
Face of Death (2014)

Curse of the Granville Fortune (January 2014: Month9Books)

The Monster Within (April 2014)
The Darkness Within (2014)

Chapter 1

A red light means stop. I learned that long before I got my license, but I kept going through the traffic light anyway. It had been broken for weeks and no one really knew why the light was there to begin with. The only thing on the back road was a cemetery that had gone to hell a long time ago. The caretaker had died a few years ago, and no one had taken over after him. So, I didn't see any reason to pay attention to the traffic light today, especially since I was late for school. After being homeschooled for most of my life, I still hadn't gotten used to having to get up early and drive to school five days a week.

I flipped through the radio stations and cringed. Static, news, phone prank. Didn't anyone play music on the radio anymore? I sighed and hit the power button, deciding silence was better than middle-aged people pretending to be young on the air.

I was reaching for my cell on the passenger seat when a flash of brown caught my attention. I dropped my phone and grabbed the steering wheel as the deer slammed into my car. I screamed and stomped my foot on the brake. The deer flipped over the hood and landed in a heap on the ground by the passenger side of the car.

"Oh, God!" I gripped the steering wheel tighter. I could barely breathe, barely move. "Please, don't be dead. Please, don't be dead."

I'd never hit an animal before. Well, a snake once, but that didn't count—who likes snakes anyway? I leaned my head back against the seat and closed my eyes. Mom was going to kill me. I'd just gotten this car for my birthday two months ago. Sure, it was used, but it was still expensive, and we didn't have a lot of money. I released my death grip on the steering wheel and opened my eyes. I had to see how much damage there was. I said a silent prayer that the deer had magically gotten up and pranced away while I'd had my eyes closed.

I pushed the door open and stepped outside. The cold February air swirled around me and made my cheeks tingle. Luckily, it was an unusually mild Pennsylvania winter because I wasn't exactly wearing a warm coat. Shivers ran up my spine as I saw the huge dent in my hood. Yup, Mom was going to kill me. Streaks of blood stained the car in a strip, like an arrow pointing to the deer's body. I took another deep breath before convincing myself to see if the poor thing was dead. My stomach lurched when I saw it, lying there with blood on the side of its face. Its mouth hung open, and its legs were bent underneath it. Warm tears trickled down my cheeks. I'd killed it. Why had I reached for my phone? Why hadn't I been paying more attention to the road?

I bent down next to the deer. Its eyes stared out into nothingness. "I'm so sorry. You poor thing. I never meant to hit you." Something came over me, and I felt like I had to touch the deer. I reached out and gently patted its head. Two tiny nubs made me wonder if this buck would've grown huge antlers if he'd had the time. If he hadn't met me—or should I say my car? But that only made everything that much more real, and I started to cry all over again, my tears dotting the deer's back. I heard a car coming down the road, so I wiped my face. Warmth trickled from my right nostril. Brushing it away, I noticed a touch of blood on my hand. Another nosebleed, thanks to my allergies. I wiped the blood on the deer's back, not knowing what else to do with it, and stood up. That was when I saw the deer move. Glassy brown eyes stared up at me, and the furry chest rose. I stumbled back, not believing what I was seeing. I blinked several times. Was I dreaming? No way could the deer be alive, but, snorting loudly, it sprang to its feet and tore across the street and into the trees.

I stared after it in shock. A black sedan pulled up alongside me. I recognized it right away: Mr. Leeman, my next-door neighbor. "Jodi? Are you okay? Did you have an accident?"

"Yes, I hit a deer. Or a deer hit me. I'm not sure which." I wasn't sure of anything right now.

"Where is it?" Mr. Leeman got out of the car and looked around. "That's one nasty dent in your hood. I doubt the deer got very far before it died."

I shook my head, hoping to jumble my thoughts until they made sense. "It got up and ran away." I pointed to the woods. "There."

He narrowed his eyes at me and walked toward the trees. "I don't see it." He turned back to me. "Are you sure you're okay? Did you hit your head or anything? Were you wearing your seatbelt?"

"I'm fine." I was still dazed.

"You heading to school?"

School! I had to go. I was already late. "What time is it? I have to get to school."

"Whoa, calm down. You were in an accident. I think the school will understand if you're a little late." He took my arm and helped me back to my car. "Can I call someone for you? Have someone pick you up?"

"I have my cell. I'll call my mom." I sat down in the driver's seat and picked up my phone. Thank goodness for speed dial because I couldn't even remember my own phone number. Mom answered on the third ring.

"Hello?"

"Mom, it's me."

"Did you forget something? I was on my way out the door."

"No, I hit a deer. My car is… well, it's pretty banged up. I don't know if I should drive it."

"Are you okay? Where are you?" Her voice was frantic.

"Mom, relax. I'm fine. Mr. Leeman's here. He stopped to see if I needed help. I'm by the old cemetery on Willow Drive."

"Stay put. I'll be right there." She hung up before I could answer. I let my phone drop into my lap.

"Do you want me to wait with you until your mom gets here?" Mr. Leeman asked.

I shook my head. "No, that's okay. Thanks for stopping, though."

3

"No problem. You be careful, okay?"

I gave him a small smile and watched him drive away. I turned toward the woods. How had the deer gotten up and run away? I had been sure it was dead.

Mom got there in a matter of minutes. She pulled me into a hug and squeezed me until I gasped for air. "Sorry, sweetie," she said, finally releasing me. "I called a tow truck. They'll take the car home. And I called the office to tell them I'd be late. Are you sure you don't want to see a doctor?"

"No, I want to go to school. Second semester just started, and Mr. Quimby said this unit on mythology in literature is going to be really tough. Plus, trigonometry is brutal so far. You know how I am with math. I don't want to get behind already."

"All right," Mom said, as we got into her car and headed to school. "But if you start feeling bad in any way, you call me, and I'll come get you. Sometimes injuries don't surface right away after an accident."

"Really, I'm fine." She gave me a stern look. "I promise I'll call if I don't feel well."

We pulled up to the front of the building, and I mumbled a quick thank you and goodbye before jumping out and heading straight to the office for a late pass. Mrs. Thompson peered at me over her glasses. "Reason?" I swore they purposely hired people with no personal skills to work as receptionists.

"I hit a deer. My car had to be towed."

She raised her glasses and looked me over. "You need to see the school nurse before going to class. She needs to clear you."

"Clear me for what?"

"The school can't be held responsible for you passing out in class or suffering from a concussion." She spoke with no sensitivity whatsoever. "See Ms. Steingall, and then come back for your late pass."

I sighed and headed for the nurse's office. Giving a quick knock on the door, I stepped inside. Jimmy Benton was lying across a padded bench, faking a stomachache. He did it every time he had a test.

Ms. Steingall shooed him with her hand. "Mr. Benton, I've told you twice. You don't have a fever. Go to class."

Jimmy punched the bench and mumbled a few curses before leaving.

"What can I do for you, Miss...?"

"Marshall. Jodi Marshall."

She wrinkled her brow like she was trying to place my name. "Are you new? I've never seen you before."

"I started in September. I used to be homeschooled."

"Oh, well it's nice to meet you." She sat down at her desk and pointed to a chair. "What can I do for you this morning?"

"Mrs. Thompson said I had to come see you. I got into an accident on the way to school. Hit a deer. Nothing major." I decided to leave out the part about the mangled deer getting up and running off.

Ms. Steingall stood up again. "I see. Well, let's take a look at you." She flashed a light in my eyes, making them fill with tears. I apologized when a few ran down my left cheek and onto her hand. She shrugged it off and asked me a few questions. That was about the extent of checking me out. "You look fine to me, but if you should start to feel strange in any way, I want you to come see me, okay?"

"Sure." I gave a quick wave and headed back to the office.

Mrs. Thompson raised an eyebrow at me. "Everything in order?"

I couldn't help thinking that the system was a little screwy. I mean, I could've pretended I went to the nurse and got checked out. She was just taking my word for it. "All good," I said. She handed me a late slip, and I headed to English lit class. Mr. Quimby was in the middle of a lecture. He held his hand out for my pass and put it on his desk without looking at it. He didn't stop his lecture. Just kept droning on and on about Zeus. Why was mythology always about Zeus? Weren't there other gods? Maybe some that were a little more interesting than a guy with a giant lightning bolt?

I took my seat next to Melodie, who frantically whipped out her phone and started texting me. Mr. Quimby didn't tolerate talking in class, but he was oblivious to texting under our desks.

My phone vibrated. "What happened?"

"Hit a deer," I texted back.

"Miss Marshall," Mr. Quimby said, making me drop my phone in my lap. He paused to make sure he had my attention.

"Yes?" I fumbled under my desk and slipped my phone into my purse.

"Since you were late, I think you should pay extra attention to the next part of the lesson. There will be a test at the end of next week, and it will count for thirty percent of your semester grade."

I nodded.

"Good. Well, moving on from Zeus, we'll be talking about something a few of you may find more interesting." Mr. Quimby's eyes met mine. "If I consulted my class roster correctly, someone in this class has a birthday that falls between November 29 and December 17. Is that correct, Miss Marshall?"

I sat up straight. "Um, yeah. December eighth, actually."

Mr. Quimby smiled. "Very good. Now, how many of you have heard about the thirteenth sign of the zodiac?"

A few people raised their hands.

"Those individuals born between November 29 and December 17 are actually born under the sign of Ophiuchus, not Sagittarius."

"Ophi*yuck*is?" Kyle Erickson asked. He eyed me up and down. "Sounds appropriate."

No one laughed but Kyle. He wasn't exactly well liked, and right now I was thankful for that. After the morning I'd had, I couldn't deal with being the butt of any jokes.

Mr. Quimby gave him a stare that I wouldn't want to find myself on the end of. "As I was saying, Ophiuchus has a place in mythology. He was the son of Apollo and Coronis. His mother was killed because she was unfaithful to Apollo, but her unborn child was rescued from the womb."

An echo of "Oh, gross!" rang through the room, but Mr. Quimby kept right on going. "After Apollo cut the baby from Coronis' womb, he brought the boy to the centaur Chiron, who raised him and taught him the art of medicine."

"So, the people born under this Ophi guy's sign grow up to be doctors or something?" Melodie asked.

"Not exactly. You see the goddess Athena gave Ophiuchus a gift. Two vials of blood."

More sounds of gagging.

"The blood was from the Gorgon Medusa; Medusa, you might recall, was killed by Perseus, thanks to Athena's aid." Again Mr. Quimby's eyes bored into me, and I felt like slinking under my desk. "The blood from the right side of Medusa's body was said to have the power to restore life, while the blood from the left side of her body was poisonous. Now, some people say that Ophiuchus got his power to restore life from a serpent, which is why his constellation in the sky is sometimes referred to as the Serpent Bearer or Serpentarius. In my opinion, the blood was a much more likely source for his power." He spun on his heels and began pacing the front of the room. "But moving on. Ophiuchus mastered the act of restoring life so completely that Hades, the god of the underworld, became angry. He didn't like his dead being raised by Ophiuchus, so he complained to Zeus."

I rolled my eyes. It always came back to Zeus.

"Zeus decided he had to do something to appease his brother, Hades, but at the same time he didn't want to offend Apollo by killing Ophiuchus. So, Zeus struck Ophiuchus down with a thunderbolt and placed him in the sky as a constellation where he could be honored." Mr. Quimby stopped pacing and turned back to me. "Does anyone need clarification on the details?"

Kyle raised his hand. "So, this Ophi guy had the power to raise the dead?"

"That's correct," Mr. Quimby answered.

Kyle raised his hand again. "But he could've used the Gorgon blood from Medusa to kill people if he wanted, right?"

Mr. Quimby nodded. "That is also correct."

The P.A. system crackled. "All teachers, please keep your students in class until you are instructed otherwise. If any students are in the hallways, please report to the nearest classroom immediately."

"What's that about?" I asked Melodie.

She shrugged. "It's probably a lockdown drill. They do them every once in a while. It's no big deal. We just sit here while the administrators walk through the building and make sure it's safe."

Even after five months, I still wasn't used to being in a regular high school. The only lockdown drills I'd had while I was homeschooled were if I was grounded or when Grandma would give me time-outs at the kitchen table on days when Mom couldn't work from home.

The classroom door opened, and a girl walked in. "Mr. Quimby, the announcement said to go to the nearest classroom."

"Take a seat," he said.

T

She walked over to the empty seat behind me and sat down. I'd never met her before, but that didn't stop her from leaning forward and whispering, "This isn't a drill. I was in the hall, and I saw the school nurse being carried out on a stretcher. She collapsed in her office. Jimmy Benton told me he found her lying on the floor."

I couldn't believe it. I had been there only twenty minutes ago. Ms. Steingall had looked fine. "Do you know what happened to her? Why she collapsed?"

She shook her head. "Not really, but it must have been a heart attack or stroke or something."

"Why do you think that?"

"Because she's dead."

Chapter 2

"Dead? She can't be dead." My head was spinning.

The girl nodded. "Believe me, she's dead. I saw her myself. They had a sheet over her face, and her arm was hanging off the stretcher."

"That's awful," Melodie said.

I felt sick. First the deer, and now Ms. Steingall. My stomach couldn't take it. The faint sound of sirens made me turn toward the window. Did they use sirens when the person was dead? I got the eerie feeling that someone was staring at me. One row over and three seats back sat a guy I hadn't seen before. He had dirty blonde hair and piercing green eyes that were locked on me. I wanted to turn away, but I couldn't. He was studying me so closely. Did he know I had been with the nurse before I got there? Did he think I had something to do with her death?

"Jodi." Melodie tugged on my sleeve.

"Huh?" I turned back toward her.

"What's up with you? You spaced out or something."

"I guess I'm in shock. I mean, Ms. Steingall is—was too young to have a heart attack, wasn't she?"

Melodie shook her head. "I don't know. Maybe she had a weak heart."

"Maybe." I glanced back over my shoulder. Green Eyes was still staring at me. "It's just creepy is all."

Someone knocked on the door, and Mr. Quimby got up from his desk. He'd been working at his computer, occasionally flipping through his grade book. It sort of looked like he was entering grades or attendance, but I had this feeling that he was emailing or something else totally not school-related. The teachers tended to go off-duty any chance they got. Plus, he looked annoyed at having to get up to answer the door.

Mrs. Thompson stepped into the room and looked around. Her gaze stopped on me. "Miss Marshall, would you come with me, please?"

"What's this about, Mrs. Thompson?" Mr. Quimby asked.

"Miss Marshall is needed in the office."

Mr. Quimby gave me a small smile. "If there's a problem, I can vouch for Jodi's presence in my class. She even contributed to part of the lecture."

Confirming my birthday wasn't exactly contributing to the lecture, but I was grateful for his concern. No one wants to be called down to the office, especially during a situation like a lockdown. Even more so when someone had died.

"I can assure you that Jodi is not in any trouble." Mrs. Thompson's tone implied a "yet" attached to the sentence.

Mr. Quimby nodded at me, and I stood up. "Should I bring my books?"

"That would probably be best," Mrs. Thompson said.

Melodie gave me an encouraging smile that also said, "Fill me in later." I nodded and followed Mrs. Thompson out of the room. We walked in silence. I couldn't help glancing into the nurse's office as we passed. The door was open, and a chair was overturned. Had Ms. Steingall fallen out of the chair or knocked it over when she collapsed?

"Miss Marshall?" Mrs. Thompson gave me a stern look, motioning for me to hurry up.

"Sorry." I stopped short when we reached the office. A uniformed police officer stood with his hands on his hips. The gun on his belt seemed to stare right at me.

"Are you Jodi Marshall?" the officer asked.

"Um, yes. Am I in trouble?" Nothing says guilty like asking if you're in trouble. The only thing that would've been worse was if I'd said, "I didn't do it."

"I need to ask you a few questions. Why don't we step into the principal's office?" He motioned for me to lead the way.

I hugged my books to my chest as I stepped into the corner office. I'd only ever been in here once, when I'd first started here. I sat down in the leather chair and placed my books on my lap. The officer sat down in Principal McMichael's chair.

"I'm Officer Adams. I was told you were one of the last people to see Ms. Steingall alive."

"I guess. I mean, I was sent to her office when I got to school. I had an accident. A deer ran out in front of my car. Mrs. Thompson, the receptionist," I added, figuring he probably didn't have clue who Mrs. Thompson is, "said I had to get cleared by the nurse before I could go to class."

Officer Adams scribbled in a notepad as I talked. I waited for him to finish. "I'm going to need you to tell me everything you remember from your visit to her office."

There wasn't much to remember, yet somehow my brain had trouble focusing. "Um, she asked me some questions about the accident. Whether I hit my head, if I was wearing a seatbelt, questions like that. Then, she used that little flashlight thingy to look in my eyes. She said that, other than being a little bloodshot from crying, everything looked fine. Then, she sent me to class."

"Was anyone else in the office?" Officer Adams furiously wrote every word I said.

"No, just me. Well, after Jimmy Benton left. I guess he thought he might have a fever, but Ms. Steingall said he didn't, and she sent him to class."

"And how did she seem to you? Was she slurring her words at all or moving any slower than usual?" He stopped writing and studied my face.

"Not that I noticed. She seemed fine."

"Did you go straight to class after that?"

"Well, I had to get a late pass from Mrs. Thompson first. Then, I went to class."

"Did you walk past the nurse's office on your way to class?" He was staring so intently at me that I swallowed hard. I hadn't done anything wrong, but he was making me feel like I had.

"Yes."

"Did you look into the office as you passed by?"

"No."

"Are you sure?" He leaned over the desk. "This is very important, Miss Marshall. Did you look into the nurse's office and notice anything strange?"

"No." The word was barely a whisper. "Why? Did someone do something to her?"

"I can't say." He stood up, glaring down at me. "But my instincts are telling me that Ms. Steingall was already dead when you walked by her office."

The hair on my arms stood on end. I had to get out of there. "May I go now?"

He pointed toward the door. I didn't hesitate. I scooped my books in my arms and rushed out of there as fast as I could without looking too suspicious. I didn't know where I was going or if the lockdown was over. My legs were moving on their own, without any direction from me. I turned the corner and saw Green Eyes. What was he doing out of class? He was leaning against the lockers with his cell phone in his hand like he'd just finished texting someone. When he saw me, he flipped his phone shut and shoved it in his pocket. He pushed off the lockers and started toward me.

I lowered my head and turned down the next hall. I was practically power-walking, his footsteps quickening behind me. I started to run when a door opened in front of me.

"Jodi, hey," Matt said. "What's the rush?" He grabbed my arm, and my books toppled to the ground. "Sorry." He bent down to pick them up.

I turned and looked for Green Eyes, but the hallway was filling up with students. The lockdown was over.

"Are you all right?" Matt asked, handing me my books.

"Yeah. Rough morning. I hit a deer with my car and then—"

"You hit a deer? Are you okay?" He grabbed my arms and looked me in the eyes.

"I'll be better once everyone stops asking me that." I smiled at him. His beautiful brown eyes and warm smile instantly calmed me.

"Did you hear they're letting us go home early?" He walked me to my locker.

"Really?" Nothing would've made me happier than going home and pretending this nightmare of a day had never happened.

"Yeah, some emergency with the school nurse or something. I don't really know all the details. But the buses have been called, and we've been dismissed for the day."

"Ugh, the bus. I have to take the bus because my car was towed."

"I'll give you a ride. We can even grab lunch."

I didn't exactly feel like eating after all I'd been through, but I couldn't say no to Matt. We'd just started dating, and we hadn't even kissed yet. He was the sweetest guy I'd ever met, *and* a total gentleman. Sometimes a little too much of a gentleman. "Sounds great."

I put my books in my locker and followed Matt to his car. He drove a blue Mustang. It wasn't new, but it was gorgeous. I had always had a thing for Mustangs. Plus, it was way better than my Civic. I was starting to feel better by the time we pulled out of the parking lot. Then, I saw Green Eyes. He was in a gray boat of a car, tapping his finger against the steering wheel like he was waiting for something—or someone. I had a sinking feeling I knew who that someone was. As Matt turned onto the main road, Green Eyes followed.

I tried to stay calm. I mean, Matt was with me, and he was bigger than Green Eyes. I didn't have anything to worry about. Only, I was still worried.

"Where do you want to go?"

"Huh? Oh, I don't care. Wherever you want to go is fine."

"I'm strangely in the mood for venison."

I thought of the deer from this morning and turned toward Matt in horror. He flashed me a smile and laughed. "Sorry, I couldn't resist. Besides, you said you wanted people to stop asking if you're okay."

"So, you thought you'd make fun of me instead." If it were anyone else, I probably would've gotten at least a little mad. But it was Matt, and he could do no wrong in my eyes.

"How about Alberto's?"

"My favorite," I said.

Matt reached his hand over and laced his fingers through mine. Yes, my day was starting to get a whole lot better. I even forgot about Green Eyes.

We got a table in the corner. My stomach didn't feel like it could handle much, so I ordered a plain bagel and a vanilla milkshake. Matt ordered a foot-long sub and ate every bite.

"Where do you put it all?" I asked as he swallowed the last of his sandwich.

"Good metabolism runs in my family." He pointed to my half-eaten bagel. "Do you always eat so little?"

"No, I have a pretty good appetite most of the time." I cringed. I'd dated a few guys, but I still wasn't sure where they stood on the whole girls and food issue. Did they want us to have good appetites?

"Okay, I know I'm not supposed to ask, but your day's been kind of—"

"Crappy? Yeah." I smiled at him. "But it's getting better."

The bell above the door jingled, drawing my attention. Green Eyes walked in, scanning the restaurant.

"Do you know that guy?" I asked Matt, nodding toward the door.

Matt turned slightly to look without being obvious. "No. Do you?"

"He was in my English lit class today, but I don't think I've ever seen him before."

"Maybe he's a transfer."

"Maybe." I sipped my milkshake. "He likes to stare."

"At you?" Matt glanced at him again. "Is he bothering you?"

I put my milkshake down. "No, not really. I'm probably imagining it. My mind's been a little crazy since the accident."

"Come on, I'll take you home. You look like you need some rest." He grabbed our trash and headed for the garbage.

I got my coat, my gaze wandering over to Green Eyes. He was still standing by the door, but now he was texting. We were going to have to walk right past him. Matt helped me put my coat on and gave me his arm. I squeezed his well-toned bicep. He couldn't get more perfect. We walked to the door, and Matt opened it for me. He nodded at Green Eyes. It was only a nod, but it spoke volumes. Matt was letting Green Eyes know I was with him. Part of me wanted to spin around and kiss him right there. But I kind of wanted our first kiss to be more special than in the doorway of Alberto's with Green Eyes staring at us.

Matt opened the car door for me. "You're right. He *does* like to stare at you." He leaned down and kissed my forehead. "Not that I can blame him."

He drove me to my house and parked in the driveway. My banged-up car was sitting there looking pathetic. Who knew how long it would be before we had enough money to have it fixed? Matt turned in his seat so he was facing me. "Thanks for going to lunch with me. I know you weren't really feeling up to it."

My heart raced even though I was only sitting there. "I had fun." I was too nervous to think of anything better to say. It was silly. I'd kissed guys before, but Matt was different. He was sweet and funny and perfect.

"I don't believe it." Matt sounded really annoyed. He was looking past me, out the window.

"What?" I spun around to see what he was staring at. Green Eyes was standing between the trees by the side of my house. "Did he follow us?"

"Go inside and lock the door. I'm going to have a little talk with this guy." Matt got out of the car and came to get my door. He opened it and helped me out. He kissed my forehead again and nodded toward the front door. I went inside, locking the door behind me. I didn't know if Green Eyes was a real threat or not, but with the way my day was going, I wasn't taking any chances.

I went to the living room window and peered through the curtains. Matt and Green Eyes were talking. Matt didn't look happy, but Green Eyes was smirking. Then, he snapped. He shoved Matt. I ran for the door, not having a clue how I was going to help. I couldn't break up a fight between two guys who were much bigger than me. My five-foot-four frame was no match for either of them. Still, I flung the door open and ran outside.

"Matt!"

Green Eyes froze when he saw me. Matt swung at Green Eyes, who dodged the hit, stumbling backward.

"Stay away from her! If I see you around her again, I'll call the cops."

I grabbed Matt's arm and pulled him toward the house. He came with me willingly. Green Eyes watched us go, but he didn't leave. Matt locked the door behind us and went to the window. "What the hell is he doing?"

I joined Matt at the window. Green Eyes stared back at me. I didn't know what I'd done to make this guy stalk me like this. All I knew was I was really freaked out.

Chapter 3

"You need to call the cops," Matt said. "He's not going to leave on his own." He turned away from the window. "Jodi? Are you listening to me?"

I started laughing. I felt like a lunatic, but I couldn't help it.

Matt hugged me, somehow understanding that I was falling apart. I squeezed him until I was calm.

"Thanks." I stepped out of his arms and reached for the phone. I dialed 911. I'd never actually called the police before and couldn't believe I had a reason to now.

"911. What is your emergency?"

"Hi, this is Jodi Marshall. Um, this guy has been following me all day. He followed me home and attacked my boyfriend. He's standing outside my house, and he won't leave." I pushed the curtains back. Green Eyes was gone. "Where is he?"

"Excuse me?" the operator asked.

"He's gone. I don't see him anymore."

"Would you like me to send an officer out to your house?"

"I don't know. I guess. I mean, I don't know if he really left or if he's hiding in the bushes or something."

"What's your address?"

"118 Pine Street."

"I'll send someone out now. Please, stay in your house with the doors locked until an officer gets there."

I hung up. Matt hugged me again. I wished I could stay in his arms all the time. I felt safe there. I made us some iced tea and popcorn—Matt was hungry again—and we watched TV until the police arrived. I wasn't really watching; I couldn't focus on anything except the lunatic outside. I answered the door, half expecting to see Officer Adams. That would've been the perfect ending to my perfectly awful day. It was a woman standing on my porch.

"Are you," she consulted her notebook, "Jodi Marshall?"

"Yes, that's me."

"And you called about a stalker?"

Stalker? It sounded so awful, but Green Eyes was stalking me. "Um, yeah. Come in."

"Actually, I prefer to stay out here. You reported that the man was watching you from your yard, correct?" she asked, without even telling me her name.

"Yes, but he's gone now. I think." I leaned out, searching the yard.

"Do you know the man?"

"No, and he's not really a man. He's a student… at my school. Maybe. I don't know. I've never seen him before today, but he was in my English lit class. And he's been following me ever since."

Matt put his hand on my shoulders for support. The officer looked at him. "Who's he? Your boyfriend?"

"Yes." I felt my cheeks blush. We hadn't officially started calling each other that yet, but this was the second time today it had come up. Matt squeezed my shoulder, letting me know he was okay with it.

"Did you see this guy?"

"Yeah." Matt nodded. "He was here when I brought Jodi home. I told Jodi to go inside and lock the doors, and I went to talk to him. He got all cocky and said he hadn't done anything wrong. I told him stalking a girl and totally freaking her out was definitely doing something wrong. Then, he attacked me. He pushed me, and we got into a fight."

"Have you seen him before?"

"No. Never."

She took out a notebook and pen. "Can you describe him?"

"Dirty blonde hair, green eyes, about six feet—maybe a little shorter." I shrugged.

"Build?" she asked.

"He wasn't that muscular, or at least I couldn't tell from the clothes he was wearing. But he looked like he was in pretty good shape." I shook my head, trying to get the image of Green Eyes out of my head.

"Any distinguishing marks, tattoos?"

I shook my head and checked with Matt. "Not that I saw," he said.

She flipped her notebook closed and stuffed it in her jacket pocket. "Okay, well, I'll check the area and keep a car here tonight to make sure you're safe. If I were you, I'd ask around at school tomorrow. See if anyone knows who this guy is. If you get a name, you call me." She handed me a card and left.

I closed the door behind her. Matt put his arm around me and led me to the couch. He pulled me closer to him, and I breathed in his scent. I wanted to get lost in him and forget about the rest of my day, but since we had never officially done anything, that was a little tough. I tilted my head back and looked him in the eye. He stared back at me for a minute before leaning his face toward mine. I closed my eyes and reached my hand to his cheek.

"Jodi!" Mom yelled, bursting through the front door.

I jolted back in the seat, and Matt dropped his arms to his sides. "Mom." I stood up and motioned toward Matt. "This is Matt. I've told you about him."

She looked at Matt for a second before turning her attention back on me. "I was just stopped by a police officer. She said she was called here about a stalker." She looked at Matt again. "What is going on?"

She'd given me an out for having a boy in the house when she wasn't home. It was one of her rules. No Mom, no boys. "Matt and I grabbed some lunch because they let us out of school early. He brought me back here, and this guy was following us. Well, actually he'd been following me all day, starting with lit class and then again in the hallway after Ms. Steingall—Oh my God, did you hear about Ms. Steingall?" Yes, I was a babbling idiot, but Mom was looking at Matt like he was the one I'd called the cops on.

"Maybe I should go," Matt said. "It's been a crazy day, and you two probably need to talk."

Mom looked at Matt and nodded. "I think that would be best. Thank you."

Matt smiled at me and headed for the door. I followed him, with Mom glaring at me. "Sorry."

"No problem. Stay safe, okay?" He squeezed my hand quickly before stepping through the door.

"Thanks for everything," I called after him.

"Jodi?" Mom called.

I shut the door and plopped down on the couch.

Mom took her coat off and motioned to the iced tea on the coffee table. "How long was he here?"

Seriously? I'd hit a deer, wrecked my car, had my school nurse die moments after I was in her office, and been stalked by a creepy guy, and she was asking me about Matt? "Mom, Matt didn't want to leave me home alone with that guy staring in the window. He was seriously creepy. Besides, I told you about Matt. You know we're just starting to date."

"Yes, I do know, and that's what worries me."

I sighed.

"But," she paused and let out a long sigh, "given the circumstances, I guess I'm thankful you weren't home alone." She sat down and wrapped me in a hug.

"Thank you."

"Do you have any idea who this guy is? The one who's been following you?"

I took another sip of my tea and shook my head. "I saw him in class for the first time today, and he's been following me ever since."

Mom slumped back on the couch. "It's been some day, huh?"

"You have no idea."

"How about pizza and a movie? A quiet night at home."

"Sounds good. I think I'll go shower while we're waiting for the pizza. I need to get the awfulness of the day off my skin." I stood up and Mom did the same. She pulled me into another hug.

"You want to go back to homeschooling?"

"No," I answered without any hesitation. "I like being around other people my own age. Sure, things are crazy in high school, but I'll deal with it."

She nodded and went for the phone. I climbed the stairs, heading for the bathroom. I took the hottest shower I could ever remember taking. I couldn't seem to wash the events of the day off of me. Finally, I gave up and headed to my room. I listened to music while I slipped on my pajamas and combed my hair. As the song ended, I heard a thump outside my window. I froze with my comb halfway down my head and listened. Nothing. When the next song started, I put the comb down and slipped over to my window. I didn't want to turn the music off in case Green Eyes was lurking. I wanted to catch him off-guard. I grabbed my cell phone and dialed the number on the card the officer had given me. I didn't press send though. I just wanted to be prepared in case I had to make the call.

I stood to the side of the curtains, out of view. I didn't really have much of a plan. Take a quick peek and hit send if I needed to. I counted to five and swung myself in front of the window. A brown bird was perched in the tree, looking dazed. It must have flown into the glass. I unlatched the window and raised it slightly. The cool air rushed into my room. I reached out toward the branch and shook it gently. The bird didn't move. It had to be alive though. It couldn't stay perched there if it were dead. I reached further and did something really stupid. I poked the bird with my finger.

That got a response. The bird flew right at me. I yanked my hand back in the window, cutting my finger on an exposed nail. "Ow!" I squeezed my finger to stop the bleeding. There was another thud. I looked down and saw the bird lying motionless on the ground. Shaking my head, I shut the window. I'd had enough dead things for one day.

After bandaging my finger, luckily on my left hand and not the one I write with, I headed downstairs. The doorbell rang as I was turning toward the kitchen. "I'll get it," I called to Mom, who was setting up plates at the coffee table.

"There's money in my coat pocket."

I stuck my hand in the left pocket of her coat and found a twenty. That would cover it. I swung open the door and, without even looking at the delivery guy, said, "How much do I owe you?"

"I'll settle for twenty minutes of your time."

I jerked my head up and saw Green Eyes. "You." My first instinct was to slam the door in his face, but he was holding our pizza. "How did you manage this? Did you jump the pizza delivery guy?"

Green Eyes smirked. "I gave him a really good tip to let me deliver the pie to your house."

"Well, I hope you tipped yourself, too." I grabbed the pizza from him and slammed the door shut. I nearly dropped the pie, trying to lock the door.

"What was that all about?" Mom asked, steadying the pizza for me.

I didn't want to freak her out any more than she already was, so I lied. "Nothing. I know that guy from school. He's a real jerk."

I shoved the twenty in the waistband of my pajama bottoms before she could notice I was still holding it.

We ate dinner and watched some sappy love story Mom had lying around. It was awful, but I didn't care because I wasn't really paying attention anyway. I kept sneaking glances out the window, looking for any sign of Green Eyes. How had he pulled off the pizza delivery? I mean, he didn't even know we'd ordered pizza. Or did he? I got goose bumps. And where was the police officer? She said she was going to hang around tonight and keep an eye on things.

"Well, I'm beat." Mom yawned as she turned off the movie.

"It's over?" I asked.

"Yup, you missed the whole thing. You were in your own little world. You didn't even hear your phone ring." She patted my knee. "Is there anything you'd like to talk about before I go to bed?"

"No, I'm pretty tired, too." I stood up, grabbing the pizza box from the coffee table. "I'll clean up and then head to bed."

"Thanks, sweetie." She checked the lock on the front door. "I saw the police car go by a minute ago. That officer is still out there patrolling, so no need to worry, okay?"

"Great." I gave Mom a smile. She said a quick goodnight and disappeared upstairs.

I brought the pizza into the kitchen and put it in the fridge. Then, I checked the back door. It was locked, and the deadbolt was in place. I wondered if that was enough.

I went upstairs and crawled into bed, placing my cell on the nightstand. It beeped to let me know I had new voice mail. The first one was from Melodie. "I heard you had lunch with Matt. I guess your day took a turn for the better. I want details tomorrow at school." Melodie had a way of knowing everything. She probably had people texting her from Alberto's while Matt and I ate.

The next message was from Matt. "I didn't know if I should call. Your mom didn't seem too happy to see me in your house today. I hope you didn't get in too much trouble." I smiled. It was sweet of him to call. I wasn't sure he'd want to see me again after the day we'd had. I saved the message.

The mechanical voice told me I had one more message. "We need to talk. One way or another, you'll listen to what I have to say." The phone fell from my hand. How did he get my cell number? Had someone at school given it to him? I picked up my phone and went to my missed calls. The number he'd called from was blocked. I still didn't have any leads on who he was or what he wanted from me. I put the phone on my nightstand and hugged my knees to my chest. Outside my window, I saw the flashing lights of the police car. Officer Whoever was still out there, yet I didn't feel much better knowing that.

If Green Eyes had managed to get past the cop once, what was to stop him from doing it again and finding a way into the house while I slept?

Chapter 4

Mom drove me to school the next morning. She didn't want me standing around at a bus stop with Green Eyes still on the loose. She was trying to pretend she wasn't scared for me, but I could tell she was. She hadn't even mentioned the incident with the nurse, but that didn't really involve me. So what if I'd been one of the last people to see Ms. Steingall? It wasn't as if I had anything to do with her death.

I walked into lit class and took a seat by Melodie. "Tell me everything!" She was so excited I thought she'd fall out of her seat. "I know you went to Alberto's, but then what happened?"

I couldn't resist. "I ordered a bagel and a milkshake, and he ordered a foot-long sub. It was pure magic." I batted my eyelashes at her.

"Very funny," she said. "Seriously though, did he kiss you yet? Tell me he kissed you."

I shook my head. "He almost did, but my mom walked in on us."

"Oh, ouch. You got caught with a boy in your house without your mom home."

"We didn't plan on going back to my house. He took me home after lunch and," I lowered my voice, "this guy was there." I looked over my shoulder one row and three seats back. The desk was empty. Where was Green Eyes today?

Melodie snapped her fingers in front of my face. "Who was there?"

"Sorry. A guy from this class. He was staring at me yesterday, and then he followed me down the hall after Nurse Steingall died, and then he showed up at Alberto's."

"Whoa, you have a stalker? And he's in this class?" She looked around the room. "Well, who is he? I have a few things to say to this guy."

I shook my head. "He's not here. But believe me, you don't want to meet him. I had to call the cops on him, and an officer patrolled my street all night. But he still got past her. He conned the pizza delivery guy to let him deliver the pizza to my door. And he left a message on my cell. How did he get my number? It's unlisted." My voice was shaking.

"Calm down." Melodie reached out and grabbed my hand. "If he's in this class, then Mr. Quimby will know who he is. Let's ask him."

Mr. Quimby. He'd have a class roster. Even if Green Eyes was a transfer, Mr. Quimby must have some paperwork on him. A name at the very least. "I'll go ask him." I got up from my chair. Melodie nodded and let go of my hand.

Mr. Quimby was reading the paper at his desk when I approached. "Um, good morning, Mr. Quimby."

He looked up briefly and then glanced at the clock as if to point out that he wasn't on teacher duty until the bell rang.

"Sorry to bother you before class, but I was wondering if you knew the name of the new student. The guy who was in the back of the class yesterday."

He met my eyes for a second before returning to the paper. I'd never noticed his eyes were green. I mean, who really looks at their teacher's eyes? "I wasn't told about a new student. You must be thinking about another class."

"No, this was the only class we had yesterday. We were let go early because of…" my voice trailed off. I didn't want to relive the other events that had happened. "He was sitting one row over and three seats back from me. He had dirty blonde hair and green eyes."

The bell rang. "Sorry, Miss Marshall, but you must be mistaken. Now, if you'll please take your seat, I need to begin my lesson."

I scrunched my forehead. How could Mr. Quimby not know about Green Eyes? Teachers should know the students in their classes. I walked back to my seat. Mr. Quimby was already picking up with the lecture from yesterday, droning on and on about Hades and the underworld.

"Well?" Melodie asked.

"He said he didn't have a new student. He didn't know who I was talking about."

The rest of the school day was a blur. Matt had a doctor appointment, so he missed the morning classes. I met up with him at lunch briefly before he had to take a make-up test. "Hey, we didn't get to really say goodnight yesterday with everything that was going on. Think we could maybe try it again tonight?"

I smiled, and Melodie kicked me under the table. "Yeah, we could do that. What did you have in mind?"

He squatted next to me, giving us more privacy. "Let's check out the new club in town. Serpentarius."

Melodie leaned across the table, trying to hear.

"We're not twenty-one. We're not even eighteen." Boy, did I sound like a big dork. Melodie must have heard because she kicked me again, but this time a lot harder. I widened my eyes at her, and she nodded toward Matt.

He laughed. "My cousin's the bouncer. He just got hired about two months ago. We'll get in."

I shrugged. "Why not?"

He stood up and adjusted his backpack on his shoulder. "Great. I've got to run. Do you need a ride home after school?"

"Oh, um, no. Melodie said she'd take me." This time I knew the kick was coming. Hell, I wanted to kick myself. Why was I turning down a ride from Matt?

"Okay, well if you change your mind, let me know." He gave my shoulder a squeeze and left. I watched him go and tried not to drool.

"What is wrong with you?" Melodie flung a French fry at my head.

"I don't know," I whined. "He's just so—"

"Perfect and totally kissable. But you turned him down for a ride. Alone. The two of you. In his car."

"Yes, I get it. I'm an idiot." I took a bite of my peanut-butter sandwich and sighed.

I spent the afternoon thinking of believable excuses for why Melodie had to suddenly back out of driving me home so I could ask Matt for a ride instead. They all sounded completely lame. Last period study hall arrived, and I still hadn't come up with anything. On the positive side, I hadn't seen Green Eyes either.

I tapped my pencil eraser on my desk and stared at Mr. Quimby. Lucky me, I had him twice a day thanks to study hall. He spent the period ignoring us, as usual. Maybe he didn't know who Green Eyes was. Maybe he tried not to pay too much attention to his students. He might feel guilty for ignoring us if he actually knew all our names. Just because he didn't know about the new student, though, didn't mean no one did.

I gathered my books and walked up to Mr. Quimby's desk. "Mr. Quimby, I was wondering if I could go to the office."

He stopped typing on his computer and looked at me. "What for?"

"Well, you may have heard I was in an accident before school yesterday. I hit a deer with my car. I was supposed to get a ride home from Melodie, but she got called in to work." Matt would never fall for the "called in to work" excuse because he knew Melodie didn't have a job. Matt and Melodie had been friends for a long time. She was the one who had introduced us. "So, I need to take the bus home. I figured since I haven't taken the bus in a while, I might need a bus pass."

He studied me like he was trying to decide if I was telling the truth. I smiled, trying to look innocent. "Very well. You may go."

"Thank you." I hurried out the door before he could have second thoughts.

I took the long way to avoid going by the nurse's office. There'd been a sign on the door all day saying, "Emergencies only"—with "only" in big letters—"should report to the main office." I guessed they didn't have a substitute nurse on hand. I cringed at the thought of Mrs. Thompson taking care of sick students. I'd rather throw up in class than have her glare at me for an entire period, but right now I needed her help. So, I put on my best smile and walked right up to her desk.

"Good afternoon, Mrs. Thompson." I faked as much cheerfulness as I could.

She raised her eyes without lifting her head. The effect was unnerving, and I swallowed hard. She didn't say anything, so I continued. "Um, Mr. Quimby sent me. I have study hall with him this period. He had a student missing from class today. Not from study hall. From lit class."

"Lit class?" she asked, as if I was speaking another language.

"Literature. First period."

"Uh huh."

"Well, he had a new student yesterday. A boy. But he—the boy—never gave Mr. Quimby his transfer slip. You see, Mr. Quimby was in the middle of a fascinating lecture about mythology, and since this unit counts for so much of our semester grade, he didn't want to interrupt the class to get this boy's name." I paused to see if she was buying any of this. Her expression was stone cold, but since she wasn't yelling at me to go back to class, I decided to keep going. "Um, so Mr. Quimby wanted to know if you could give me this boy's paperwork, so he could enter it in his grade book."

My fingers were laced in front of me in an attempt to look innocent, but I was clenching my hands so tightly my knuckles were turning white. I quickly unlocked my fingers and put my arms down at my sides. I knocked over the nameplate on her desk in the process, and jumped when it landed with a thud. "Sorry," I mumbled, bending to pick it up. I expected Mrs. Thompson to tell me that Mr. Quimby would have to come get the paperwork himself because she couldn't hand it over to another student for confidentiality reasons. At least, that sounded like something a school should do. Instead, she typed something into her computer.

"We've only had one new student in the past two weeks. A girl, and she's not listed on any of Mr. Quimby's class registers."

"What? That can't be right." I leaned toward her computer screen, trying to read it.

She removed her glasses, something I'd never seen her do before. "Excuse me, young lady, but school files are not for the eyes of students."

I backed up again. "But you don't understand. This boy was in class yesterday. I saw him. He has—"

"Look." Mrs. Thompson put her glasses back on. "I've heard Mr. Quimby isn't the most exciting teacher we have here. Isn't it possible you were daydreaming about this new boy?"

Daydreaming? Who daydreamed about a stalker? "No, I—" She glared at me, and I knew the conversation was over. "Thank you for your help."

"Tell Mr. Quimby to come see me if he thinks there's been some sort of mistake."

I nodded and left the office. Nothing was making sense. Green Eyes wasn't a figment of my imagination. I'd seen him in class. Matt saw him at Alberto's and fought with him in my yard. He'd delivered pizza to my house. Something was wrong. Really wrong.

The bell rang and students rushed out into the halls. The end of the day was always a scramble. I went to my locker and exchanged some books before heading to meet Melodie. Luckily, driving to school, or getting a ride from Melodie, meant I didn't have to rush like everyone who rode the bus. Having been homeschooled for most of my life, I'd only taken the bus a handful of times. And for that I was thankful. It was nothing but loud, obnoxious, pent-up kids who really needed to let out some aggression after being herded around school all day like a bunch of lab rats.

I turned the corner, trying to put my jacket on as I walked, which isn't easy when you're carrying a bag full of books. I dropped my shoulder bag, spilling my books and pens all over the floor. "Great."

A hand reached out and picked up my bag. I turned to see Green Eyes. "You!"

"Is that going to be your new greeting for me?" he asked.

"Give me my bag." I yanked the strap, but he held on tight.

"First, we need to talk."

"Fine. How about you start with what you're doing here? You don't go to this school. I know. I asked around." I tugged on the bag again, with no luck. This guy was stronger than he looked.

"You asked about me?" He smiled.

"Don't flatter yourself. I only wanted to know your name so I could tell the cop I called last night."

"So, you want to be on a first name basis, is that it?"

I couldn't believe him. He was beyond cocky.

"Hey!"

I let go of my bag and turned to see Matt rushing toward us.

"We'll talk later." Green Eyes tossed my bag to me, running in the opposite direction of Matt.

I hugged my bag to my chest, staring after him.

"Did he hurt you?" Matt reached out to me.

"No, he was just a jerk. I'm fine. Really." Matt helped me stuff my books back into my bag.

"Come on. I'm taking you home." He put his arm around me.

"Hey, Jodi, there you are. I've been waiting for you." Melodie stopped and looked at Matt. "Oh, um, you know I have this thing I have to go to."

"A thing?" Matt asked.

"Yeah." Melodie nodded. "It's totally last minute. I only found out about it last period. So, um, Jodi, I can't drive you home. I'm so sorry." She winked at me, the most wicked, obvious wink in the history of winking.

I rolled my eyes and looked at Matt. "She was your friend first."

Matt laughed. "Yeah, but I can't remember why."

Melodie shook her head. "Oh, just get out of here, you two."

I smiled at her and mouthed, "I'll call you."

"Have fun," she called after us in a singsong voice.

"You really don't mind taking me home?" I asked as we got into his car.

"Not at all. In fact I'll feel better knowing that creep isn't hanging around outside your house."

Boy, I really hoped Green Eyes wasn't waiting for me. "Are we still on for tonight?"

"Absolutely. I talked to my cousin. He said to come by around nine, and he'd get us in. So, I'll pick you up around 8:45."

"Sounds great."

We pulled into the driveway. "Stay in the car while I go check for loser boy."

"You know, I don't think he wants to hurt me. I think he just likes to scare me."

"Well, I don't want him doing anything to you."

I waited while Matt circled the house. He came back and shrugged his shoulders. I got out of the car. "All clear." He smiled.

He walked me to the front door, and I hesitated with my key in my hand. "So, 8:45 you said?"

"Yeah." He leaned forward, and the front door swung wide open.

"Hi, honey!" Mom said. "Matt, is it?"

"Yes, ma'am." Matt nodded. "Nice to see you." He turned to me again. "I'll pick you up later."

All I could do was nod. How many times was my mother going to ruin my first kiss with Matt? I pushed by her and went straight to my room. She called up that dinner would be ready at five. I didn't even answer. I flung open my bedroom door and nearly screamed.

My room had been torn apart. Things were scattered everywhere. I knew exactly who had done it. Green Eyes had been in my house. He'd gone through my room. And probably while my mom was downstairs.

Chapter 5

I dropped my bag in the doorway. My chest felt like a sumo wrestler was sitting on it. I couldn't hide from this guy. There was nothing I could do to stop him from getting close to me. He wasn't a student at Lambert High, yet he had somehow managed to get inside the school and into one of my classes without being caught. Now, he'd broken into my house and ransacked my room.

"Jodi, are you okay? What was that banging?" Mom yelled up the stairs.

"I dropped my book bag. Sorry!" I yelled down, scooping up my bag and rushing into my room. I closed the door and leaned my back against it. I couldn't let Mom see my room like this. She'd make me quit Lambert and go back to homeschooling. And she'd never let me go out with Matt tonight. With all the crap I'd been through, I needed one night of fun. One perfect night with the perfect guy and the perfect first kiss. That was all I wanted.

I raced to my bed and started making it. One of my pillows was sliced open, but I shoved it in a pillowcase and put it back in its place. Then, I went to my desk and closed all the drawers, tossing the contents of them back inside, not caring if things were in their proper places. I had to get it off the floor before Mom came upstairs. My dresser was next. Clothes spilled out. I shoved them inside and threw myself at the closet. I heard

Mom's footsteps on the stairs. She probably wanted me to set the table or make the salad. I got down on my knees and literally swept the shoes and clothing into my closet with my arms. I was shutting the doors when Mom knocked.

"Honey?" She opened the door and stepped inside, glancing around the room. "It's getting a little messy in here, don't you think? You should spend some time cleaning it up this evening."

"Mom, I have a date with Matt tonight." She already knew that. She'd heard our conversation on the front porch when she'd so rudely interrupted us.

"Oh, well, see what you can do before you go out."

I nodded. "Sure."

"And I'd love it if you could set the table for me. Dinner will be ready soon."

"Be down in a sec." I kicked a pillow feather under my bed.

As soon as she left, I flopped down on my bed. Things were getting too complicated. Dodging stalkers, keeping secrets from Mom, and I didn't have a clue what I was going to wear to the club tonight.

Dinner was uneventful. I didn't mention the break-in or the surprise run-in with Green Eyes at school. Mom seemed to be tiptoeing around the subject of the nurse. The funny thing was that no one was really talking about it at school either. There had been an announcement in first period letting everyone know about the funeral arrangements. Other than that, no one had mentioned it.

After dishes, I went upstairs, showered, and called Melodie. "You have to help me pick out an outfit. I've never been to a club before, and I want to look amazing tonight," I blurted without even saying hello.

"Don't you mean you want to look kissable?"

"Exactly. See, this is why I called you."

"Okay, go to your closet and start describing what you have."

I went to the closet and opened the doors before I remembered the break-in. My clothes lay in a heap on the floor. "Maybe I should call and cancel."

"No way! I'm not letting you do that. Give me a second to think." I could hear Melodie tapping her finger on the side of the phone. "Got it! Wear those dark jeans you got last week. The ones I picked out."

"They make me look—"

"Kissable," Melodie interrupted. "Put them on. And then find your black top with the lace neckline. It's dressy casual. Plus, you'll easily be able to dance in that outfit."

"Okay. Thanks, Mel."

"No problem. Now, hurry up. You only have a half hour before Matt picks you up."

What? When did that happen? "Thanks, again. Love you. Bye," I rambled into the phone before tossing it on the bed. I scrambled through the closet and found the black top. Then, I raced to the dresser and searched for the jeans. They were hidden in the back with the tags still on. I never would have bought them if Melodie hadn't made me. They hugged a little tighter than I was used to. But Mel was the fashion expert, not to mention the dating expert, so I slipped them on. Well, I tugged them on.

Shoes. Crap, I'd forgotten to ask what shoes I should wear. I went back to my closet and searched for something to match. I was flinging shoes all over my room. So much for cleaning up. I reached for another pair when my hand touched something furry. I screamed when I got a good look at it. A rat. A big dead rat. I screamed again, pulling my hand away. As I did, I pricked my right index finger on a pin in the shirt I was holding. A single drop of blood dripped onto the rat. Mom raced into my room wearing her bathrobe and a towel on her head. She must have come straight from the shower.

"What?" Her eyes fell on the rat, inches in front of me. "Jodi!" She pointed, and I looked down as the rat rolled onto its feet and ran under my bed.

I jumped on top of my bed, shrieking. Mom screamed and joined me. We huddled together.

"What do we do?" I gripped her tightly.

"Okay, okay… We need to calm down and think."

"Right." I nodded. Think about the dead rat that got up and ran under my bed. Nope. Thinking wasn't working.

"Um, where's your tennis racket?" Mom asked.

"I'm not going to hit that thing with my tennis racket. Besides, it's under my bed."

"All right. New plan." Mom looked around the room. "The trash can. We'll trap it under the trash can."

"But how do we get it to come out from under the bed?"

Mom shook her head. "Don't suppose you have any cheese hidden in your nightstand?"

I gave her a look that said, "Be serious."

"Okay." She picked up the hanger I'd thrown on the bed when I'd gotten dressed. "I'll go on one side of the bed and start banging the hanger on the floor. You go on the other side of the bed with the trash can. When the rat runs out, you drop the trash can on him and trap him under it."

It was a plan straight out of a blooper reel of one of those funny home video shows, but since I didn't have any better ideas, I couldn't object. I scooted to the foot of the bed and reached for the trash can. "It's too far away."

"Here, use the hanger." Mom handed me the hanger, and I reached it out, hooking it on the can and dragging it to me. The rat squeaked under the bed. I screamed, and the hanger raked across the Band-Aid from the night before when I'd cut my finger on the window. The Band-Aid fell off, and I saw my finger was bleeding again. I dropped the hanger as blood dripped on my off-white carpet. Just great.

"Got any more hangers?" I already knew the answer.

"Time for a new plan?"

"No. I think I can reach the hanger without getting off the bed. Can you hold on to me so I don't fall on the floor?"

Mom bent down and grabbed my calves. "Got you." It was times like this that I was glad my mom was so young. She didn't think twice about doing crazy stuff. Of course, when it came to me dating, she was very overprotective. But if I'd had a baby at sixteen, I probably would've been a little overprotective of my teenage daughter, too. That reminded me that I still hadn't come up with a good lie about where Matt and I were going. Mom would never let me go to a club, especially one like Serpentarius that was for twenty-one and up.

"You having second thoughts?" Mom asked.

Apparently I'd been hanging half off the bed, contemplating my dating situation and completely forgetting about the rat for too long. "Working up the courage."

"Let me know when you've found enough. I want to make sure I have a good grip on you. No rat is going to chew on my daughter."

"Thanks for that image." I shuddered. "Okay, here I go." I held my breath—not for any real reason, it just seemed like the thing to do—and reached my arm out, snatching the hanger. "Pull me up!"

Mom tugged on my legs. The rat gave another squeak, but this time I held on to the hanger. "Good job," Mom said, sounding as out of breath as I felt.

"I got blood on the carpet." I held my finger up.

She waved it off. "Don't worry about it. I'll take blood on the carpet over a rat under the bed any day. Let's trap that disgusting thing and get it out of here."

"Right." I still had the box of Band-Aids on my nightstand from last night, so I put a new one on and got a good hold on the hanger. "Take two." I positioned myself on the end of the bed again. I hooked the trash can and pulled it close enough that I could grab it. "Got it!" I lifted it onto the bed.

Mom took a deep breath. "Now, the hard part."

Like that had been easy? "Are you sure you don't want to trap the rat while I bang the hanger on the ground?"

"I'm going to have to hang off the bed and spook the thing. All you have to do is drop the trash can on it. Do you really want to trade jobs?"

I had visions of the rat attacking the hanger. "Never mind. I'm good."

I got on one side of the bed, and Mom moved to the other. "Ready?" she asked.

"What if it runs out the bottom of the bed?"

"Let's hope all that noise you made down there with the hanger and trash can was enough to scare it away from there."

I nodded. We were putting a lot on hope. "Here it goes." Mom leaned over the side of the bed. I waited for her to start banging the hanger. As soon as she started, the rat squeaked. I held the trash can between my hands, ready to slam it down on top of the vile rodent. But Mom screamed. "It's coming this way!"

I scrambled over to her side, pulling her up and out of reach of the rat's sharp little teeth and claws. Its head poked out from under the bed, and then it disappeared again.

"Okay, so now we know the rat is going to attack the hanger." Mom breathed heavily.

"I say let's move to the foot of the bed. That way we can lie down on the bed and only hang over as much as we need to. We'll be more steady than trying to lie across the bed since we don't totally fit."

Mom sighed. I could tell she didn't want to try this again, but what else were we supposed to do? We couldn't get out of the room, and I didn't want to sleep with a rat underneath my bed either. "Okay, let's get this over with before I completely lose my nerve." She pointed the hanger at me. "But once this is over, you are cleaning this room. If it wasn't so dirty, you wouldn't have attracted a rat in the first place."

I didn't think the rat was attracted to the mess in my room. Not even after Green Eyes had rummaged through it. I had this disturbing feeling that Green Eyes had left the rat for me. A little token of his hatred.

"I promise I'll clean my room," I said. "But not tonight. Matt will be here soon to pick me up for…" What had I decided on? "For the movie."

"Well, I hope he gets here soon enough to help us dispose of the rat." It wasn't exactly welcoming Matt into our home or being happy I was dating a nice guy, but it was something.

I scooted down to the edge of the bed and extended my legs for balance. Mom did the same beside me. She lowered the hanger and banged it on the box spring. There were a few squeaks and squeals—squeaks from the rat and squeals from Mom and me. The rat ran right at the hanger. Mom lifted the hanger, and I slammed the trash can down.

"We did it!" I cheered.

Mom squealed again, but this time it was with excitement. She threw her arm around me.

"Easy." I pressed down on the trash can. "He's really going nuts under there." I felt him ramming into the sides of the can, looking for a way out.

Mom hopped off the bed. "Hold on. I'm going to get something to weigh it down so you can let go." She went for my heavy book bag next to the desk and placed it on top of the trash can, balancing it before letting go.

"Okay, that should be good." She took a small step back, holding her hands out in case the rat moved the trash can and toppled the books. Nothing happened. The rat didn't even squeak in protest.

I sighed and swung my legs off the bed. My relief lasted a whole ten seconds before the doorbell rang. "Matt's here!"

"Well, bring him up here. He can help us get rid of this thing."

I looked around at the state of my room.

Mom saw my hesitation. "Too bad, young lady. Maybe this will teach you to keep this place clean."

I sighed and headed downstairs. I opened the door, and a huge smile crossed my face. Matt was standing there, looking absolutely gorgeous in a dressy casual sort of way—I was really going to have to hug Melodie for picking out my outfit—and he was holding a single pink carnation. He held it out to me, and I saw that it was fake. I must have looked confused because he laughed and tucked it in my hair.

"My sister told me to bring it. She said girls love flowers, but since I didn't have time to stop at the florist, and it's February so the garden's bare, I had to settle for silk. At least Amber said it was silk."

"I love it."

"You look amazing." He stepped toward me. "Uh, is your mother home?"

"Actually, yes. And we need a little favor." I brought him upstairs without explaining.

Mom was guarding the trash can. "Hi, Matt. You're right on time. We have a little unwanted visitor."

Matt looked at me. I knew he was thinking of Green Eyes. If only he knew.

Mom pointed to the trash can. "We've got a rat trapped under there."

"Oh." Matt sounded relieved. He walked over to the trash can and removed the books. Mom and I huddled together while Matt slowly lifted the can. "No problem. This guy looks like he's been dead for a while."

I stepped closer. That couldn't be possible. He had been running all over before we caught him. Matt took the bag from the trash can and scooped the rat into it. He was right. It was definitely dead. I stared at the bloodstain on the carpet, thinking about how odd it was to see the drop of my blood where the rat had died.

Chapter 6

I was still shaken up over the whole rat incident. Mom didn't give the thing another glance, so she didn't see how bloody and decayed it looked. There was no rational explanation for how it could've been running around under my bed minutes before, but I didn't say a word. Mom was freaked out enough, and nothing was going to keep me from going on this date. I was determined to have my perfect night out with Matt. No way was I letting a dead rat, or even Green Eyes, ruin this for me.

"So, is your room always that messy?" Matt asked as we drove to the club.

"Let's just say it's been a crazy week." I shifted uncomfortably in my seat.

"I kind of like that you're not a neat freak. Amber's room is spotless. She's always on my case to pick up my things." He turned and smiled at me. "Did I tell you that you look amazing?"

"I think you might have mentioned it." My heart beat faster, but for a much better reason this time.

We pulled up to Serpentarius and found a parking spot around back. There was a line to get in, but Matt took my hand and led me straight to the door. He shook hands with the bouncer. "Jodi, this is my cousin, Jared."

"Hi," I said, standing up straighter so I looked older. Well, at least taller.

"Have fun," Jared said.

Matt slipped him a twenty, and we walked inside.

"You have to tip your own cousin?" I asked, practically having to yell over the band.

"Jared's got to give his boss some reason for letting us in."

The club was dark and loud, but Matt seemed to know where he was going. He led me to the bar and ordered us two bottles of water. He handed me one, leaning in close so we didn't have to shout. "I know not to push my luck. That's why Jared's boss looks the other way when I'm here."

"So, you come here often?" I asked, taking a sip of water.

"That didn't quite come out right. Can I try that again?"

"Oh no, you don't get off that easily." I gave him a playful smile. "How many girls have you brought here? And don't try to tell me I'm the first."

He put his free hand to his chin and tapped it like he was thinking. I smacked his arm, making him spill some of his water.

"What? It's not easy keeping track of all those girls."

"Very funny."

He stepped closer to me. "Seriously, I've brought two girls here."

Two. I wondered who they were.

"Amber and you." He leaned closer to me. Our faces were just inches apart. He smelled incredible.

"I guess your sister doesn't really count, huh?" The water rippled in the bottle as my hand shook. My nerves were getting the better of me.

"No, she doesn't. But you do." He leaned down.

This was it. My eyes fluttered shut, but not before I saw him. Green Eyes. Right next to me. He yanked my elbow, pulling me away from Matt and into a crowd of people.

"Let go of me!" I yelled, though it lost all effect with the music blaring.

It took Matt a second to realize what happened. He stepped toward us, having to push past people trying to get to the bar. Green Eyes let go of me and disappeared into the crowd.

Matt grabbed my arms. Somehow in the commotion, we'd both dropped our bottles of water. "What did he do to you? Are you okay?" I wanted to get through one day where he didn't have to ask me that.

"He yanked me away from you. I guess…" I shook my head. "I guess he didn't want us kissing or something."

"That's it. I've had it with this guy. He's obsessed with you, Jodi." Matt was so angry, angrier than I'd ever seen him get. He was always so nice and friendly. This was a side of him I wasn't used to seeing. I was glad I hadn't told him about Green Eyes ransacking my room. "Listen, I want you to go to the ladies' room. Stay there until I come get you."

"What are you going to do?"

"I'm going to find that guy and get his ass tossed out of here."

I nodded, and Matt pointed to the bathroom. He watched me go inside before he turned to find Green Eyes. I almost felt sorry for Green Eyes. Matt was fuming. And since his cousin was the bouncer, Green Eyes didn't stand a chance.

I went to the sink and stared at my reflection. I almost expected to see a wrinkle or a gray hair after the couple days I'd had. But I still looked like me, and I had to admit Melodie was right about this outfit.

I washed my hands out of boredom. What else was I supposed to do while I waited for Matt? The stall behind me swung open, but I didn't think anything of it. I reached for a paper towel. After I dried my hands and threw the towel in the garbage, I went back to the mirror to check my makeup. My reflection wasn't the only one in the mirror.

"Looks good to me," Green Eyes said behind me.

I whirled around, my heart in my throat. "How did you get in here? This is the ladies' room!" But he was Green Eyes. What made me think a little sign on a door would stop him?

"Like I told you before, we need to talk."

"Talk, huh? Is that why you left the dead rat in my bedroom after you rifled through it?" I crossed my arms in front of me, trying to pretend I wasn't terrified of him.

"Was the rat dead?" he asked, not denying any of it.

What a weird question. "You left the stupid thing there. Shouldn't you know if it was alive or dead?"

"The question is, do you know?"

"What?" This guy was one riddle after another.

"Algernon didn't get up and run across your room or anything, did he?" He said it like he knew it was true. Like he knew the rat had come back from the dead or something. I stepped closer to the door, not answering him. He followed me. "We really need to sit down and talk. Somewhere else. Somewhere people can't walk in on us."

"I'm not going anywhere with you. You've been stalking me and leaving dead rats in my closet."

"I have to explain a few things to you. Starting with this place. Do you know where you are?"

"Do you?" I motioned to the ladies' room we were standing in.

He smirked. "Cute, but we need to be serious. This place, did you notice the name?"

"Serpentarius. So what?" I wasn't sure why I was even still talking to him. I should've bolted for the door, but I had a feeling he'd beat me to it.

"Don't pay attention in school, do you?"

"Speaking of school, what were you doing there? I know you're not a student. Mr. Quimby had no idea who you were, and the front office didn't either."

"Mr. Quimby knows who I am. He's the one who told me about you. He's the one who asked me to follow you."

"What?" I shook my head. "This is crazy. I'm leaving." I turned for the door, but he grabbed my arm, twisting me around to look at him.

"Do you know what will happen to your boyfriend if you get too close?"

"Are you threatening him?" I tried to yank my arm free, but his grip was too tight.

"Actually, you are. One kiss and he's history. He'll be as stone cold as the nurse who examined you after your accident."

My stomach dropped. What exactly was he saying? The bathroom door opened, and a girl in a leopard print halter top walked in. "Oh, sorry. I didn't mean to interrupt anything."

I shook my arm free from Green Eyes. "You're not interrupting anything. I was just leaving." I glared at him one more time as the girl stepped out of my way.

"The name's Alex," he said. "I know you've been wondering."

The girl squinted at me. Great, now she thought I was hooking up with a random guy in the bathroom. A guy I hadn't even bothered to ask his name. I was so not that girl. I shook my head and bolted through the door.

I saw Matt heading this way. "I couldn't find him. It's like he disappeared."

"Yeah, he disappeared in there." I motioned over my shoulder to the ladies' room.

"What?" Matt started toward the door.

I grabbed his arm. "Please, don't. Let's just get out of here." He was gritting his teeth and breathing heavily. "Please, Matt." I pulled him toward the exit, and luckily he let me. We got in the car without saying a word. Matt waited until we were halfway to my house to start asking questions.

"What happened back there?"

"Alex—that's his name—was waiting for me in the bathroom. Somehow, he knew I'd go there. I don't know how. Nothing's making sense." I wanted to tell Matt about my room and the rat, but I couldn't relive it all right now.

Matt pulled into the driveway. It was only 9:45. Home way before curfew. Wouldn't Mom be proud?

I turned to face Matt. "How long has Mr. Quimby been teaching at Lambert?"

"Mr. Quimby? Why? What made you think about him?"

"Something Alex said." I shook my head. "Never mind. It doesn't matter. It was probably all lies anyway." I reached over and touched his hand. He pulled back slightly. "Sorry about tonight." I stared into his eyes. "I don't suppose you want to try again sometime?"

He lowered his head and laughed. "I think I'm crazy for saying this." He looked at me and smiled. "But yeah, let's try it again. Tomorrow?"

I nodded. I thought about kissing him goodnight, but somehow it didn't feel right to have our first kiss on the same night that all this had happened. "Call me," I said, opening my door.

Matt opened his door, too, ready to walk me to the porch, but I reached for his arm. "Stay. It's starting to rain."

He nodded. "Tomorrow," he said with a smile.

"Yeah, tomorrow." I got out of the car, amazed at my bad luck. So much for my perfect night out with Matt. I turned and waved to him before I went inside.

"Home already?" Mom asked, walking into the living room, holding a cup of steaming hot tea.

"Any more of that?" I pointed to her mug.

"Yeah, I'll pour you a cup. Go sit."

I flopped down on the couch. Why couldn't I be like every other girl at Lambert? Out with the guy she likes on Friday night. Was it too much to ask?

Mom returned with two mugs of tea this time. I sat up and took one from her. I sipped it, loving the feeling of the scalding hot tea on the back of my throat.

Mom sat next to me. "Now, tell me what happened. Did you two break up or something?"

"We aren't even officially together. I mean we've been out a few times, but can you really call someone your boyfriend if you've never even…" I took another sip. Mom and I talked about everything, but was kissing boys too much for a mother-daughter relationship to handle?

"Oh," she said, hiding her smile behind her cup of tea.

"It's not funny, Mom. Matt must think I'm a complete dork."

"Well, honey, if you aren't ready to kiss Matt, then he'll just have to wait."

Of course, that wasn't the problem, but I wasn't about to tell her that I was dying to kiss him. I finished the rest of my tea in three big gulps.

"You know you're supposed to sip tea. Enjoy it."

"I like it hot. If you don't drink it quickly, it gets cold." Like my relationship with Matt was going to get if I didn't kiss him soon. I put my mug on the coffee table and stood up. "I'm going to bed."

"This early?" Mom looked at her watch. "Why don't you stay up with me? We can talk more. Or watch a movie, if you'd rather."

"Thanks, but I think I'm going to let this day end." I hugged her and went upstairs. I didn't even feel like showering, but I didn't want to add "dirty" to the list of adjectives that described my life lately. I made it quick and kept the water scalding hot. I threw on my pajamas and checked my cell. No call or text from Matt. But why would there be?

He was probably talking to some other girl from school. One who didn't have a stalker and one who'd kiss him the first chance she got.

No, I didn't really believe that. Matt was nice. He wouldn't date someone else without telling me first. Although, I really wouldn't blame him if he did.

My phone vibrated in my hand. Melodie. "Hope you're having fun!" the text read. Yeah, fun. I vaguely remembered what that was. I didn't respond. I was supposed to be on my date, so she wouldn't expect a response anyway. Of course, she would expect a call at the end of the date. I really wasn't up to that. I put my phone down and walked over to the window. I needed some air. I had to sidestep the faint bloodstains on my carpet. Mom must have tried to get them out while I was gone. Any excuse to wear latex gloves—the woman loved to clean. I could still see some discoloration. Just what I needed. A constant reminder of the present Alex had left for me.

Luckily, it had stopped raining, so I opened the window and let the cool air hit me in the face. It felt great after the hot shower. I heard shouting and realized the Sandersons must have been having another one of their fights. They were the two most miserable people on the planet. All they did was fight, but they refused to get a divorce. They thought they were doing the right thing by staying together for the sake of their kids. Somehow, they missed the fact that their kids were never home. They did everything they could to avoid being around their parents.

My eyes fell on my car. I had totally forgotten to ask Mom if she had any idea when we could get it fixed. I was sure the tow truck alone had cost a small fortune. I made a mental note to refuse my allowance this week. If Mom even offered it. She might not have enough cash after the tow truck expense. I turned back to the Sandersons. I could see them in the downstairs window now. Maybe they were right to stay together. At least they didn't have money problems to worry about.

My parents hadn't tried to stay together. I didn't even know my dad. According to Mom, he'd left right after he found out she was pregnant. She said being a teen parent was too much for him to handle. Like it was easy for her? She did the best she could, and I did my best not to complain when I couldn't have the things other kids my age had. Grandma and Grandpa had surprised me with the car for my birthday, and Mom had started giving me an allowance to cover gas money.

I sort of zoned out, but something moved by the bushes. At first, I thought maybe it was a bear. We had a resident black bear that liked to go through our trash sometimes, but then I remembered it was February. The bear usually only came around during the summer. I squinted to get a better look. That was when he stepped into full view. Green Eyes. Alex. We stared at each other, neither of us moving.

I didn't know what scared me more—the fact that he was standing there watching me or the fact that I wasn't calling the cops on him.

Chapter 7

Alex took out his phone and started texting. My cell vibrated on my nightstand. "You've got to be kidding." I shook my head at him and went for my phone. I flipped it open.

"Come outside."

I didn't want to text him back. He might take it as me talking to him. So, I flipped the phone shut again and went back to the window. He stared up at me. I slammed the window closed and pulled the curtains together. I let out a deep breath. This had to stop.

I didn't sleep well at all. I kept having nightmares about rats with green eyes. They chased me throughout the house, and all I had to defend myself was a stupid trash can. I was actually glad when the sun came up. I threw the covers off and got dressed. Mom was already drinking her morning coffee in the living room. We never sat at the kitchen table. Every meal happened in front of the TV. Some people may think that's weird, but it worked for us.

"You're up early," Mom said, putting a waffle on a plate for me.

"Couldn't sleep." I sat down next to her and saw she was watching the news. Normally, I'd change the channel immediately, but the reporter was talking about a rabid deer. I turned up the volume.

"Last night a deer terrorized the animals at Stanton Farm, leaving nothing but destruction everywhere it went." The camera panned out, showing a broken fence and patches of grass covered in a reddish black substance that could only be dried blood.

"Ugh," Mom said, "turn that off." She reached for the remote, but I moved it away.

"Hang on."

"The deer is assumed to be rabid or suffering from some other disease, as its stomach was extremely swollen and its mouth was dripping thick saliva," the reporter continued. "Cameramen were able to get these close-up shots." The screen switched to still pictures of the deer. The first one was of the deer's side. All bloated and discolored. That was bad enough, but the next one was the deer's face. Blood was caked on its cheek and white foam oozed from its mouth. I could just make out two stumps on its head. I turned away in disgust, thankful that I hadn't touched my waffle yet.

"Footage indicated that the deer was most likely hit by a car. It runs with a severe limp in its right leg, and there's a definite gash across its shoulder." That got my attention. I whipped my head back toward the TV. A video of the deer half running, half hobbling through the farmer's field was on the screen.

"Oh, God," I gasped. "I think that's the deer I hit."

Mom took another sip of coffee. "Impossible, honey. But speaking of the deer, your car is going to the body shop today."

I forced myself to look away from the TV. "Can we afford that right now?" I'd expected to be without a car for a while. Like months, not a few days.

"We'll manage." She moved her waffle around on her plate, avoiding my stare.

"You don't want me taking the bus to school, do you?"

She put her fork down and laid her hands on her lap. "After you had to call the police because of that boy following you around... well, I'll feel better knowing you're not taking a bus that he could get on, too."

"I could get rides with Melodie or Matt." At least, I hoped Matt was still up for giving me rides.

"I thought about that, but what if they're busy? I don't want you getting stuck at school or having to take the bus." She brushed her hands across her pants. "I've already made the arrangements with the body shop. I'll drop your car off on my way to work today. The mechanic said it would be okay to drive it that short distance."

"How will you get to work?"

"Martha said she'd pick me up at the body shop and take me to the office. She even offered to drive me home after work, too." Martha was the only person at the office that Mom actually liked.

"You don't need to do all that. I can take the car to the body shop."

"Absolutely not. The car will have to be there for a few days, so you'd need a ride home. And besides, you're busy today."

"I am?" I didn't remember her asking me to do any chores around the house today. Saturdays were usually my lazy days.

"Did you forget you volunteered to help rebuild the community center? You said you needed more community service to put on your college applications next fall."

"Ugh, I completely forgot." I looked at my sweater and favorite comfy jeans. Not exactly construction site appropriate. I'd be devastated if my favorite lounging outfit got paint splattered on it or torn on a nail. I checked my watch. "I should go change."

"And I should get moving if I'm going to drop the car off before work." Mom grabbed her car keys from her purse by the door and tossed them to me. "Be careful. And look out for rabid deer." She smiled.

"Funny. Really funny." As soon as she left, I focused on the TV again.

The farmer was being interviewed. "It killed two of my sheep. Just attacked them. There's definitely something wrong with that deer. Something really wrong."

It couldn't be the same deer. Could it? I sighed and turned off the TV. I had to get changed. I put on a pair of old faded jeans and a long sleeved t-shirt I got at the one and only 5K race I ever ran. Stupid college applications. Why did they insist on their students being well-rounded? I layered Grandpa's old plaid coat over it. He used to leave it here for working around the house in the winter. But then his back started acting up, and he stopped doing work for us, so I had claimed the jacket for shoveling snow and things like that. Thankfully, we were having the mildest winter in a long time and hadn't had a snowstorm in over a month.

Melodie knocked on the door. We'd planned to walk to the community building together. I'd conveniently forgotten to tell Mom about that. I'd be home before her, so she'd never know.

"Why didn't you call me last night?" she asked the second I opened the door. I knew she wasn't going to let me answer, so I locked up while she ranted. "I stayed up until two A.M. Do you see the bags under my eyes? Not pretty. I used half a bottle of concealer, and I still look awful."

"You don't even wear makeup." Melodie had never worn makeup. Well once, but that was on Halloween. She hated the feel of it on her face.

"Fine, but I thought about it." She elbowed me, her hands shoved in her coat pockets. "So, what happened? I want details. Were you too exhausted from making out to call me?"

I wished. "Not exactly."

"Please, tell me you guys kissed. It's physically impossible to not have kissed after the number of dates you two have had."

"Trust me, it's not impossible."

She looked at the ground and shook her head. "Spill."

"Remember that guy I told you about? The one who was following me?"

"Did you kiss *him*?"

"What? No! Would you focus?"

She shrugged. "Sorry."

"Okay, well, his name is Alex. He showed up at the club, and he cornered me in the girls' bathroom. Matt got really mad. I've never seen him that upset. But I convinced him to take me home instead of pounding on Alex."

"You almost had two guys fighting over you?" She had way too much excitement in her voice.

"You're kidding, right? Alex totally ruined my date with Matt. We were this close to kissing." I held my index finger and thumb an inch apart. "And then Alex grabbed my arm and pulled me away from Matt."

"Whoa! So, this Alex guy likes you?"

"If by 'like,' you mean broke into my house, trashed my room, and left a dead rat in my closet, then yes, he likes me."

Melodie stopped short. "He did what?"

I nodded, not about to repeat any of that.

"You're the only one I've told. My mom thinks the rat got in my room because it was such a mess. I tried straightening it up before she saw it, but then I found the rat and… well, Mom and Matt helped me get rid of it."

Melodie squeezed her head in her hands. "Information overload, Jodi. What are you going to do?"

"I don't know. I tried calling the cops on him, but he found a way around that. I'm not sure there's anything I can do to stop him."

We turned down the next block.

"What does he want? Has he told you?"

"Yeah. He said he wants to talk to me."

"So, maybe you should talk to him. It might be the only way to get him to leave you alone. I could come with you if you want."

"He wants to talk to me alone. He said we needed privacy."

"No way. After all he's done to you, you can't talk to him by yourself. It's crazy."

"I know. But what else am I supposed to do?"

We reached the community center and walked inside. There were volunteers everywhere. Who knew this many people would willingly give up a Saturday to fix an old, falling-down building?

A man carrying a clipboard greeted us. "Names?"

"Jodi Marshall." He flipped through his list and checked off my name.

"Melodie Sinclair."

"I'm Mike, but you can call me Chief. Have either of you girls done any construction before?"

We shook our heads.

"No problem. Most of the volunteers we get don't have experience." He looked around. "I'll need one of you to help remove the rusty nails and the other to sweep up the sawdust."

"I'll sweep," Melodie said.

Mike, or Chief as he wanted to be called—although I doubted anyone really used his nickname, pointed to a broom in the corner. "Have at it." Melodie waved to me and went to work. "Okay, so hammers are over there on the table. You do know how to remove a nail, right?"

"I've done it a few times."

"Great. Have fun."

"Fun. Sure." I grabbed a hammer from the table and brought it to the first of many boards. It wasn't hard to pull the nails, and I got into a pretty good rhythm after a while.

"Look out!" someone yelled.

I'd heard that anytime someone yells at a construction site, you're supposed to drop what you're doing and cover your head. So, I dropped my hammer and threw my arms up, shielding my head.

I heard a sickening thud. Not at all the sound a hammer would make falling on wood. I uncovered my head and looked down. The hammer had fallen on a squirrel.

"Ooh," Mike said. "Well, this is why animals shouldn't be on jobsites." He put his hands on his hips and looked around. "Someone want to clean this mess up?"

I watched the blood pool on the floor. "I-I didn't mean to hurt it. I didn't even know it was there."

Mike waved it off. "Don't sweat it. Tommy over there should've yelled 'squirrel' instead of 'look out' when it ran out from behind those boxes. Not your fault at all. In fact, you did the right thing protecting your head. Smart girl."

Not my fault? I'd dropped a hammer on the poor thing. How many animals was I going to injure or kill this week?

Mike pointed to my hammer on the ground. "You better get that before the squirrel bleeds on it anymore. You can rinse it off in the portable sink we have in the next room. I'll get one of the guys to get rid of the squirrel for you."

I nodded and bent down to get the hammer. I didn't take my eyes off the squirrel. I felt terrible. Mom and I always fed the squirrels in our yard. We loved watching them with their bushy tails and tiny paws. I felt the coldness of the hammer and closed my fist around it, stabbing myself in the side of my pointer finger with the last nail I'd removed from a board. "Ow!" I yanked my hand back, dripping blood.

"You okay?" Mike asked, looking completely panicked. "I had you sign a release form, right?" He flipped through his clipboard. "Oh, good. It's here." He sighed. "Come on over to the medical kit. We've got antiseptic and some other stuff."

I followed him to a card table set up by the door. He opened a red medical kit and rummaged through it.

"Hey, Mike," another guy called. "Where's this squirrel you want me to take care of?"

Without looking, Mike pointed to the area where I'd been working. "Over there. Right by the hammer on the ground."

I applied some pressure to my finger, trying to stop the bleeding.

"There's nothing here but a hammer and some blood," the guy said.

"What?" Mike and I exchanged a glance and walked over to the guy. "Tommy, I don't have time for games. I've got to—" He stopped and stared at the ground. Tommy was holding the hammer, and the only thing on the floor was the pool of blood from the squirrel.

"Where did it go?" I asked.

Mike shrugged. "Guess someone else picked it up already." He turned back to me, dismissing the squirrel. "You should go get that finger checked out by a doctor. Rusty nails can mean tetanus."

"I'm pretty sure I got that shot in September, before school started, but I'll double-check after I finish here."

Mike considered it for a second and then handed me a Band-Aid. "All right. We've got a lot of work to do here, so I'll let you stay. But I need you to promise me that you'll go to the doctor as soon as you're done here."

"I promise."

"Oh, and I'll need to you to sign another form for me. An accident report, stating that you refused immediate medical attention."

Boy, this guy was afraid of lawsuits. "Sure. No problem." Of course, I wasn't sure how I was going to sign since the cut was on my right hand, my writing hand.

Someone screamed. We all turned to see what had happened. Melodie shrieked and pointed at a volunteer, a middle-aged guy who was swatting at his shoulder. He had a brownish lump on him. The lump moved, giving us a better view of its matted fur. The bloody squirrel was digging its claws into the guy's back. Foam sprayed from the squirrel's mouth as it sank its teeth into the guy's neck.

Chapter 8

I didn't know why, but I grabbed a coat off the table and threw it over the guy's head. Melodie and Mike were yelling at me, but I couldn't even process what they were saying. All I cared about was getting that squirrel off this guy's neck. He fell to the floor, gripping a lump under the coat. He had the squirrel. With a sickening ripping sound, which could only be the sound of his flesh tearing, he pried the squirrel off himself. He cried out, almost dropping the coat and squirrel. I reached for a toolbox on the floor and opened it wide.

"Here!" I yelled over his screams. "Put it in here."

He held the coat over the toolbox and dropped the squirrel inside. I snapped the box shut, locked it, and backed away like it was a bomb.

The squirrel chattered and must have been going crazy locked up in there, because he was actually moving the toolbox, even with the tools in it. I wasn't sure how the squirrel even fit in there with all the hammers, screwdrivers, and other things inside. If it didn't quit moving around, it might end stabbing itself to death.

"Jake, are you okay?" Mike asked.

Jake had his hands pressed to the back of his neck. Blood spilled out around them, soaking his beige Carhartt jacket. His eyes rolled back, and he collapsed, taking out a table on his way down.

"Someone call 911!" Mike yelled.

Melodie already had her phone out and was giving an address to the operator. "They're on their way."

Mike was practically cradling Jake in his lap. His jacket was off, and he was using it to soak up the blood. "Okay, everyone else clear out. We're done for today. Leave your tools where they are."

"What about the squirrel?" I pointed my foot at the toolbox.

A kid from school—Brian something or other—said, "My dad's a vet. I'll call him."

"Just kill the thing." Tommy grunted. "Look what it did to Jake."

"No," Melodie and I protested. Mike and Tommy looked at us like we were crazy.

I was still shaking, but I couldn't stand the thought of Tommy or Mike smashing the squirrel with a hammer. "You can't kill it. It's a squirrel. It got spooked or something."

"You call that getting spooked?" Tommy asked.

"It probably freaked out because it got in here and couldn't find a way out. Animals act really weird when they feel trapped," I insisted.

Brian flipped his phone shut. "My dad's just around the corner. He said he'd be here in a minute."

That made me feel a little better. At least if the vet decided to kill the squirrel, he'd do it in a humane way. One that didn't involve a hammer or a two-by-four.

Sirens blared in the background, and brakes squealed as the ambulance pulled up to the building. We stood around staring at each other as the paramedics took Jake out on a stretcher. They said he'd lost a lot of blood and would need a series of rabies shots, but he'd be okay. Mike's brow was sweating, probably because he was going to have to fill out another accident report. I swear I overheard him ask Tommy if he thought Jake would sue.

Brian's father got there right after the paramedics left with Jake.

"Luke Hemshaw, veterinarian." He reached out and shook Mike's trembling hand.

Mike pointed to the toolbox. "It's in there."

Dr. Hemshaw carefully opened the box. He gasped when he saw the squirrel and quickly slammed the toolbox shut again, which made the thing start chattering like crazy. He reached into his medical bag, muttering, "This is impossible. It can't be."

"What?" I asked. "Does it have a disease or something?"

He turned and looked at me. "No, it's not sick. It's dead."

"It isn't dead," Mike argued. "It attacked Jake. Ripped the back of his neck right off."

I felt the two bites of waffle I'd eaten for breakfast coming back up.

Dr. Hemshaw took a syringe from his bag. "I'm going to sedate it and show you what I mean."

Sedate it? He just said it was dead. Melodie looped her arm through mine, squeezing me in fear. I watched Dr. Hemshaw open the toolbox just enough to stick the needle inside. After a few seconds, he pulled the needle out and put a latex glove on his hand. He reached into the toolbox and pulled out the squirrel. It was covered in blood, Jake's blood. Dr. Hemshaw turned the squirrel over in his hand. "Have a look." No one wanted a better look at the thing. We stood still. Finally, Dr. Hemshaw stepped forward and showed us the squirrel. The back of its head was smashed in from where my hammer had hit it, and its brains were leaking out.

Melodie covered her mouth and ran from the room. Mike wasn't far behind her. I was frozen in place, not able to move or talk.

"There's no possible way this animal is alive." Dr. Hemshaw shook his head. "Yet, it attacked someone, and I had to sedate it." He sighed, unable to make sense of it.

"What are you—?" I gagged, my throat constricting from the sight of the squirrel.

"Sorry." He covered the squirrel's head with his other hand so I couldn't see its brains anymore.

"What are you going to do with it?"

"The only humane thing to do is euthanize it. It's clearly in pain, and it can't survive like this. Another animal would pick it off in a matter of minutes."

I wasn't so sure about that. I'd seen what the squirrel could do, even with the contents of its head spilling out.

Dr. Hemshaw took another syringe from his bag. Taking one last look at the squirrel, he euthanized it. "I'm going to take this to my office, check it for rabies and other diseases so I can let the hospital know how to treat... Jake, is it?"

I nodded as Dr. Hemshaw walked to the door. I was still in a daze. My life couldn't get more bizarre.

"You should really go get that hand looked at," Mike said after Dr. Hemshaw had left. He was writing on his clipboard.

"Yeah, I'll go now. I just need to find a ride. I walked here because my car is in the shop." I thought about the deer and how it had looked dead, but then it got up and ran off. Ran off and terrorized a farm, killing two sheep. The reporter said the deer was probably rabid. Images of the deer popped into my head. It had looked… well, like the squirrel did. Diseased. Dead. What was going on in this town? And why did I always seem to be around when it happened?

"Want me to get one of the guys to drive you?" Mike asked.

"No, that's okay." I didn't know these guys. They seemed nice enough, but Mom would kill me if I got in a car with a strange guy like that. It wasn't like my injury was life-threatening.

"Come on, let's go home." Melodie still looked green.

"I have to get my hand checked out and make sure my tetanus shot is up to date."

"My car's at home. How are you going to get there?"

It was too far to walk to the clinic. "Mom left me her car, but I'm not good at driving stick. I hate to ask, but could we walk to your house and you maybe drive me? You can drop me off if you don't want to wait around for me. I'll call Matt or someone for a ride home."

"Yeah, okay. Maybe the doctor will have something to settle my stomach."

We walked back to Melodie's house, and she ran inside to get the keys to her car. I leaned against the passenger side door. The sun was bright, and it felt good. My entire body was chilled to the core, and not because of the February weather. I heard a noise in the bushes and jolted upright. Dirty blonde hair stuck out from the top of the closest bush.

"Alex?" Normally, I would've been freaked out, but I had had enough for one day. "I can see you. Enough with the games. I'm not in the mood."

He stepped into the open. Finally, we could get this over with. But Melodie came rushing out of the house with the car keys. "Sorry that took so long, I—" She stopped when she saw Alex.

"Melodie, this is Alex, my personal stalker."

He glared at me, not even glancing at Melodie. "Another time." He turned and disappeared behind the bushes.

Melodie unlocked the car. "Get in. Let's get out of here before he comes back."

"He's not coming back." At least not now. He wanted me alone.

We drove to the clinic. Melodie insisted on waiting for me while the doctor examined my finger and checked my files. "It will give me a chance to catch up on all these ancient issues of magazines no one but a doctor would ever subscribe to."

I smiled at her and followed Nurse Bennett into one of the back rooms. I'd known her all my life, which was the only reason she took me in despite the fact that the clinic was closing for the day. She took my blood pressure and then un-bandaged my finger. The cut was deep and embedded with flecks of rust. That couldn't be healthy.

"Jodi, you cut yourself on a rusty nail, didn't you?"

"Yeah, I was helping rebuild the community center this morning."

She put on a pair of gloves, sat down on a swivel chair, and wheeled herself over to me. "Rebuilding the community center, huh?" She took my hand in hers. "Let me guess, college application time is coming up and you're lacking in community service?"

If it hadn't been true, I would've gotten offended. It's not like I was against doing community service. It's just I spent my free time helping Mom around the house. She worked so much. It wasn't easy for her to support the both of us and keep the house clean.

I turned away, not wanting to watch Nurse Bennett remove the rust. Warm blood ran down my finger. She pressed a piece of gauze on the cut and applied pressure. I winced. "Hold this for a second." I took over, not putting anywhere near as much pressure on my hand. The cut on my left finger stung. The stupid thing wouldn't heal. It was bleeding through the Band-Aid again. Now I had a matching pair. Nurse Bennett came back with a tray at the same time Dr. Alvarez came in. She filled him in on my situation.

Dr. Alvarez sat in front of me. "Okay, I'm going to put some dissolving sutures on this finger. It's not that bad, but since you're probably going to want to use your hand in the next few weeks, this will help it heal quicker."

"Thanks," I said.

He worked quickly. "There, that should do." He put his instruments down on the tray, and Nurse Bennett carried them out of the room. As Dr. Alvarez removed his gloves, his eyes fell on the bloody Band-Aid on my left finger. "Another cut? Let's get a fresh Band-Aid for that." He changed the bandage, getting some of my blood on him in the process.

"Sorry," I said.

"No worries. We have disinfectant soap, and exposure like that is pretty low risk. It happens a lot." He went to the sink. "We don't need to worry about—" He gagged, like he was choking on water.

I hopped down from the examination table. "Dr. Alvarez, are you okay?"

He reached a soapy hand to his chest and fell to the floor, his head landing at my feet. I jumped back, knocking over the tray and the chair. Nurse Bennett knocked on the door and peeked her head in. "Is everything—" her eyes darted from the mess to me to Dr. Alvarez. "What happened?" She rushed to him, but looked surprisingly calm.

"I-I don't know. He was washing his hands." I pointed to the faucet, which was still running. "And then he started choking like he was having trouble breathing. I asked him if he was okay, but he clutched his chest and collapsed."

Nurse Bennett bent down and listened for sounds of breathing. She pressed two fingers to the side of his neck. "Call 911 and have Helen get me the AED now." I grabbed my cell from my back pocket, but Nurse Bennett pointed to the phone on the wall. "Use the landline." I grabbed it and dialed.

"911. What is your emergency?"

"Dr. Alvarez collapsed. I think he had a heart attack. We're at the clinic on Seventh Street. Nurse Bennett said they're going to use something called an AED." I had no idea what that was.

"Foxmoor Clinic on Seventh Street?"

"Yes. Please, send someone," I pleaded before hanging up the phone.

"What can I do?" I asked.

"Jodi, please go in the waiting room. I need room to operate the AED." Her voice was calm and composed, as Helen rushed in with what looked like a black box in both hands. She must have overheard Nurse Bennett ask for the AED.

I nodded and stepped around her. Melodie was reading a magazine, completely oblivious to what was going on. "Hey, did you know eating corn makes your stomach look fat?" she blurted the second she saw me. She flipped the page before doing a double take in my direction.

I broke down, tears streaming down my face.

Melodie put the magazine aside. "What happened? Do you have to get rabies shots? They don't have to amputate your hand or anything, do they?"

I grabbed a tissue from the receptionist desk. "It's Dr. Alvarez. He collapsed. I think he had a heart attack."

"Seriously?" Melodie asked. "Like an actual heart attack?"

I nodded and threw my tissue in the garbage. "I called 911. Nurse Bennett is trying to help him."

"Come, sit down." Melodie patted the seat next to her. I didn't want to talk anymore. It was way too scary. Melodie seemed to sense that because, for once, she wasn't grilling me with questions.

We sat there in silence, watching the paramedics rush into the waiting room. I pointed to the examination room. "He's back there." Two of them went on ahead while the third, a guy in his twenties, held back for a minute.

"Everyone okay out here?"

"Yeah. Shaken up, but okay. I was with him when it happened."

"Can you tell me exactly what happened? How he acted? What he did?"

More questions. Everyone kept asking me to relive the scariest moments in my life.

"I'm sorry," he said. "I know this is tough, but anything you can tell me may help save his life."

I took at deep breath and swallowed hard. "He was putting a new bandage on my finger and I bled on him, so he went to the sink to clean it off, and then he started to choke. He reached for his chest and fell to the floor." I was breathing heavily, but managed to hold back the tears.

The paramedic nodded. "Thank you." He stood up, probably to join the others in the back room, but Helen came into the waiting room. Her face was blank. We stared at her, waiting for the word on Dr. Alvarez. She shook her head and stepped aside as the paramedics wheeled a stretcher into the back room. The silence was deafening. A few minutes later, the paramedics brought the bed back out, but this time there was a covered body lying on it.

"He's dead." I barely recognized my own voice.

Chapter 9

The paramedic we'd been talking to practically pushed us out the door. If he was worried about us being traumatized at the sight of a dead body, he was a little late. I'd seen more dead bodies in the past couple days than a mortician. The deer—I still swore he'd been dead—the rat, the squirrel, and now Dr. Alvarez. But I still let him usher us outside. I had to practically beg him to let us go home on our own. He wanted us to call a cab or one of our parents, but neither Mel nor I had money on us and our parents were working. I didn't want to give the paramedic time to change his mind, so we hopped into Melodie's car and got out of there.

Melodie was in a daze and not paying much attention to anything. I didn't have the heart to tell her she was only doing twenty-five miles an hour in a fifty zone. I left her to her thoughts, letting her deal with Dr. Alvarez's death in her own way.

I stared out the window, watching the scenery crawl past. We came to an intersection, and the light turned red. Melodie didn't seem to notice. Traffic was coming from both sides of us. "Mel, the light!" I yelled. She slammed her foot on the brake, tires screeching as the car came to a stop inches from a white pickup truck. It had come so close to barreling into us. My hands were pushing against the glove compartment. It was a knee-jerk reaction to our almost collision. One of those stupid things you do even though you know it won't help. All it did was hurt my cut-up fingers.

Melodie leaned her head back on the seat and cried. "I'm so sorry. I was completely zoned out. I didn't even see the light change."

I doubted she'd seen the light at all. "It's okay. No one was hurt. And after the day we've had, it's a miracle we're both still sane."

The light turned green, but Melodie didn't move. "Hey, would you mind driving? I'm not feeling all that great."

Cars honked behind us. They were not going to be happy about us getting out and switching seats, but I didn't think Melodie should drive anymore. "Sure. No problem." We changed seats to the sound of more honks and a few choice words from the SUV behind us. I smiled and waved at the driver. Mom always said nothing annoys a jerk more than you being nice to him. Apparently, it was true. He started yelling comments that didn't make much sense at all. I guessed I'd confused him with my reaction.

I put the car in drive and got through the light just before it turned red again. The driver of the SUV waved his fist out the window at us. Even with everything going on, I was able to find some humor in that. I drove down Fifth Street and decided to take the back roads the rest of the way home. I was halfway down Willow Drive when I saw the deer. My deer. Or at least the one I'd hit. No doubt about it. It looked… well, dead. I pulled over and jumped out of the car.

"Jodi!" Melodie yelled, lowering her window as I ran to her side of the car. "What are you doing?"

"The deer. The one I hit. It's right there." I pointed to the trees. The deer stood still, watching me.

"So? What are you going to do, ask it to hop in the car so we can take it to the vet?" Melodie squinted at it. "Ugh, that thing is nasty. What's wrong with it?"

"It was hit by a car, remember?"

"Yeah, but look at it. Its skin is practically falling off." She leaned out the window and threw up all over the side of the road. I turned away. I never could stomach the sight of someone else puking.

The deer stepped closer to me, and I saw that Melodie was right. Its skin was sagging, and its fur was falling out in clumps. I didn't know much about rabies, but I had a feeling this deer's problem made rabies look like a jog in the park.

Melodie moaned and pulled her head back through the window. "Can we please go?"

"Yeah." I headed back to the car, keeping my eyes on the deer. It watched me, creeping closer with every step I took toward the car. "Sorry, buddy, but I already have a stalker, and one's all I can take right now." I got in the car and slammed the door shut. The deer kept coming.

"Go!" Melodie screamed.

I threw the car into drive and floored the gas. In the rearview mirror, I saw the deer dash into the road and stand there, staring after us. "Now, that was really creepy."

"Don't talk about it. I have to get the image of that thing out of my head before I throw up again."

I sped the rest of the way home. I didn't even care if I got pulled over. I wanted to get away from the deer. I wished I could get away from all the awful stuff that was happening in my life, but for right now I'd settle for losing the deer. I pulled into the driveway and turned off the engine. I leaned forward, resting my head on the steering wheel. Melodie wasn't in any shape to drive home, so we just sat.

The silence was interrupted by the buzzing of my cell phone in my pocket. I pulled it out. A text from Matt read, "Be by at five to pick you up." It was three-fifteen already. I wasn't sure how that had happened.

"Is that Matt?" Melodie asked, her eyes still closed.

"Yeah. We're supposed to go out tonight. He said he'd pick me up at five."

Melodie leaned forward and opened her eyes. "Are you really going out with him after everything that's happened today?"

She had a point, but my other option was to sit at home and think about all the awful things I'd been through today. "I need to clear my head. Forget about… everything."

"And what better way than by making out with the boy you like?" Melodie said, sounding more like herself.

I laughed, and it felt really good. "Yeah, that would cheer me up."

We laughed until our stomachs hurt. Not because what I'd said was funny, but because we needed to laugh. When I finally stopped, I flipped open my phone. "I should call him and tell him I'm running a little late." Melodie continued to giggle in her seat.

"Hey," Matt answered. "I wasn't expecting a call back. I thought you might still be doing your community service gig."

Did everyone but me remember I'd signed up for that? "No, we got out early. It's kind of a long story."

"Well, then you're in luck. It takes surprisingly little time for me to look amazing."

I laughed. "Is that so?"

"Yup. Good genes I guess. So, tell me what happened."

I sighed, not sure if Melodie could handle listening to me recount the events of the day. "Um—"

"Oh, just tell him." Melodie sighed. "If you don't, he'll ask me, and I can't handle talking about it."

"There was an incident at the community center. A squirrel got in the building, and it kind of freaked out. Someone yelled to watch out, and I thought I was about to get clobbered with a board or something, so I dropped my hammer and covered my head."

"Seems like a smart thing to do," he said. "Unless you dropped the hammer on your foot."

"No, not on my foot. On the squirrel."

"Ouch, that had to hurt it."

"You could say that. We all thought it was dead, but then it attacked a guy."

"Attacked him? Like starting clawing at him?"

"More like ripping his neck to shreds with its teeth." My stomach churned, and I was grateful I'd missed lunch. I wasn't eating much at all these days.

"Are you pranking me?"

"I wish. The thing went ballistic. But we trapped the squirrel, and the vet came and... put it to sleep."

"Sounds like an exciting day."

"That was just the morning." I told him about my finger and Dr. Alvarez and the deer. I blurted it all out, barely pausing to breathe.

He was completely silent on the other end. My eyes darted back and forth. Had he hung up? I wouldn't blame him if he thought I was crazy or a magnet for trouble. It certainly seemed that way. Finally, he spoke.

"I'm coming over now. We don't have to go out. We'll stay in and talk until you feel better."

"No, I'm okay. Really. Besides, Melodie is with me. She'll keep me company until our date."

"Are you sure you still want to go out? Because we don't have to. I'll completely understand if you want to cancel."

"Actually, I think I need to go out. And I really want to see you."

"Good." He paused. It was one of those awkward moments at the start of the relationship where neither person knows what to say and worries about freaking the other one out. "I, uh, want to see you, too."

"Good. Then five?"

"Five. See you then." He hung up.

"Want to come inside?" I asked Mel.

"Depends. You got anything that will erase my memory? Just for the past six hours or so?"

"If I do, you'll have to fight me for it."

We went inside. Mom would be home soon, and I had to get ready for my date, but there was still time for some cookie dough ice cream to numb the pain of the day. Without a word, we headed straight for the kitchen. Melodie got the spoons, while I grabbed two pints from the freezer. Mel was strictly a chocolate girl. I put them on the table, and Mel stuck the spoons right in. Times like this called for eating right out the container—no need to be bothered with bowls. I scooped a big spoonful and put it in my mouth, letting it dissolve on my tongue.

"Much better," Melodie said, with her mouth full.

We made it through half our containers before Mom walked in on us. "Girls, girls, girls," she scolded, grabbing a spoon from the drawer. "Don't you know ice cream can't solve your problems?" She took the rainbow sprinkles from the cabinet and dumped them right into the containers. "Ice cream and sprinkles, on the other hand, can solve just about anything." She took a heaping spoonful of chocolate—like Melodie, she wasn't a fan of cookie dough. She'd been taking a lot of heat from her boss. Apparently, his boss was on *his* case, and he was taking it out on Mom. I hated that. She worked so hard for the little money she made. I knew she only kept the job for the medical benefits. There was no way she'd put up with her boss' idiotic behavior if she didn't have to take care of me. The thought brought another big helping of cookie dough to my lips.

We had almost finished the ice cream when we heard a noise upstairs. "What was that?" Melodie asked, looking at the ceiling. "Did you guys get a cat or something?"

"No," Mom said. "Jodi, did you leave any windows open?" Even in the dead of winter, I liked fresh air. I was about to say no when I realized what had made the noise.

"Um, you know, I think I did. I bet the wind knocked my stuff off my desk again. I'll go close it."

Mom and Melodie got back to the ice cream while I headed upstairs. I went slowly, making sure I didn't make any noise on the stairs. I didn't want to let Alex know I was coming. I had to catch him off guard, see what he was looking for in my room and whether he'd left me any more presents.

I hesitated when I got to the door. I'd left it open, but it was shut now. Apparently, Alex needed privacy for whatever it was he was doing in there. I wrapped my fingers around the doorknob, being careful not to let it jiggle at all. I held my breath and silently counted to three before swinging the door wide open.

Alex threw himself down on the other side of the bed. I was a little disappointed. For a stalker, he wasn't very stealthy.

"Looking for something? Or are you planting another dead rat in my room?"

He stood up and brushed off his shirt. "Sorry about the rat, but I had to make sure I was right about you. You wouldn't talk to me, so I had to resort to other methods of confirming my suspicions."

"Confirming your suspicions? *You're* the one who's sneaking around and acting all suspicious."

"I'm doing what I have to. If you would've talked to me in the first place, you could've saved us both a lot of trouble."

"I could've saved us a lot of trouble?" I lowered my voice, realizing I was talking way too loud. If Mom or Melodie heard me, they'd come upstairs to see who I was talking to. I couldn't exactly explain having Alex in my room. "You're the one causing all the trouble here. And how did you get in my room? Do you pick locks?"

"You're wasting time with all these questions."

I looked at the clock on my nightstand. "You're right about that. I have a date to get ready for."

Alex's face turned cold. "You can't go out with Matt."

"Is that what this is about? Because Matt and I *are* dating, and you don't really get a say in the matter. So, if you've got some kind of bizarre crush on me, you're going to have to get over it."

"Don't flatter yourself, Jodi." He turned toward the window and gazed out it. "Like I've been trying to tell you, we need to talk."

"Then, talk." I held my arms out at my sides. "We're alone. You got your way. So, talk."

"Do you know what's been happening to you? The things with the animals?" He turned back around and faced me.

"What do you know about that?"

"The deer you hit. It died. Until you bled on it and brought it back to life."

"Brought—"

"And the rat I left in your room. It was dead, Jodi. Until you bled on it. Just like the squirrel."

"Stop!" My voice was getting loud again.

"And then Dr. Alvarez. You weren't expecting that one, I'm sure. The cut on your finger infected him. Your blood poisoned him, turned his own blood toxic and killed him."

"Stop! I didn't kill anyone!"

"Jodi!" Mom yelled. I heard her feet on the stairs. "Are you okay?"

I whipped my head toward the door and then back at Alex. Mom couldn't find him here. I rushed over to him and grabbed his arm, shoving him toward my closet. "Get in, don't move, and stay quiet." I shut the door, not sure what was happening to me. I mean, what kind of girl hides her stalker in her closet?

Chapter 10

"Jodi?" Mom walked into the room and looked around. "Who were you talking to?"

I reached into my back pocket and took out my phone, trying to act like it had been in my hand this whole time. "Some guy from school. He keeps asking me out, and he can't take a hint. He's really getting on Matt's nerves."

Mom frowned. "Honey, just because you're seeing Matt doesn't mean you should be mean to other boys. Especially ones who like you. Think of how you'd feel if the guy you liked was dating someone else and kept turning you down."

I wasn't in the mood for a Mom lecture, so I nodded. "You're right. I'll try to be nicer to him."

She walked over and kissed my head. "That's my girl. Melodie said Matt's coming by at five. You better hurry up and get ready."

I smiled and watched her leave. As soon as she was out of sight, I shut the door and headed for the closet. Alex was already stepping out of it.

I crossed my arms in front of me. "What did you mean about my blood poisoning Dr. Alvarez?"

He walked over to my bed and sat down. "You told Mr. Quimby your birthday was December eighth."

"So?" I didn't see how my birthday mattered.

"So, you were born under the thirteenth sign of the zodiac. Under Ophiuchus. That makes you different. It makes you dangerous."

"Dangerous." I almost laughed. I was the least dangerous person I knew; I hardly raised my voice. At least I hadn't before I met Alex. "You don't know anything about me."

"I know you have Gorgon blood running through your veins. I know that blood has the ability to bring the dead back to life. And make the living fall dead." I started to protest, but he grabbed my left hand just below the Band-Aid. "How long did it take for Dr. Alvarez to collapse?"

I didn't answer.

"I'm guessing not long at all. Just long enough for your blood to work its way through his system, shutting down every part of his body."

Tears welled up in my eyes. "I called 911, and the nurse used that AED thing almost immediately."

"It doesn't matter. Modern medicine is useless against Gorgon blood."

"What do you mean Gorgon blood? Gorgon like as in Medusa?" I pulled my hand back from his.

"Weren't you paying attention to Mr. Quimby's lesson? The whole reason he focused on mythology this semester was for you. To teach you about who you really are."

"How long has he been teaching at Lambert?"

"He started the same time you did. In September. He needed to be able to watch over you. We knew you'd be coming into your powers soon. It was the absolute worst time for your mom to stop homeschooling you. You were going to be around regular people all the time. We had to get someone in that school to protect you. And to protect others *from* you."

I squeezed my hands against my head, ignoring how much it hurt my cuts. "No, this is crazy." He stood up and placed his hands on top of mine. His touch was gentle, sympathetic.

"I know what you're feeling." I looked up at him. "I'm like you, Jodi. We're necromancers."

"Necromancers bring the dead back to life. They don't kill the living." I'd read enough books to know that. All the books I'd read had been fiction, but I didn't mention that.

"We're part of a special group of necromancers called the Ophi. We have more power than a normal necromancer because of the Gorgon blood in our bodies."

"Ophi like as in Ophiuchus?"

"Yes. Ophiuchuses doesn't have the same ring to it." He smiled. "So, we shorten the term. There's a group of us in this area. That club you went to the other night, Serpentarius—that's one of our places."

"Your places?"

"We have to make a living somehow, right? I guess we could work as hired hit men, but that's not exactly on the up and up."

"And you call raising the dead and killing non-Ophi people on the up and up?"

He laughed. "Not really, but that's why we formed our group. We have safe places, like Serpentarius, and you wouldn't believe how much money that place brings in."

"Why does that name sound so familiar?" I knew I'd heard it before, and not just when Matt took me to the club.

"It's another name for the constellation Ophiuchus. He holds the constellation Serpens in the sky. So, he's known as the Serpent Bearer or Serpentarius. It was all in Mr. Quimby's lesson."

"Okay, see, that right there is proof I'm not one of your Ophi. I hate snakes. I always have."

"Please, do you really think a snake knew how to use herbs to heal people? That myth was created to cover up the truth. To hide it from non-Ophi. We have Gorgon blood in us. The same blood that was given to Ophiuchus by Athena."

"Mr. Quimby said there were two vials of blood."

"Yes. The blood from Medusa's right side had the power to restore life."

"And the blood from her left side was poisonous." I wondered if Alex was telling the truth about Mr. Quimby and the lesson being for my benefit. "You said Mr. Quimby told you to follow me. That he took the job at Lambert to keep an eye on me." He nodded. "That means he's an Ophi, too."

"Yes. He wants me to take you to one of our safe places."

"Serpentarius?"

"No, that place wouldn't be safe enough for you. There are too many humans. The Ophi there know how to keep their distance and not hurt anyone. They usually don't even work on nights they let humans into the club, which isn't very often."

I shook my head, trying to process all this. Matt's cousin worked there. "So, there are humans who work there, too?"

"Yes. On different days, but the place I'm taking you is a sort of school so we can teach you how to control your power. It's triggered by your emotions and transferred through your blood and... other bodily fluids." Oh yuck! I must have looked horrified because he quickly added, "Like your tears or your saliva. That's why you can't date Matt. If you kiss him, you'll kill him."

I remembered what Alex had told me in the bathroom at Serpentarius. *One kiss and he's history. He'll be as stone cold as the nurse who examined you after your accident.* The nurse. I'd forgotten about her. "I killed Ms. Steingall. She looked in my eyes with that flashlight thing. It made my eyes tear. She apologized for making me cry and wiped my cheek."

Alex put his hand on my shoulder. "You didn't know. I should have gotten to you sooner."

My legs felt weak, so I walked over to the bed and sat down. My shoulders slumped forward.

"I promise it will get better. We can help you, Jodi. We'll show you how to control your power and even put it to good use."

I wasn't sure how something so awful could be put to good use. But then I thought of something. "You mean I could bring things back to life? Animals and even people? And they'd be normal. No foaming mouths or bloody skulls."

"They'd be exactly how they were when they died. Maybe some blood and guts, depending on how they died."

"But they'd be themselves?"

"Yes. They'd be themselves."

I wasn't sure if I believed him, but I wanted to. I couldn't deny the things that had happened. The deer. The nurse. The rat. The squirrel. The doctor. I was the thing they'd all had in common. Me. As much as I didn't want to admit it, it had to be true. I'd been responsible for what happened to all of them; I'd done it without knowing. Learning to control this power wasn't a bad idea.

"Where is this safe place—the school?"

"I can take you there now. Pack a bag, and we'll go."

I stood up. "Pack a bag? Where exactly are we going?"

He stepped closer, taking my hand in his. When had he gone from psycho stalker to... sweet? "Jodi, you can't stay here anymore. Your powers are active now. If you're around regular people, you'll be putting their lives in danger."

Okay, forget sweet. He wanted me to leave home. Leave Melodie, Matt, and Mom. I couldn't do that. "You can't just rip me out of my life. What would I tell my mom? How would I explain any of this to her?"

"You can't." He let go of me and walked to the window. "We have to sneak away. It's the only way."

"Not say a word? My mom will call the cops. She'll have a search party looking for me. It would break her heart." He turned around and sighed. "Not to mention they'd all be looking for you. Matt and Melodie have both seen you. They'd hunt you down."

"Is that really what you're worried about?" His eyes bored into mine. "Or is it that you don't want to leave your boyfriend?"

I didn't want to leave Matt, but that wasn't it. "I'm not that shallow. I don't need to have a boyfriend. I just can't leave knowing that I'll be hurting all the people who care about me. They wouldn't know what happened to me. They'd assume the worst. That I was dead."

"I can probably arrange for you to call your mom. At least to tell her you're safe." He stepped toward me. "Jodi, please. I'm trying to help you. If you don't come with me, they'll—just trust me, it's easier this way."

What was he trying to say? That I'd end up killing everyone I loved? Or that the other Ophi would come after me?

"I need time to process this. You can't dump it all on me and expect me to run away with you, no questions asked." Okay, so it wasn't exactly no questions asked, but still.

"You want time to say goodbye," Alex said.

I wasn't convinced I was leaving, but if he was going to give me an out, I was going to take it. "Yeah." I lowered my eyes, avoiding his stare.

"Okay. But you have to promise me you won't kiss Matt. You can't go out with him tonight. It's way too risky."

"I have *some* self control. I'll be fine going out with Matt. It's pretty easy not to kiss someone." I'd sure had plenty of practice not kissing Matt.

Alex crossed his arms. "I don't like this at all. I should take you with me right now."

"Take me with you? As in throw me over your shoulder kicking and screaming? Is that really the guy you want to be?"

"Goodbye, Jodi." Alex went to the window and opened it. Finally, I knew how he'd been getting inside my room. "This lock is broken, by the way."

"Good to know." I followed him, watching him crabwalk out onto the slanted roof and shimmy over to the tree. Stopping for a second, he looked like he was going to say something. "Don't even think about telling me to be careful."

He smirked and climbed down the tree. Jumping to the bottom, he disappeared off to the right, heading for the backyard.

"Jodi." Mom knocked on the door. I closed the window before letting Mom in. She took one look at me and gasped. "You're not dressed. Matt will be here any second. You haven't even showered."

"Um…" I couldn't even think of an excuse. The doorbell rang. "Oh no!" I looked around for my towel. "Five minutes. Stall. Please." I grabbed my towel and ran past Mom straight to the bathroom. I jumped in without even letting the water warm up. If I was freezing, I'd get out faster. I splashed cold water all over me, washing my hair like a crazy person. After a quick rinse, I toweled off. With one towel on my head and the other wrapped around me, I dashed to my room.

Melodie was sitting on my bed with an outfit already picked out. "Here. Get dressed and dry your hair. I'll tell Matt you're almost ready."

"Thank you. You're a lifesaver."

"Don't you forget it. My birthday is right around the corner."

"Got it." I nodded. She left, and I threw my clothes on. I used the blow dryer for a whole three minutes. For once, I was happy I had thin hair. It dried quickly. I put on some lip-gloss and looked at my reflection in the mirror. Not great, but not bad. Definitely not kissable—or at least I hoped.

I ran down the stairs, stumbling on the last step. Matt jumped up from the couch when he saw me slip. I reached for the banister and stopped myself from face-planting. "I'm okay." I smiled at Matt. "Would it be okay if we had a small change of plans?"

"Uh, yeah, I guess. What did you have in mind?"

I looped my arm through his. "Let's go out back." I turned to Mom. "We'll be on the bench swing." Mom nodded, narrowing her brows at me. I could tell she wanted to know what was up, but she didn't want to embarrass me in front of Matt.

Melodie, on the other hand, looked like her eyes were going to pop out of their sockets. She rushed over to me, giving Matt a quick smile. "Can I talk to you for a second?" She tugged on my free arm, not giving me a choice. She pulled me into the kitchen. "What are you doing? You are going to completely screw things up with Matt. He likes you, and he's put up with a lot from you. Please, don't tell me you are cancelling your date tonight."

"Weren't you the one who asked me how I could even think about going out tonight after everything that's happened?"

"That was before Matt showed up looking…"

Oh, God. How had I not seen it before? Melodie had a thing for Matt. When I'd met them, they'd said they were friends. They'd grown up together. I never thought Melodie had feelings for him, but looking at her now, there wasn't a doubt in my mind. What kind of friend was I? She'd set us up because it was what *I* wanted. She'd rooted for us because she's a good friend. Unlike me. I felt like dirt.

"Mel—"

"Don't. It was a long time ago. Before I met you. I kissed him once. That was it. He said he didn't think of me that way." She was talking fast, like she had to get it all out before the pain set in. "It's fine. I can't force him to like me. But he *does* like you, and he deserves to be happy."

I didn't know what to say.

"Go. Don't keep him waiting." She gave me a small push toward the living room, but I turned and wrapped her in a hug.

"You're the best friend I could ever ask for."

"Yeah, yeah. Like I said, my birthday's coming. You can thank me with a really big present."

We both laughed, and I went to rescue Matt from time alone with Mom. We headed outside to the bench swing on the back patio. We sat down, and I didn't know where to begin. I had to break up with him. If what Alex had said was true, he'd be in real danger dating me. And now that I knew how Melodie felt… well, I had to end this.

"Matt, listen," I began.

But before I could get any further, he leaned over and kissed me.

Chapter 11

Matt was kissing me! Matt was kissing me! It was everything I thought it would be. I leaned into him, kissing him back. Then, it hit me. Matt was kissing me! Oh, God, no! I pulled back, knowing it was too late.

"I'm sorry," Matt said, the terrified look on my face registering with him. "It's just I've been wanting to do that for days, and well, I had to do it before I lost my nerve."

I stared at him, waiting to see what would happen. But he looked okay. He looked like Matt. For a split second, I thought maybe Alex had been lying. Maybe he really was a crazy stalker guy who just wanted to break Matt and me up. I relaxed, letting go of the tension in my shoulders. I smiled at Matt. "No, I'm sorry. I've been wanting to kiss you, too."

Matt leaned toward me again, and I met him halfway, but before we got our second kiss, his face turned red and he started choking.

No. Please, no. Please, be a coincidence. He could've choked on his gum. But he brought his hands up to his throat. He couldn't breathe. His hand reached for his chest. I watched the life drain out of his eyes, knowing I was the cause of it. He slumped forward, and I caught him in my lap. I didn't know what to do. I couldn't give him mouth to mouth, could I? My mind went into overdrive. Alex said I'd brought the deer, the rat, and the squirrel back to life. Could I bring Matt back?

Tears spilled from my eyes, and I let them soak the back of Matt's neck. I didn't know how my power worked. So far, it had been calling the shots, and that wasn't going too well for me. But I couldn't control myself. Matt was my boyfriend. We'd only gotten one kiss. He was dead, and it was because of me. Because I had been stupid enough to let him kiss me, to kiss him back. I had to try to fix this.

I stared at Matt's limp body in my lap. Nothing was happening. He wasn't jerking back to life the way the deer had. Maybe my tears weren't enough to bring back a human being. Then I remembered I'd bled on the deer. I looked around. If my blood was the source of my power, then I'd have to use it to fix what I'd done. I lifted him off me and rested him on the bench, then got up and dashed to the tool shed. I went straight to the hedge clippers hanging on the wall. Grabbing them, I ran back to the bench.

Matt was gone. I panicked, spinning around in a circle to search the entire backyard. Had Alex seen what I did? Maybe he took Matt before I could bring him back. Or had my tears worked? No, I needed blood. Didn't I? "Matt?" My voice was shaky. "Matt, please, if you can hear me, say something. I can help you. Just tell me where you are."

I had no idea what waking up from the dead would be like for a person. The animals I'd brought back acted crazy, confused. Matt might be feeling the same way. I had to find him and fast. "Matt?" I ran to the bench, looking for signs of where he might have gone. I checked the back door. It was still shut, but that didn't mean he hadn't gone inside. Still, that would be my last option. I couldn't go in there without Matt. Mom and Melodie would ask too many questions that I couldn't answer.

I checked the bushes and the front yard. He wasn't anywhere. I walked back up the driveway, deciding to head to the backyard again. But as I passed Melodie's car, I jumped. Matt was sitting in the passenger seat. His expression was vacant. He stared straight ahead at the garage door. I tapped on the car window, trying to get his attention, but he ignored me. My hand shook as I reached for the door and opened it. My instincts told me to hold on tight to the hedge clippers, and I hated myself for thinking that.

"Matt? Are you okay?" I bent down, hiding the clippers behind my back. "What are you doing in here?"

He wasn't answering, so I touched his arm. He looked down at my hand and sniffed the air. I didn't know what that was about. What was he smelling? Finally, he raised his eyes to my face.

"Why don't we go in the backyard again? We could talk some more." I had to figure out what was wrong with him, if anything *was* wrong with him. I had no clue why he'd gotten in Melodie's car, especially since his was parked right behind it. All I knew was that I couldn't have Melodie come out to her car with him still sitting here. "Come on." I took his hand in mine and gently tugged. My right hand hurt, and I noticed my sutures had split. I must've bled on him when I moved him off me on the bench. That was how he'd come back to life. He came with me, staring at everything in a daze. I closed the door as quietly as I could. I didn't want to make noise and draw attention to us. We walked around the side of the house, and I heard Mom calling my name. I stopped short. Matt walked right into me and grunted.

"Sorry," I whispered and put a finger to my lips. Mom couldn't see us. Not until I did something about Matt. Only I had no idea what that something was going to be. We waited there, on the side of the house, until Mom finally gave up and went back inside. I peeked around the corner to be sure. We couldn't go back to the bench swing. It was too much in the open, and Mom or Melodie could walk out and find us. I headed for the trees lining our property. Still holding Matt's hand, I crept along the trees and came out behind the tool shed. No one would see us here.

"Matt?" He stared past me. Tears spilled over my cheeks again. "Oh, Matt. What have I done to you?" A bunny hopped across the lawn behind him. I wouldn't have even noticed if Matt hadn't whirled around, practically yanking my arm out of the socket. I let go of his hand and rubbed my shoulder. "Ouch. What are you doing? What's wrong?" What was wrong was that he was dead. I knew that.

Matt eyed the bunny, and his face contorted into a tortured expression. His top lip curled up on one side, and he let out this guttural sound. "Matt," I said a second too late, not that my talking was having any effect on him. He lunged and scooped the bunny off the ground. He brought it to his face and sank his teeth into the bunny's back. "No!" I yelled in complete horror. This couldn't be happening. I fell to my knees, dropping the hedge clippers, and covered my face with my hands. Matt grunted, and I heard slurping sounds that made me gag. The next thing I knew, I was puking. I tried to stand, but my legs wouldn't support me. Matt tossed the bunny on the ground in front of me, like a cat that brings its leftover food scraps home to its master. I cringed and crawled backward, trying to get away from Matt.

He stared down at me with his head cocked to the side, blood splattered all over his face and neck. He stepped toward me, and I scrambled back until I was pressed up against the shed. Matt raised his arm like a club, and I shielded my head from his oncoming attack. Before I could scream, Alex grabbed Matt around his waist and knocked him to the ground.

"It's not his fault!" I yelled.

Alex kept Matt pinned beneath him.

"I didn't mean to," I sobbed. "I was going to break up with him. Tell him I couldn't see him anymore. But before I could say a word, he kissed me. I was caught off guard, and I kissed him back. I didn't even realize what was happening until it was too late."

Alex struggled to keep Matt down. Even dead, Matt was strong. "Stupid!" It took me a minute to realize Alex was talking about me. "Why would you go somewhere private to break it off with him? It's like you were inviting trouble." He kneed Matt in the stomach, and Matt groaned. "Look what you've done, Jodi."

"I know," I said, more angry at myself than at Alex. "Please, can't you do something? Help him?"

Alex shook his head. "I can't fix this."

"Yes, you can. You can kill him and bring him back the right way. You said there was a trick to it. That I needed to learn how to do it right. You can do it. You can put him back the way he was." I was begging, but I didn't care.

Matt gritted his teeth and growled. Blood and spit flew out of his mouth. Alex shoved his face to the side so Matt was looking at me. It only made me cry more. "This isn't your boyfriend, Jodi. This is a—for lack of a better word—zombie. You don't know how to use your power, so you didn't put all of him back into his body. He's almost an empty shell. No brain, no thoughts. Only animal instincts." Alex nodded at the bunny, shredded on the grass. "I'm guessing he did that."

I couldn't bring myself to answer, but I didn't need to. Alex knew everything. He may not have been here to witness it all, but he knew enough about raising the dead to put the pieces together. "Please," I begged, "there must be something you can do. We can't leave him like this."

"No, we can't. We have to kill him, Jodi. But this time for good."

I started to protest again, but Alex interrupted. "You didn't know what you were doing when you brought him back. You did it wrong. When you bring someone back—the right way—they come back exactly as they were before they died." He gestured to Matt, still growling and dripping blood from his mouth. That was how Matt would come back, even if Alex did everything right, because that was what I'd turned him into.

"You mean he'll still be like a zombie?"

"Yes. I'm sorry."

I lost it, sobbing so hard I could barely breathe. My nose ran, and my eyes stung. I hated myself for bringing Matt back in the first place. If I hadn't brought him back, if I had waited, Alex would've been able to bring him back the right way. I still wouldn't have been able to date Matt, but he'd be alive.

"Go," Alex said. "You don't need to watch this. I'll take care of Matt and get rid of his body."

"What do you mean 'get rid of his body'?"

"We can't let anyone see him like this. He's covered in blood."

"Then we'll clean him up. I'm not letting his family wonder what happened to him. I'm not going to put them through even more hell than his death will already cause." I stood up. "I did this. I have to take responsibility for it, and I have to do what I can to make up for my mistake." It felt idiotic to call murdering the guy I liked a mistake. Mistakes were cheating on a test or lying to your parents. Killing a person wasn't a mistake. It was inhuman.

Alex nodded. "Fine. We'll clean him up and make his death look like an accident. Although, the effect our blood has on humans is most like a heart attack. Do you know if he had a history of heart problems in his family?"

I ignored the question. Matt was seventeen. He was healthy. No one would believe he'd had a heart attack. And besides that, I was caught up on something Alex had said. "We're not human, are we? Ophi, I mean."

Matt was getting really restless trapped beneath Alex. "There's too much to explain right now. We need to get this over with. Fast."

"How will you do it?" It was an awful question. One I didn't really want to know the answer to. But I didn't want Matt to suffer, and I didn't want Alex to do anything that would raise even more questions about Matt's death.

"I'll use the power of my blood." He removed a knife from his pocket.

"Wait!" I said. "Maybe we should use my blood. I'm the one who did this to him in the first place. I should be the one to clean up my mess."

"Sorry, but you can't. I appreciate you wanting to take responsibility, but you don't have control over your powers yet. You may end up making things worse."

I couldn't imagine how things could get any worse. But I lowered my hand.

"I need to spill my blood if I'm going to fix this. An adult Ophi can release souls by commanding them, but I don't fully have that ability yet, so I have to poison him again. I'll explain how it all works later. But for now, I need you to step back, and no matter what happens, don't touch Matt or me. Got it?"

I swallowed my fear and nodded, taking a step back. It was hard to watch Alex slice his left palm with his knife. I winced at the sight of his blood. He held Matt's mouth open and dripped the blood inside. For a second, Matt welcomed the blood, and that made me cringe. He really *wasn't* human anymore. But then his body went completely stiff. Alex stood up and nodded to me. "It's done."

The tears came again. I was surprised I had any left. Alex stepped forward and wrapped me in his arms. It felt strange to have him hold me. He'd completely freaked me out before, but now he was saving me… from myself. I cried on him for a few minutes, relieved that my tears couldn't harm him. I could be myself around Alex.

"Jodi, we have to get him cleaned up and work out a story before your mom or Melodie finds us." His voice was soft, comforting.

I pulled away from him. "There's a hose at the back of the house, but someone might hear or see us."

Alex put his hands on his hips and wrinkled his forehead. "Okay. I need you to go back inside. Tell your mom and Melodie that Matt broke up with you. Tell them he found out you liked someone else."

"No. They'd never believe that. They knew I was crazy about Matt. There was no one else." I cringed, realizing I was already talking about him in the past tense.

He sighed. "Fine. Tell them he was tired of all your drama. Dating you was too much work."

That was believable. Especially with the way my life had been lately. I nodded.

"Good. I'll clean him up. Give me five minutes or so. That's all I'll need. Then come back outside. I'll handle the rest."

I was afraid of what he'd do, but Matt was already dead. Nothing Alex did now was going to hurt him. I headed back to the house and hesitated at the door. I took a deep breath and went inside. Mom and Melodie were in the living room. Mom was on the phone.

"There you are!" she said. "I've been trying to call your cell. Where did you go?"

I fought back the tears. I couldn't have any more accidents. I summoned all my strength and opted for a stoic misery. It must have been convincing because Mom and Melodie rushed to me and brought me to the couch.

"What happened?" Melodie asked.

"Matt," I said. "He broke up with me."

Mom looked angry, while Melodie looked almost relieved. They both waited for me to go on.

"He said dating me was too much work. Things were too hard, and he needed to move on."

Melodie turned and peered out the front window. "Where is he? His car's still out front."

"We took a walk, but he was in the backyard when I left him."

Melodie got up and stormed out of the room. Mom and I followed her. We went out the back door. "Matt!" Melodie yelled, sounding like she was ready to give him an earful. But she stopped short when she saw the pool of water on the back patio. Matt was lying in the middle of it with the neighbor's snapped power line next to him.

Chapter 12

"Oh my God, Matt!" Melodie shrieked.

"Stop!" I grabbed her arm. "That's a power line. If you go near it or the water around Matt, you'll get electrocuted."

"We can't leave him there and do nothing!" Melodie cried. "Jodi, he's my best friend." She broke down, and I couldn't take it. I turned and ran back into the house yelling something about 911. I ran right into the kitchen table and doubled over it. My breathing was labored. I looked up to see Alex in my kitchen. He dialed the phone for me, but then he held it out.

"If I call it in, the police might ask about me. They'll want to talk to everyone who was here. You have to do it."

I took the phone.

"911. What is your emergency?" the operator said. I really hated the sound of that.

"This is Jodi Marshall. There's been an... accident." I choked on the word. "A power line snapped. My boyfriend's been electrocuted."

"Miss Marshall, can you please confirm your address for me?"

Why was it that I could call for pizza delivery and they could tell my address from the phone number, but 911 needed me to confirm it for them?

"118 Pine Street."

"I'll send someone out right away. Please, stay away from the power line and the body. Do you understand me? If your boyfriend's been electrocuted, then the wire is live, and it will electrocute anyone else who comes in contact with it."

"I understand." I hung up the phone before she could lecture me anymore.

Alex was gone. I was surprised that I wanted him here, but he knew the truth. He understood how I felt. Right now, he was the only one I wanted to talk to.

The back door opened, and Mom led Melodie in by her shoulders. She sat her down at the kitchen table. I turned away from her. How could I look Melodie in the face after I'd killed the guy she was secretly in love with? Mom made tea for everyone, not that we touched it. The paramedics and the power company arrived, and Mom showed them to the backyard. We stayed inside. Mom asked the paramedics to take Matt's body around the side of the house. She didn't want us to have to see him.

I sat at the table, across from Melodie, who was still in shock. Mom called Melodie's parents and explained what had happened. Mom offered to let Melodie spend the night, but her parents insisted that they'd come get her. They wanted her home so they could make sure she was okay. Her dad showed up fifteen minutes later and took her home, saying he'd come back for her car in the morning. The house was eerily quiet after that. The silence of death hung in the air, and I'd put it there.

"Can I get you something, sweetie?" Mom asked.

"No."

She sipped her tea, which must have been ice cold by now. "The guy from the power company said the wire looked like it had been snapped by a tree branch. They found one down in the woods behind the house. It must have been struck by lightning or something during the last storm. It was weak, and it finally gave."

I wondered how Alex had done all that in a matter of minutes. Unless he had been working with a tree that really had been struck by lightning. Maybe he'd seen it during one of his stalking sessions. He'd certainly spent enough time hanging around my house to know if there was a tree that had been hit by lightning.

"The power company said this kind of thing is more common than you'd think. It—"

"Mom." I raised my hands in frustration. I couldn't listen to this. I didn't want to think about Matt or the stupid fake story Alex had concocted to cover up the real way Matt had died. "Please, I can't. Not now."

"Sweetie, I'm sorry. I just don't know what to say."

"Let's not say anything. Okay? Nothing we could possibly say is going to bring Matt back or change what happened." But Alex had changed what happened. He'd covered for me, made it look like a freak accident. "I want to go to bed. Sleep the day away and escape this nightmare."

Mom looked lost. "This is one of those times when I really wish I was older. That I hadn't had you at sixteen. Maybe if I was older I'd know how to make you feel better right now. How to protect you from things like this."

"Mom." I hugged her, and she cried on my shoulder. "There are some things you can't protect me from." Like myself. "I'll be okay. I just need time."

She nodded and wiped her tears. "You go to bed. I'll lock up down here."

I knew she was going to sit at the table and cry for at least another twenty minutes. And the worst part was that she was feeling like she had somehow let me down because she couldn't shield me from the bad things in life. She had no clue I was one of those bad things. She didn't really know who I was at all. Hell, *I* didn't really know who I was.

I slept late into the next morning, completely wiped out from the day before. But the first thought that popped into my mind when I opened my eyes was that Matt was dead. I'd killed him. I'd brought him back, and I'd turned him into a monster—an animal that tore a cute little bunny to shreds. I felt tears well up in my eyes.

"Don't start that." Alex's voice made me sit up abruptly.

"What are you doing here? What time is it?"

"Almost noon." He was leaning against my windowsill. "Your mom came to check on you about an hour ago. You were out cold."

I looked at the nightstand. Mom had brought me a muffin and some coffee. There was also a note. "Jodi, I hate to do this to you, but I got called in to work. I told them I couldn't stay long. That I had to be home for personal reasons. They weren't happy, but I insisted. Please, eat something, and call me when you wake up. I love you. Mom."

I sighed. "She went to work."

"Probably better that way." Alex pushed off the windowsill and sat at the end of my bed. "How do you feel?"

"Like I killed my boyfriend."

He frowned. "I meant, do you feel drained in any way? Sometimes using our powers drains our energy. At least, when we're first learning to use them. It doesn't take nearly as much energy once we get used to it." He ran his hand along the edge of my bed. "You've been using a lot of your power lately, without knowing it."

"Thanks for the reminder. I guess to clarify my response to how I'm feeling, I should say I feel like I killed my boyfriend, a doctor, a nurse, and a bunch of innocent animals. Yeah, that's more accurate." I slumped back onto my pillow.

"I can help you pack if you want." Alex looked around my room.

I covered my face with my hands, careful not to reopen any of my cuts, and shook my head. Was he seriously doing this to me now? I felt his eyes on me, so I sat up again and met his stare. "I'm not going anywhere. My boyfriend isn't even in the ground yet. Everyone will expect me to be at his funeral. The police may even call me in for questioning. Who knows? I mean, I told Mom and Melodie that Matt had broken up with me. What if the police think we were fighting and things got heated? What if they think I had something to do with his death?"

"You did have something to do with it." The words stung. "But the police will never know that. The power company said that tree had been hit by lightning. That Matt's death was an accident. No one is going to believe you had anything to do with Matt's death."

Except, I did have something to do with it. "Was that tree really hit by lightning or did you do something I'm not aware of? Do you have other superhuman powers?"

He smirked. "It was hit by lightning. I actually saw it get hit last week in that bad storm we had."

"Last week?" My mind started spinning. "You were spying on me last week? I thought Mr. Quimby just told you to start watching me a few days ago."

Alex turned toward me, bending his right leg up onto my mattress more. Our legs touched, and I couldn't help looking at our limbs resting against each other. God! What was I doing? Matt just died yesterday, and I was getting excited about my stalker touching my leg?

"Jodi, I was sent to watch you in September. After Mr. Quimby confirmed our suspicions—that you were an Ophi—I started camping out in the woods behind your house. Monitoring where you went, when you came home, who you went out with." He said the last part like the words were painful on his tongue.

"September? You've been watching me for five months?" I felt violated. I was finally starting to kind of like him, to not mind having him around, and now this. We were right back where we'd started. I pulled my leg away from his, curling it under me and as far away from his body as it could get.

"I'm sorry that bothers you, but you have to remember we're trying to do what's best for you. Asking you to come with me is part of that."

"Asking me? So, I can say no and that would be that?"

He hesitated. Somehow I knew it wasn't that simple. Alex may not have wanted to force me into anything, but that didn't mean the other Ophi wouldn't. "I want to help you, Jodi, but you have to let me. I won't force you."

I knew it was childish, but I crossed my arms and turned away from him. "I'm not going with you. This is my life. I'm not leaving Mom and Melodie. I'm not missing Matt's funeral. I owe him at least that much."

Out of the corner of my eye, I saw Alex get up and go to the window. "If you need me, you have my number in your phone. I'm willing to bet you haven't deleted my texts."

He was right. I hadn't. But why hadn't I? Who kept messages from their stalker? Maybe to use as evidence, but I'd kept them hidden from everyone. I unfolded my arms and turned to the window, but Alex had already gone out it.

I couldn't eat. The day passed, and I let it. Mom got home around four-thirty.

"Sorry, sorry," she said, practically running through the door. "I was all set to get out of there after an hour, but there was a major crisis. The company is being sued, and if I didn't pull my weight they were going to fire me and find someone who was willing to work on a Sunday."

"Is that what they said?" I asked, staring at the blank TV screen, realizing for the first time all day that I'd forgotten to turn it on. I didn't even remember coming downstairs.

"Oh, yeah. They said that. Can you believe it?" She hung up her coat and purse and sat down next to me. "I was thinking I'd make pot roast for dinner. If I start now, it will be ready for a late dinner, and we could throw in a movie and stay up all night. What do you think?"

She was doing her best to avoid the subject of Matt. I had to give her credit, but there was actually something I needed to know. "Have you heard from his parents?" Matt's car wasn't in the driveway, so they must have come for it at some point.

Mom sighed. "I guess you didn't talk to Melodie today?"

I shook my head, feeling my throat close up. "I didn't know what to say to her, and I guess she didn't want to talk to me either."

"Matt's parents called me today. I was able to sneak off to the bathroom long enough to get the details." She squeezed her knees. "They've already made all the arrangements. They don't want to hold things up. They said it's too painful, and they need closure."

I stared at her, waiting for what I needed to hear.

"The funeral is tomorrow night. There's not going to be a service before it."

"No service? They're just going to shove him in the ground and be done with it?" It was outrageous. "What kind of parents are they? What does Amber have to say about it? She and Matt were really close."

"Jodi." Mom put her hand on mine. "People grieve in different ways. I don't know how I'd—" She choked on the words and had to blink back tears. "We have to respect what the family wants. Maybe it's too painful for them to see Matt this way. Maybe they want closure so that they can remember him the way he was when he was alive."

I stood up. "I'm going to bed."

"What about dinner?" Mom called after me.

I stormed upstairs, slammed my door shut, and flopped face first onto my bed. I squeezed the pillow in my fists and screamed until my lungs ached. Mom didn't check on me. My phone didn't ring once. And Alex didn't show up lurking in my closet or anything. I was alone. Me and my poisonous Gorgon blood. Toxic to those I loved. Had I loved Matt? Probably not. I'd never really been in love, but I definitely had strong feelings for Matt. When he kissed me, it was electrifying. I'd never felt so completely alive. It was why I'd kissed him back—why I hadn't pulled away sooner. That kiss could've stopped time; instead, it stopped Matt's heart.

By the time I picked my head up, my pillow was drenched in tears and my room was dark. The sun had set. I went to the window and searched for Alex. Was he still watching me? I guessed he was, but he wasn't letting me see him. It didn't seem fair. He was the only one I could talk to right now. Yet, I knew if I broke down and called him, he'd try to get me to leave again. I wasn't ready to do that. I had to say goodbye to Matt first. Then, I had to find a way to tell Mom what I am, tell her that the daughter she gave birth to was really a monster.

I stayed in bed all night, staring at the ceiling and wondering how to do that. By the time the sun came up, I still didn't have an answer. I heard Mom get up and shower for work. The smell of coffee drifted up to my room. My alarm buzzed in my ear, but I hit it until it gave up. Finally, Mom came in my room.

"I didn't know if you were up."

"I never fell asleep," I said, continuing to stare at the ceiling.

Mom let out a long breath. "Do you want to stay home from school today? I think your teachers would understand."

I didn't feel like moving. I wanted to lie there completely still, like Matt was right now. I wondered if his body was already in the casket.

Mom looked at her watch. "Listen, I have to go or I'll be late. Text me and let me know if you decide to stay home. I can call the school for you from work." She bent down and kissed my forehead. "I think it's a good thing the service is tonight. You'll feel better when it's over. I promise."

Somehow I doubted that.

Chapter 13

I didn't get up all day. Didn't eat. Didn't sleep. I stared. A lot. But the day managed to pass anyway. My cell vibrated more than once, and I knew it was Mom checking on me. I never called her to say I was staying home. I couldn't face everyone at school, though. All the questions about Matt's death, about our break-up. I'd break down and cry and who knew how many more deaths that would lead to. Maybe Alex was right. Maybe it was too dangerous for me to be around people right now. Or ever again.

Mom stormed into my room the second she got home from work. Saying she looked mad was an understatement, and I could imagine what all her voice mails sounded like. "You don't get to do that to me! I get that you're upset. I get that you're hurting. But you are my daughter. Do you have any idea what it was like for me at work today? I was a wreck. I screwed up a major computer file. I almost lost my job. The only thing that saved me—that saved us—was me telling my heartless boss what happened Saturday."

I sat up and pulled my knees to my chest. "You told him about Matt to avoid getting fired?" I didn't want Mom to lose her job, but blaming her screw-up on Matt's death seemed a little too convenient.

Mom looked horrified. "Tell me, what we would do if I lost my job? You know how hard I worked to get that position. I never went to college, Jodi. I don't have the degree to be doing half of what I do." She threw her hands in the air. "So yeah, I did use Matt's death to save my job today. And you know what? It *was* the reason I screwed up. Matt's death made you shut down. You wouldn't answer a single one of my calls. Then, your school calls and tells me you never showed up. I had no idea if you were okay. That's why I screwed up, Jodi." She sat down on the edge of my bed and cried. Big sobs that made her shoulders shake uncontrollably. I wanted to wrap my arms around her and hug her. Tell her how sorry I was that I'd made her worry. Tell her... the truth.

But I couldn't. I'd cry. I'd cry, and she'd be dead. And Alex was keeping his promise by staying away, so he wouldn't even be here to bring her back. I hated my life. All of it. There was no way I could go to the funeral. Not unless they had a few extra caskets lying around to bury all the other people I'd end up sending to their graves.

I jumped up from the bed and ran to the door. Mom looked up at me, totally confused.

"Mom," I sniffled. "I can't do this." She stood up and reached her arms out for me, but I took a step back and held my hand up to stop her. "Please. Don't touch me, okay?" She stood still, staring at me like she didn't even know who I was. "I can't go to the funeral. I can't face those people. I need to get away. Be by myself."

"Honey, you were by yourself all day. This isn't good for you. You can't isolate yourself. You'll never heal like that."

"I need time, Mom. This is all happening too fast for me. I need time to process everything. Please."

She nodded. "Okay, we don't have to go to the funeral. We can stay home instead. We'll cook a nice dinner. You always love when we cook a big meal together, and we haven't done it in a long time."

How was I supposed to leave her? How did you say goodbye without actually saying goodbye?

I had to make it through dinner. One last family dinner before I broke her heart and left for good.

"Yeah, dinner would be nice. Um, there's just something I need to do first. Somewhere I have to go."

"I'll take you. Your car's still in the shop."

"No, I can walk."

"I don't like that idea. After the incident with that guy following you—" She shook her head. "I wouldn't feel comfortable with you going out by yourself."

I waved her off. "That was a big misunderstanding. He needed to talk to me. We're fine now. Friends almost." She looked skeptical, probably thinking I was only saying what I thought she wanted to hear. "Really, Mom. I promise."

She picked up my cell and handed it to me. "Take this, and answer when I call."

I nodded.

"Home by six-thirty."

I looked at the clock. It was almost five. The funeral would be starting soon. "Got it. I better go before it gets any later."

She kissed the top of my head. "If you aren't home by six-thirty, I will drive around screaming your name out the window." That made us both laugh because we knew it was true.

I half-walked, half-ran to the cemetery. We lived pretty close to it if I cut through some people's yards. I got there just as they were throwing flowers on Matt's grave. I stayed hidden in the trees, not daring to get any closer. No more accidents. Matt's parents and his sister, Amber, were huddled together at the head of the casket. They looked like their worlds had been shattered. I felt the tears sting my eyes and looked around to make sure I was still alone and it was safe for me to cry.

I waited until everyone left. Matt's body was in the ground. I walked over to his grave, picking up a stray red rose on the way. I laid it on top of the grave. "I'm so sorry, Matt." I wished I had something better to say. Something that would actually make a difference. But what did you say to the guy you kissed, killed, and turned into a zombie? Hallmark didn't make a greeting card for that, and I was at a loss. I wondered what would happen if I dripped tears on his grave. I didn't want to find out, so I backed away, right into Alex.

"You shouldn't have come." His tone wasn't reprimanding; he was genuinely worried about me.

"I had to say goodbye."

"I know." He gently turned me around to face him. "Did you figure out a way to say goodbye to your mom?"

"No." I pretended to look at a bird in the distance. "But I've decided that I owe her one last family dinner. We're cooking a big meal when I get home. Then—well, I don't know what, but I'll leave somehow. I can't risk anything happening to my mom. Breaking her heart is better than stopping it for good."

"I can help you if you want."

"How?" I faced him again. "What would you say? You're the guy who stalked me, but you only wanted to tell me that I can raise the dead and that my blood, tears, and saliva are poisonous to humans? You think that will make it easier for her to let me go with you?"

"Okay, point taken. I have my cell on me. Call me when you're ready to go." He walked away, stopping at Matt's grave and placing a rose on top. I hadn't even noticed he was holding it.

I made it home with two minutes to spare.

"You're lucky," Mom said, taking out a frying pan. "I was about to get my car keys."

"I'm surprised you weren't warming up your vocal cords." It felt good to act normally. I wanted a normal night. Something nice to remember when I was gone.

"Green peppers and onions are on the counter. Could you chop them up and fry them for me? I need to finish seasoning the chicken."

I grabbed the knife and started chopping the onion. It hurt like hell thanks to the cuts on my fingers.

"How was it?" Mom asked.

"What?"

"The funeral. I'm figuring you went and sat in the back where no one would see you."

I stiffened, jerking the knife in my hand. I felt it slice into my thumb. No! Blood dripped a thin red line down my left thumb and onto the cutting board. I stood in shock. I didn't want to make any sudden moves that would let Mom know what had happened. I had to get my blood cleaned up before she saw it and wanted to help. My heart thumped so loudly I barely heard Mom saying my name.

"Jodi! You could at least acknowledge that you heard me. Even if you don't want to talk about it."

"Talk about what?" I asked, trying to sound casual as I squeezed my finger and reached for the roll of paper towels.

"The funeral. Is everything okay? Do you need help chopping those?"

"No!" I answered, way too quickly. "I, um, broke a nail. That's all. I'll finish chopping in a second." It was the lamest excuse ever.

Mom put the chicken in the oven and then reached for the cutting board. "Here. Give me the knife, and I'll finish these. You go—" It took me too long to remember I'd bled on the cutting board.

"Mom, no! Stay back!" I grabbed the cutting board, pulling it toward me. I slid it across the counter and into the sink, onion and all.

"Jodi, you cut yourself. Let me see."

"It's nothing." I squeezed the paper towel tighter around my finger, willing my blood to clot already.

"I have to make sure you're okay. You're bleeding."

"I'm fine. I'll just go wash it off in the bathroom sink." The knife was still on the counter, and the edge was tinted red. I reached for it.

"I'll clean that," Mom said. "Go rinse your hand."

"No! Really, I got it." I grabbed the knife and put it in the sink. I ran the water, watching my blood go down the drain. It didn't look any different than normal blood. How could it be so poisonous?

Mom reached for the paper towels and started wiping the counter. "Stop!" I reached for the paper towel. As I turned, I smacked my hand on the faucet. I cried out as my thumb hit the cutting board in the sink. The paper towel fell off my thumb and landed in the sink.

Mom stopped trying to clean the counter, her eyes falling on my hand. "We have to take you to the emergency room. You might need stitches." I thought about Dr. Alvarez. He died because of me. Another one of my victims. I couldn't let that happen again. I grabbed the paper towel Mom had left on the counter and wiped the surface, making sure none of my blood was lingering anywhere. I threw the paper towels in the garbage and tried to tie it shut. I wasn't sure if dried blood would be able to kill, and I wasn't about to find out when Mom got rid of the trash. Tying one-handed wasn't easy, especially since both hands had cuts on them.

"Honey, what are you doing? Don't worry about that. I'll take care of it later. Right now I only care about getting your hand checked out."

She wasn't going to let up. I was hurt, and all she could think about was helping me. If I didn't tell her the truth fast, she was going to end up getting killed.

"Mom, there's something you don't know about me. Something you aren't going to like."

"Whatever it is, you can tell me after we go to the emergency room." She went for her purse on the kitchen table.

"No!" I had to get her attention. Make her listen. "I have to tell you now. Before anyone else dies because of me."

She narrowed her eyes at me. "I think you're losing too much blood. You aren't thinking straight. No one has died because of you."

"Yes, they have." I couldn't get into the details. I couldn't risk crying on top of bleeding. Mom came back into the kitchen. "Please, Mom. Don't touch me."

"What is with this 'no touching' thing you have going on lately? I don't understand, Jodi. Please, fill me in. What's going on with you?"

"I'm not who you think I am. I'm something called an Ophi. It means I have different blood than you do."

She shook her head, and her nostrils flared. She thought I was making this up, and she was getting angry.

I continued before she could yell at me. "Remember that guy who was following me? The one who needed to talk to me? Well, he's the one who told me this. He's like me, and he wants to help me."

Mom cocked her head to the side. "Wait, is he the reason you and Matt broke up?"

"What? No!" I squeezed my thumb in anger and winced in pain.

"We don't have time for stories right now, Jodi. You need a doctor."

"No! My finger isn't that bad."

"Then why won't you let me see it?" Mom slammed her hand down on the counter.

"Because if you touch my blood, you'll die. You'll die just like Matt did when he kissed me. Like Dr. Alvarez and Nurse Steingall. My blood is like poison." I was shaking, probably because I was holding back, fighting every urge to cry.

Loud knocking on the back door interrupted whatever Mom was about to say. I moved around her, making sure we didn't come in contact, and opened the back door.

"Now are you ready to come with me?" Alex asked.

"Were you watching me again? You're like a peeping Tom."

"I'm trying to save your life, and apparently your mother's, too. Are you going to let me in so I can help you explain all this to her?"

I stepped aside and let him pass. "Ms. Marshall, I'm Alex. I'm like your daughter. An Ophi. Only I was raised into a very different kind of life. My parents are Ophi, too. I want to take your daughter to a safe place where we can help her learn to control her abilities." He was blurting it out, like he knew he was only going to get one shot at this.

"Control her abilities?" Mom asked. "Okay, this has gone on long enough."

"She's a necromancer," Alex said. "She can bring back the dead."

Mom looked Alex straight in the eyes. "Do you know a boy died here two days ago? He was put in the ground today. How dare you make jokes about bringing back the dead after what Jodi's been through?"

"I wish I were joking."

Mom glared at Alex. "Jodi, get your coat. I'm taking you to the emergency room right now."

Alex stepped between us, blocking Mom's way. "She can't go there. She needs an Ophi to take care of her. Anyone else will die from touching her blood."

"Her blood is my blood. I'm her mother!"

"I know. And I don't want Jodi to have to live with being responsible for your death. She's already—"

"You put those crazy ideas in her head." Mom turned to me. "That's why you were so upset about Matt." She nodded her head at Alex. "He said you were to blame for Matt's death." I'd never seen Mom so angry. She lunged forward, pushing Alex out of her way, and reached for me. "There is nothing wrong with your blood. Your blood is my blood." Before I realized what she was doing, she grabbed my cut hand in hers.

"No!" I screamed, as my blood came in contact with her skin.

Chapter 14

I yanked my hand from hers and stared at the red blood staining her palm. She choked, her face turning red as if she were drowning. Alex rushed over to her, reaching his hands out as her eyes fluttered and she collapsed into his arms. He lowered her to the floor, cradling her head in his lap.

"No, no, no! Please!" I shrieked, my whole body convulsing. "This can't happen. Don't let her be dead."

Alex looked up at me with sadness in his eyes.

I bent down to him, gripping his upper arm, not wanting to touch Mom and inflict any more of my poisoned blood on her. "I'll come with you. I'll do whatever you say. Just please bring her back. Please!" My sobbing was uncontrollable.

Alex nudged me back and lowered Mom's head to the floor. "Stay back. Don't bleed or cry on her body. I need room."

I stumbled back, so grateful that he was going to save her. He reached into his pocket with his eyes still closed and pulled out his knife.

"What are you doing?" I panicked, afraid I'd been right to be afraid of him before.

He ignored me and sliced his right hand with the blade. He closed his fingers over the cut and positioned his hand over Mom's mouth. He opened her mouth with his other hand. "Stop!" I cried as he squeezed his fist and drops of his blood fell into Mom's mouth. I wanted to do something, make him stop, but it was like my body was frozen. Something was holding me back. Finally, Alex opened his eyes. He backed away. I ran to him and smacked him over and over. Instead of fighting back, he wrapped his arms around me and let me cry on his shoulder.

"She's going to be okay. Give my blood a minute to do its stuff. She'll come back."

I turned my head so I could see Mom. She was still motionless on the floor. I watched, the seconds ticking slower than I thought possible. "Maybe you did something wrong."

"I didn't." Alex sounded very sure of himself. "Patience, Jodi."

My breath caught in my throat. How long did this take? It was absolute torture. If she didn't come back... I couldn't get over losing her. Especially when it was *my* blood that had killed her.

Mom's eyes snapped open, and she choked. "Mom!" I bent down to her, but Alex stopped me, grabbing the wrist of my bloody hand.

"We don't want to go through all that again," he said. "She'll be okay. She's just having a little trouble adjusting to my blood in her system. But she'll be fine in a minute or two. That doesn't give us much time to get out of here."

"What? I can't leave. Not now. She won't even know where I am."

"Do you want her to live?"

Of course I did. There wasn't any question about that. He was right. This accident could easily happen again. I couldn't risk that. I couldn't lose her for good. Alex might not always be around to fix my mistakes. I wasn't even sure if you could bring someone back more than once.

"Let me at least tell her where I'm going."

"You can't. It has to remain a secret. You can call her later and tell her you're okay." Mom's choking was easing up. "We're running out of time, Jodi." I looked down at her through the wall of tears I'd built up.

"I love you, Mom." I turned and ran out the back door. I had to get out of there fast or I wouldn't be able to make myself leave. If Mom had seen me or called my name, that would've been it for me. I would've lost my nerve and given in to staying. That would've been selfish and stupid. I ran past Mom's car, hearing Alex's footsteps behind me. To my surprise, there was another car in the driveway.

Alex ran around to the driver's side. "Get in. It's unlocked." I listened. We peeled out of the driveway and took the back roads to the highway. I cried. I couldn't believe I'd left Mom. Couldn't believe I'd killed Mom. I looked over at Alex. He was so calm. He didn't reprimand me or tell me how stupid I was for not going with him sooner. I owed him so much. He'd brought Mom back, given her another chance. I hated feeling in debt to him. I barely knew him. But I hated myself more.

Alex kept his eyes on the road, pushing the speed limit. "You did the right thing. I know it was tough, but leaving means she gets to live."

"Is she even really alive? I mean she's not going to be like Matt was, is she?"

"She's alive. Her soul hadn't even left her body when I started the process of bringing her back. It's very similar to saving a drowning victim. They can be dead for a few minutes and still come back okay."

In a way, Mom *was* like a drowning victim. She'd drowned on my blood. It had suffocated her. And Alex was the guy who'd saved her, whose blood had breathed life back into her body. "Thank you." My voice was small. "I can't even begin to tell you how much I appreciate what you did." ·

"You're welcome." He reached across me and opened the glove compartment. He motioned to the box of Band-Aids. "Cover that cut." He didn't need to tell me twice.

"I don't know how I'll ever repay you for this."

"Coming with me now is a good start. I've been getting hell for not bringing you back sooner."

"What do you mean?"

"It wasn't supposed to take me this long. I was supposed to make you like me so that, when I told you the truth about who you are, you'd come with me right away. Only I didn't do such a good job making you like me. I scared you instead."

"Saving my mom makes me like you a lot." He glanced at me just long enough to see me give him a weak smile. Then, he turned his eyes back on the road.

"Hey," I said, "why did you come on so strong at first? I mean, the whole stalker thing isn't a great way to get a girl to like you."

"I freaked. I saw you with Matt, and I lost it."

"You thought I was going to kill him."

"Yes." He got quiet.

"And I did exactly what you thought I would."

"No. *He* did exactly what I thought *he* would."

"What do you mean?" That wasn't at all what I thought he'd say.

"He fell in love with you."

I shook my head. "Matt wasn't in love with me. He liked me, but he didn't love me."

"Yes, he did. Believe me, Jodi, a guy doesn't wait around for a girl who hasn't even kissed him unless he's in love with her."

I'd never understood why Matt was so patient with me. Was Alex right? Had Matt been in love with me?

"Remember when Melodie introduced you to Matt?" Alex smirked. "The guy practically fell all over himself."

"Wait, how do you know when she introduced me to Matt?"

"I told you. I was assigned to watch you back in September."

Right. Man, that was creepy. I wondered what else Alex had seen. I decided it was best not to think about it. We sat in silence for a while. I tried to figure out where we were going, but Alex seemed to make a lot of turns and road changes. It was almost like he was trying to confuse me. I let it go, though, figuring I'd find out where we were going once we got there. I repositioned myself in the seat, trying to get more comfortable. I hated being cramped in a car for too long. Even though I wasn't tall by any standard, I couldn't take being in one position for any length of time. I twisted sideways, stretching my back, and saw the lime-green bag sitting on the backseat.

"Oh, my God! That's my gym bag." I reached for it.

"I took the liberty of packing for you. Good thing, too, since there really wasn't time before we left."

He knew I couldn't argue with that. He'd played the "you-killed-your-mother-and-I-brought-her-back-so-you-can't-get-mad-at-me" card. I put the bag on my lap and unzipped it, curious to see what Alex had thought to pack for me. At first, it looked like all practical things. Socks, sneakers, jeans, shirts. I dug deeper. "You went through my underwear drawer?"

"And what would you have done if I hadn't?" He raised an eyebrow at me.

I let out an annoyed sigh. He was right. I didn't exactly want to go commando, so it was a good thing he'd packed underwear and bras for me. Still, the thought of a guy I barely knew going through my underwear drawer wasn't exactly comforting. I put the bag down by my feet and made a mental note to wash all these items when we got to wherever it was we were going.

"So, how is this going to work? Me coming to stay with you and the other Ophi." This was probably the kind of thing I should have asked about sooner.

"I'm taking you to my parents. They live in this huge old mansion. It was a reform school at one time, but it lost its funding, and the school was forced to close. It was left abandoned. Now, a bunch of Ophi live there. My parents own the place, so they pretty much call the shots, but everyone gets along well." He shrugged. "For the most part. Well, except—"

There was always one person who had to cause trouble. "Who is he? Older brother? Distant cousin twice removed?"

"*Her* name is Abigail." I must have looked as surprised as I felt to hear the bad seed was a girl. "Yup, she's… well, there really aren't any words to describe Abby."

"Great. I can't wait to meet her," I said with all the sarcasm I could manage.

"I should probably warn you that she likes to prey on the new ones."

"Of course she does." I rolled my eyes. "I'm sure she and I will be the best of friends." That was a bad choice of words because it made me think of Melodie. I hadn't exactly been a good best friend to her. I'd killed the guy she secretly liked, maybe even loved. Then I'd taken off without saying goodbye or telling her where I was going. I was pretty much the worst excuse for a friend, daughter, or human being ever. But I wasn't really human, was I?

Alex pulled a wrapped sandwich from the middle console. "Here, it's turkey and cheese. You haven't eaten much lately, and you need to keep your strength up."

He was right. I forced myself to eat the sandwich. "Can you tell me a little more about what we are? I mean, I know we're Ophi and we have Gorgon blood in us, but what else?" I stared at Alex. Really stared. He must have felt my eyes on him because he turned his head and looked right at me.

"I'm sure you've noticed the eyes." Yeah, I'd noticed his eyes, since I'd referred to him as Green Eyes before I found out his name. He laughed and turned back to the road.

"What?" Did he somehow know about the nickname I'd given him?

"Maybe you should check out the mirror on the back of the visor." He flipped the visor down. In the small mirror, all I could see were my eyes. My green eyes. "All Ophi have green eyes. Now that doesn't mean that everyone with green eyes is an Ophi. Not at all. There actually aren't many of us in existence."

"Why not? Wasn't there enough Gorgon blood to go around?"

"Remember Mr. Quimby said Hades got upset that Ophiuchus was bringing back all the dead and the underworld was too empty?"

I nodded. "Yeah, so Zeus struck him with a lightning bolt and put him in the sky." Good old Zeus. I wondered if being an Ophi had anything to do with my strange hatred for Zeus.

"Right. Well, Hades isn't a big fan of us Ophi."

I squinted at him. "You mean, like *now*? Hades and the other gods are still around?" This was almost too much to process. "And Hades doesn't like you guys right now?"

"Yes, the gods are still around. And Hades doesn't like you, either. You're one of us, remember?"

"So, what does that mean? Is he going to have Zeus strike us all down?"

"No, nothing like that. Hades made it so that Ophi can only procreate at the age of twenty-five, and our children have to be born between the dates of November 29 and December 17."

"That's crazy. So, you're telling me that, since I'm an Ophi, I have to have a baby at twenty-five?"

"If you want to keep the Ophi line going. Do your part."

"You mean, if I have a child any other time, it won't be Ophi?"

Alex's expression hardened. "It'll be dead."

"Are you threatening the baby I haven't even had?" Boy this guy made it hard to like him.

"No. Ophi can't have non-Ophi children. If you had a baby outside of age twenty-five and without its birth occurring under Ophiuchus' sign, the baby would die the second it took its first breath."

"What? Why?" This just kept getting worse.

"Babies feed off their mothers. The child would have your Gorgon blood in its veins. Without being Ophi, the baby would die."

"But wait. My mom's not Ophi. If only Ophi people can have Ophi children, how do you explain me?"

He looked at me, raising his brows. I shrugged. "What?"

"You can't think of where you got your Gorgon blood from? Anyone else who might have passed it down to you?"

"My dad?" I'd never met my father. I didn't even know his name. "You're telling me my dad's Ophi?"

"He has to be."

"But how is my mom alive then? Wouldn't he have killed her when they—" I couldn't bring myself to finish that sentence.

"How old is your mom?"

"Why?" I couldn't help getting a little defensive. People always made comments about how young Mom was. It wasn't anyone's business that she'd been a teen mother. The reason I ended up being homeschooled for most of my life was to avoid the heckling in school, mostly from other parents.

"I'm going to guess thirty-three or thirty-four. I bet your dad was the same age because he couldn't have come into his powers when he and your mom… got together."

"What do you mean?"

"You've kissed guys before, right?"

I crossed my arms, hugging myself. "I don't see why you need to know that."

"Come on. Don't be a prude. You're seventeen. You're hot. You've kissed guys."

I was hot?

"Oh, don't look so shocked. You own mirrors. None of those guys died because you hadn't fully come into your powers yet. It usually happens around sixteen, but your mom's not Ophi. Her blood is in your veins, diluting the Gorgon blood your dad gave you. And his blood wasn't fully Ophi yet either, so that might have something to do with it."

"Wow, that's a lot to take in." I sighed. "I guess it's good I'm coming with you. I'll be able to meet others like me. It must be harder for half-Ophi to get used to their power, right?"

"I wouldn't know. No other Ophi has ever had one human parent. You're the only one. And if the prophecy about your birth is correct, that makes you the Chosen One."

My insides tightened. How could I be the only Ophi this had ever happened to? "Chosen for what?"

"To save the Ophi race."

Chapter 15

"Whoa!" I put my hands against the glove compartment to steady myself, but all it did was hurt my cut hands. "Save the Ophi race? You have to be kidding me. Tell me this is some new kid initiation or something."

"Sorry, Jodi." Alex glanced at me quickly before turning down yet another road. "Believe me, after everything you've been through—today alone—I wouldn't joke about something like this. I hate to dump all of this on you at once, but I'm trying to answer your questions as honestly as I can."

"I appreciate that, but why didn't you tell me this sooner?"

"How would you have reacted if the first time we met I'd said, 'By the way, you're the only Ophi of your kind and that means you need to save the rest of our sorry behinds from Hades'?"

I turned to him. "From Hades? What do you mean from Hades? You said he made sure there aren't too many Ophi by controlling how we're created, when we can be born. What else does he want from us?" I was surprised how easily I was saying "us," accepting that I was one of them. It felt surreal and strangely comforting at the same time.

"Some Ophi overuse their powers. Bring back people and things that shouldn't be brought back. Hades doesn't like that. He tracks them down."

"You mean kills them."

"Yes. And it's not pleasant. Hades makes them relive the deaths of every person they brought back."

I felt the bile in my stomach churn and threaten to come up. I lowered my window and stuck my head out into the freezing cold night air. I couldn't help thinking about Hades being upset with me for all my accidental raisings. The deer, the squirrel, Matt. If Hades took my life and made me pay for all of them, I'd have to endure the torture of getting hit by a car, having a hammer smash my head in, and drowning by poison blood. Right now, Zeus and his lightning bolt were looking pretty good.

I finally pulled my head back inside the car. "Feel any better?"

"Not really. But I think your leather seats are safe for the time being. Still, I'll leave the window open for a while, just in case."

"Much appreciated."

"How do we know who we are supposed to bring back and who we're not, anyway?" I had to know how much of a problem I'd created for myself with Hades.

"Mostly, Hades doesn't want us bringing souls back from the depths of the underworld, a place called Tartarus—the lowest level of Hell. And believe me, you don't want to do that anyway. It's the scariest thing you'll ever see. Those souls are so tortured that shoving them back into their bodies is hideous and extremely dangerous. They're completely wild and animalistic. It takes a lot of concentration and power to control them."

"Why would someone do it then? If it's so difficult and it puts you on Hades' target list, why do it?"

"I can't really answer that for you." I was glad about that. If he had given me a good reason, I'd have thought I was trapped in a speeding car with a raging psycho. "The souls Ophi raise are usually in limbo or in some other part of the underworld where they aren't being tortured. They're still difficult to control, but it's nowhere near as bad."

I swallowed hard, not wanting to think about raising anything.

"Look, the drive is going to take a while and it's getting late. I know my parents are going to want to show you around and start on your training the second we get there, so you should probably recline your seat and get some sleep."

I wasn't entirely comfortable with that idea. I mean, I didn't know Alex, not really. Sure he'd saved my mom, which was the only reason I could hold it together right now after I'd been ripped from my life. But did I trust him enough to make myself that vulnerable? He carried a knife.

"Hey, why do you carry a knife? I thought only serial killers kept weapons on them at all times."

"Serial killers and Boy Scouts. I was a Scout when I was younger. Well, the Ophi equivalent, at least. I wasn't around humans much growing up."

Alex didn't have a normal life—ever. Not that my life had been so normal. Teen mom, homeschooling, and then the transformation to an Ophi. "What was it like growing up around other Ophi and not around humans?"

"Don't go feeling sorry for me, Jodi. I never knew any differently. To me, my life is normal."

"You can't miss what you never had and all that?" I wasn't buying it. "Were you ever around humans? I mean, you knew about the Scouts, so you must have been exposed to humans at least a little bit. Like the Ophi at Serpentarius."

"Yeah, some. Mom and Dad used to make me watch TV. They said it was research. I could learn about humans without actually being around them. And every once in a while, one of my instructors would take me on a field trip. Somewhere not too crowded, where I could observe humans. As I got older, I had to keep a safe distance." His voice trailed off, and his eyes glassed over. "I talked to a girl once. She was maybe a year younger than me. She was sitting on a bench in the park. It was early morning, and not too many people were there. My instructor got a phone call and told me to sit on a bench and wait for him. I did, but I stared at the girl, and she noticed me. She told me it wasn't nice to stare at people. That I should say 'hi.'" I guessed he never learned to take her advice because he'd done the exact same thing to me. "But I'd never talked to a human before, let alone a pretty one. She came over and sat with me. My instructor didn't notice because he was still talking on the phone. I tried to get his attention a few times, but I finally gave up and talked to the girl." He stopped, gripping the steering wheel in both hands.

"You don't have to tell me if you don't want to. It's none of my business really. I was just curious." I fidgeted in my seat, putting my feet on top of my bag like a footrest.

Alex swallowed so hard I heard it. "She told me her birthday was coming up, and the one thing she really wanted more than anything else was a first kiss."

My heart pounded as I put the situation together in my head. I knew what was coming, yet it didn't make it any easier to hear.

"I'd kissed a few Ophi girls by then, so I thought I'd give this girl her wish. I didn't know I was coming into my powers already. All my training so far had been preliminary, preparing me so I knew how to control my powers once they came to me. So, I kissed her. When we pulled away, I wished her a happy birthday. But before she could respond, she slumped forward in my lap. I was terrified. I looked for my instructor, but he was gone. He'd walked off to make his call more private."

I reached over and touched his hand on the wheel. He jerked his hand, making the car swerve to the right in the process. I braced myself, sure we were going to crash into a telephone pole, but Alex quickly got the car back in our lane.

"I knew my powers were working," he continued as if nothing had happened. "I held her in my arms and tried as hard as I could to bring her back. Only, it didn't work. I screwed it up, and she came back wrong."

"Like Matt," I said.

Alex looked at me for the first time since beginning his story. "Yes, like Matt. Only I'd had training. I was supposed to know how to control my powers."

"Alex, you—"

He floored the gas, and I took the hint. I shut up. He didn't say anything for a few minutes, but then he picked right up where he'd left off. "When my instructor found us, he sent me away. Told me to get in the car and wait for him. He killed her. And after that, I wasn't allowed to go on any more field trips. My parents made me study and train twice as hard."

"I'm sorry," I said, at the risk of making him angry again; I couldn't help it. I *was* sorry. I understood how he'd felt. And now I knew that, no matter how much time passed, I'd never get over what I had done to

Matt. Bringing someone back wrong was devastating. I didn't need the details of what that girl had done when Alex had brought her back to life. Without asking, I knew what she'd been like.

"It made me stronger, Jodi. Just like all you've had to deal with will make you stronger."

There wasn't much left to say after that, so I reclined my seat and closed my eyes. It was strange that a story like that would make me feel I could trust Alex. But it did. It made him almost human. Even though I was technically Ophi, I was still more comfortable with humans.

When I woke up, the clock on the dashboard said 2:15. I looked around. We were stopped at a gas station. Alex was at the pump. I rubbed my eyes, making sure there wasn't any sleep in the corners of them. I really needed to stretch my legs, so I stepped out of the car.

"Morning," Alex said. "The bathrooms aren't the cleanest, but they work if you want to go inside." He pointed to the convenience store behind me.

"How much farther do we have to go?" We'd been driving for hours already.

"Not much. If you're worried about," he lowered his voice, "being around humans in there, you might want to wait."

Worried about being around humans. It seemed absurd. I'd been around them all my life, but that was back when I thought I was one of them. Now? I nodded my head and got back in the car. We were on the road again before long. Alex kept glancing at me like he was trying to make sure I wasn't going to fall apart.

"You sleep well?"

"I guess. I'm still tired, though."

"I'll ask my parents if the training can wait a little longer, so you can get some rest once we get to the school. I'm sure they've had your room made up for you for months."

I turned to him, studying his face. "When exactly were you supposed to bring me back?"

"When you came into your powers."

"So, we're right on time then?"

"Not according to my father's standards." He sounded annoyed and a little scared at the same time.

"What do you mean?"

"Dad thinks I should've convinced you to come with me the second you came into your powers. When you brought the deer back to life."

I nodded. Of course he'd been there for that. He'd been following me for months. "Then why didn't you?"

"I was going to introduce myself to you right when it happened. But your neighbor pulled over to help you, and then your mom showed up." My heart clenched at the mention of Mom. "I had to wait. So, I watched you in school. I figured it was good for you to hear Mr. Quimby's lecture on Ophiuchus and the Gorgon blood anyway. Of course by that time, you'd already—"

"Killed Nurse Steingall." God, this past week had been a nightmare.

"When I told my parents what happened, they were furious. They told me to get you and bring you back that night, no matter what it took."

"Is that why you showed up at Alberto's looking so angry?"

He nodded. "I wasn't angry with you. I was angry with myself. Nurse Steingall's death is on my head, not yours. You had no idea what your powers could do or that you even had them. It was my job to tell you. And I failed."

"Alex." I reached for him but stopped when he pulled away. "All the texting you were always doing, you were communicating with your parents, weren't you? Keeping them updated on what I was doing."

"Them and Mr. Quimby." Of course. That explained why Mr. Quimby was always emailing in study hall and in between classes. There was something else I had to ask him. Something that had been bugging me. "Why'd you get into a fight with Matt?"

"He was always in my way. Every time I tried to approach you, there he was. It was annoying."

"But you fought him. That was dangerous."

Alex shrugged, and that's when I realized what had really happened. Aside from the initial shove, Alex hadn't touched Matt. He didn't punch him. He didn't even let Matt hit him. He dodged everything to avoid any bloodshed.

"You ducked and backed off when Matt swung at you."

"What was I supposed to do? I could've killed him… easily. I was mad, but I didn't want him dead. I let him do what he thought he had to do to defend your honor. You know, act all boyfriend-like."

Alex turned off the main road onto one I could barely make out. It might have been a fancy gravel driveway at one time, but was now more like an overgrown trail with extra rocks.

"Hang on. It gets a little bumpy up ahead."

That was an understatement. I grabbed the door handle and the edge of my seat to keep from bouncing around and bashing my head into the window. I cried out in pain from my injured fingers.

"We'll get those healed up soon enough." Alex motioned to my hands.

My seatbelt was virtually powerless against the so-called road. We passed a cemetery, and I couldn't help shivering a little. Now that I knew what I was capable of, being around dead bodies didn't seem like such a good idea.

We followed the path—I couldn't accept that it was actually a road—up a hill to where an enormous old building stood. Alex had said it was a mansion, but seriously this thing looked like a university. Maybe that was a good thing because it didn't seem like I'd be going to college anymore. Alex parked the car in the six-car garage. Six! Yes, the place could've used a facelift, but the size made it easy to overlook that.

"Ready to meet the family?" He gave me a killer smile. For a second, it almost felt like we were on a date and he was taking me home to meet his parents. I hoped they'd like me.

Alex walked back out of the garage and waved for me to follow. I looked at the door leading from the garage into the house, just a few feet away from the car, and then back at Alex.

"You can't make your grand entrance through the garage. Come on, the entryway is the best part of the house."

I followed him around to the front of the house. There was a curved stone staircase, leading up to massive wooden double doors that were probably the size of my entire house. I must have looked nervous because Alex squeezed my arm. I looked down at his hand and got a strange sinking feeling in my stomach. Oh, God, I was starting to have feelings for Alex. And not "creepy my-former-stalker-is-touching-my-arm" kind of feelings. They were "I-can-kiss-him-and-not-kill-him" kind of feelings.

The door opened without us even knocking or Alex using a key, and two people, a man and a woman, stood in the doorway. By the way the man looked at Alex like he was a major disappointment, I could only assume he was his father. Which meant the stunningly beautiful blonde woman next to him was Alex's mother. I felt myself feeling really insecure standing that close to her. My clothes were wrinkled from being in the car so long, and I was sure I had bed head. All we had in common were our green eyes. But she didn't seem to mind my appearance one bit because she stepped forward, wrapped me in a hug, and said, "Welcome home, Jodi."

Chapter 16

Home? I was home? I wondered what Mom was doing and if she was okay. Looking at Alex's mother, I knew she could never be like my mom. Still, she seemed happy to see me.

"Thank you, Mrs. uh… Alex's mom." I didn't even know Alex's last name. Alex laughed beside me, and I shot him a look.

"Please, call me Victoria. Mrs. anything makes me sound old."

"It's nice to meet you," I said before turning to Alex's father. "You must be Alex's—"

"Troy Montgomery."

The tension was thick. I looked quickly at Alex before staring at my shoes.

"Well, come in," Victoria said. "You must be hungry."

"Actually, I'm just tired." I stepped into the house. Alex hadn't been kidding. The entryway was gorgeous. It had a vaulted ceiling with a crystal chandelier hanging in the middle. The walls were a rich cream color with expensive-looking gold and silver decorative candleholders displayed on them. In the center of the room was a statue. It was a gold statue, and I was sure it was real gold. My eyes focused on the statue's head. It was a woman, and instead of hair, she had snakes frozen in various wiggly positions. Medusa.

I was strangely drawn to the statue. I didn't understand why because I hated snakes. Yet, I couldn't take my eyes off them or her. Being Ophi meant that I had Medusa's blood in my veins. I circled around her, vaguely aware that Alex and his parents were watching me. They didn't seem at all surprised by my interest in the statue. I hoped that meant I was acting normally for an Ophi. I was acting on instinct. Like an invisible force was moving my body, I reached my hand out and touched Medusa's right hand. Instantly, I felt a surge of energy. I felt alive. More alive than I ever imagined I could feel.

"Wow," I muttered.

Alex came over and stood next to me. "Incredible, right? You know why it's happening, don't you?"

I thought back to Mr. Quimby's lesson. "The blood on the right side of her body restores life."

Alex nodded.

"But this is only a statue. Why would it have this effect on me?" I still held Medusa's right hand, letting her pump life into my body.

Victoria placed her hand on my shoulder. "It's not just a statue, dear. The Ophi claimed Medusa's spirit when she died. It took the collective power of the group and killed most of the Ophi involved, but death should be expected when you strike a deal with Hades. He allowed us to use our powers to raise Medusa's spirit in exchange for the lives of several Ophi."

"But why would he care about Ophi souls when he could have Medusa's?" I asked.

"Hades prizes Ophi souls above the others. Our power becomes his when we die. He was willing to part with Medusa in order to gain more Ophi souls, and it was a price our kind was willing to pay." She paused and lowered her head, like she was collecting her thoughts. "We had Medusa's spirit sealed in this golden statue to preserve her. The statue is passed down to the most prominent Ophi family."

I dropped my hand and watched Victoria stare in reverie at Medusa. Or at least Medusa's spirit. I shuddered.

"Don't be afraid, dear," Victoria said. "In a way, Medusa is the mother of all Ophi. It is her blood in our veins. Her blood that gives Ophi life." She gestured to my hands. "See, she's even healed you."

My injuries were completely gone. If I had had any doubt about the power of this statue, it disappeared with my cuts.

I looked at Alex. He nodded. "You'll get used to it."

"And do you know what would help?" Victoria lifted my left hand toward Medusa's. I started to pull it away. While I'd enjoyed the supercharge Medusa's right hand had given me, the blood from the left side of her body was poisonous. "Relax, Jodi. Her blood is not poisonous to you."

I sighed, remembering that was true. "Sorry, this is all so new to me."

Victoria smiled, and I knew she understood. She raised my hand again, and this time I let her join me with Medusa. A strange tingling crept up my arm slowly, like a snake slithering. It didn't hurt, but it did creep me out.

"What's happening?" My words were shaky.

"Feels like snakes crawling on you, but what you're feeling is really the poison in your blood. But like Victoria said, it's not poisonous to you."

Victoria. Alex just called his mom Victoria. This definitely wasn't like my family, but they were the closest thing to family I had left now. I had an urge to call Mom. Check on her. Tell her I was okay. Then another urge came over me. Still holding Medusa's left hand, I grabbed her right.

"Stop!" Victoria shrieked, but she was too late.

My hair blew up, flying wildly all around me. My blood bubbled in my veins like boiling water, but it didn't hurt. It was the feeling of power. Too much power. My body felt like it was going to burst. Still I held on. My eyes closed, and I threw my head back. An image filled my mind. Medusa. Her snakes wriggled their bodies at me, flicking their tongues. Chills ran down the backs of my legs, but I forced my eyes away from the snakes. Lower. To Medusa's face. She smiled at me. Her face and eyes filled with warmth. She looked like… Mom.

"Do not fear me, Jodi. My blood lies in your veins and in your heart. You are one of mine. My children." Before I could react, Medusa faded away, and I felt my hands slipping from hers. I was breathing heavily, staring at the statue. While everyone else stared at me.

"Jodi," Victoria asked, "what made you take both Medusa's hands at once?"

I stared at my hands. "I don't know. It was instinctual, I guess. Something I felt I was supposed to do." I looked up at Victoria. "Why? Did I do something wrong?"

She looked confused, like I'd asked the most difficult question. Finally, she cleared her throat. "Jodi, every Ophi who has seen the Medusa statue has touched each of her hands and felt the power in each side of her body." For once, I had done the right thing. "But not one Ophi has ever held both Medusa's hands at the same time."

"Why not? It was pretty incredible."

Victoria stepped closer to me and took my hands, palms up, in hers. She stared at them like there was something written there, but nothing was there. "What was it like?"

"I felt… powerful. Like Medusa's power was rushing through me. It was a little scary because it felt like too much power. Like it was going to consume me. But then I saw—" Victoria squeezed my hands and nodded her head, wanting me to continue. I was thankful my hands were healed or it would've really hurt. "I saw Medusa. The real Medusa. Or her spirit, I think. She spoke to me." Victoria's grip was like a vice. "She told me not to be afraid of her. That I was one of her children."

As soon as I stopped talking, Victoria let go of me and spun around. She walked to the window beside the front door and stared out it. Troy glared at me, and I got the feeling that he was trying to see if I was telling the truth. Like I could've made any of this up. I turned to Alex, looking for answers.

"I don't get it. What's the big deal?"

"The big deal," Victoria said, turning back to me, "is that Medusa has claimed you as one of her bloodline."

I shrugged. "So? I thought all Ophi had Medusa's blood."

"We do," Alex said. "But that doesn't mean we're actually related to her."

"You're saying I'm *related* to Medusa? Like she's my great-great-however-many-greats grandmother?"

"We all consider ourselves Medusa's children," Victoria said, "because we share her blood. The blood Ophiuchus received from Athena. But now the prophecy about you makes more sense."

"What prophecy? Alex said something about it on the way here. Something about how I'm supposed to save you all from Hades."

"There is a reason you were supposed to bring her here immediately after she showed signs of her powers," Troy said, practically growling in Alex's face. "It would've been better for her to learn about all this in time. From us." He leaned closer to Alex. "But, as always, you are a disappointment." Alex held his ground, but I could tell it was taking a lot of effort.

"I want to know about the prophecy. I'm glad Alex mentioned it."

"Later," Troy said. "It will all make sense in time."

"No, Troy. She should hear it now." Victoria sighed. "Your father was Ophi, which is why you are Ophi. We knew that. What we didn't know right away, is that your father"—the word 'father' came off her lips like a curse—"wasn't a regular Ophi. He was descended from Medusa. He was supposed to be our leader. Our savior. Now, it looks like that responsibility falls on you."

For a brief moment, I thought Victoria was going to tell me Mom was the one who had to be related to Medusa. "There's something I don't understand." All three of them stared at me. "When I saw Medusa, she looked like my mom."

Victoria nodded. "Medusa has not blessed an Ophi with a vision of her in a very long time, but there is a rumor that her spirit can appear with the face of anyone it chooses. If she wanted to assert a connection to you, it makes sense she'd take on your mother's face to do it."

"Isn't that a little manipulative?"

"Not at all. She wanted to make you comfortable, so she chose a face you were comfortable with."

I squeezed my head in my hands. How was I supposed to handle all of this? Being chosen, descended from Medusa, a completely new life? I exhaled long and hard, trying to push the stress right out of me.

"Jodi, it's the middle of the night. You're exhausted. I think we should leave the rest of your questions for the morning." She put one arm around my shoulders and walked me to a staircase at the end of the enormous entryway. "Alex, show Jodi to her room. See that she has everything she needs, and then report to the study. There are some things we need to discuss."

"I'm actually pretty beat. That was a lot of driving to get here, and I'd love to hit the—"

"This can't wait. I'll be expecting you in fifteen minutes." Victoria gave me a quick squeeze. "We're so happy to have you here. Sleep well."

"Thank you," I said. "Goodnight." I watched Victoria and Troy walk into the room on the right. "So, those are your parents."

"Yup. Those are my parents." Alex sighed. "Come on. I know you're tired, so let's get you to bed."

"What about you? Do you think your parents will have you up much later?"

"Probably." He shrugged, trying to act like he didn't care, but I didn't buy it. "Come on. Your room is upstairs."

The staircase was narrow, and it creaked with every step. I was so tired I thought I'd collapse before I reached the top.

"I don't get it. When I was holding both Medusa's hands, I felt powerful and really alive, but now I'm wiped out."

"It's like that in the beginning. Your power will drain your energy pretty quickly. From the sound of it, you got a serious jolt from Medusa. You're coming down from it now. I'm pretty sure if we don't get to your room fast, you'll wind up sleeping on the stairs." He smiled at me.

"Funny. But since I'm the one who's supposed to save you and the rest of the Ophi, I'm thinking you should be a little nicer to me. If I collapse from exhaustion, the least you can do is carry me to bed." The second I said it, I realized how it sounded.

So did Alex, because he raised an eyebrow and said, "Very interesting. I'll make a note of that."

Wonderful. I'd accidentally come on to my former stalker.

He took me down a long hallway to the third door on the right. "This is you." He opened the door and motioned for me to go in. The room was big, which would have been a dream come true, but it was barely furnished, and all I'd taken with me was the one measly bag Alex had packed. "Oh, I forgot my bag in the car."

"We had it brought up for you." Alex pointed to my bag on the floor by the bed.

"What, do you have maids and butlers in this place?"

"Something like that. Will you be okay or is there something I could help you with?"

"I'm just going to change into comfy clothes and hit the sheets."

"And what's the verdict on whether or not you want my help with that?" He flashed a cocky smile at me. He was undeniably sexy, in an "I-have-poison-blood-in-my-veins" sort of way. Which, for me, was the only way I could handle it, thanks to my Ophi powers. Still, I couldn't think of him that way. I had to stop thinking of him as a guy altogether. He was Alex, my Ophi tutor. A tutor who had said I was hot. No, I wouldn't think about that. I couldn't.

"Should I take your silence to mean you're thinking it over?"

"What? No! I-I'm tired. I zoned out for a minute." I crossed my arms and turned away from him slightly, catching my reflection in the mirror. My hair had this windblown effect going on, most likely from my encounter with Medusa. My loose curls had a snake-like quality to them. "Oh, this is pretty. Remind me never to try that double hand holding trick again." I patted my hair down.

"I kind of like it," Alex said. "It makes you look a little wild."

"You like girls to be wild, huh?" Ugh, why did I say that out loud?

He laughed. "Depends on the girl."

Things were getting more awkward by the minute. I picked up my bag and placed it on the bed. "You did pack clothes for me to sleep in, right?"

"Um, actually, I didn't."

I tore my clothes out of the bag, which wasn't the best idea since one of my bras went flying across the room.

"I'll get that."

"No!" I put my hand up to stop him. "You stay there. I got it. It's bad enough you went through my underwear drawer. I don't need you picking up my bra for me." I grabbed it and shoved it in the top dresser drawer. The drawer was empty except for a locket lying in the middle of it. "What's this?" I picked it up and held it out to Alex.

"I don't know. I've never seen it before."

"Well, whose room was this?"

"No one's. No one's lived in here for as long as my parents have owned the house."

"Hmm." The front had a reddish stone, but the center was green. It almost looked like a red veil wrapped around the green in the middle, and as I stared at it, I swore the red part swirled almost like blood. I blinked, thinking it was just my tired eyes playing tricks on me, and turned the locket over. The letter M was engraved on the other side.

"Does it open?" Alex asked. "Aren't lockets meant to hold pictures inside?"

I looked for a way to open it. "Yeah, but this one doesn't seem to. Strange. I guess I'll put it back where I found it." I turned back to the drawer, but instead of putting it inside, I closed my fingers around it and kept it hidden from Alex.

"Sorry about forgetting to pack some pajamas for you. I have a long sleeved t-shirt you can borrow. The heating in this place is crazy. We keep it on low, and it still gets scorching hot at night. You should be plenty warm enough in the shirt, and I'm betting it would look like a dress on you." He was a lot taller than me.

"Okay, yeah. Thanks."

"I'll be right back." He left the room, and I looked at the locket again. Just like with the Medusa statue downstairs, I had this feeling. This locket was meant for me, so I put it on and hid it under my shirt before Alex came back.

Chapter 17

I woke the next day, feeling pretty good. I'd slept well, snuggled up in Alex's long sleeved gray t-shirt, breathing in his scent. Why did he have to smell so good? I felt guilty for sniffing the shirt first thing when I opened my eyes. Matt hadn't even been in the ground for twenty-four hours and I was moving on? I wasn't, really. The thing with Alex was more like me latching on to him because he was the only somewhat familiar face in my new life.

I had no idea what was in store for me today. Alex had said his family would teach me about my powers, so I figured I was in for boring information dumps. For some reason, I wasn't all that eager to get started. I remembered the locket and reached for it, pulling it out from under my shirt—Alex's shirt. Something about the locket screamed, *I'm yours!* I really hoped Alex wouldn't mention it to his parents. I didn't want to find out that it belonged to someone else. It felt at home around my neck.

Someone knocked lightly on the door, and I stuffed the locket back under my shirt. "Who is it?"

"Alex."

Oh no! I was sure I looked like a car wreck. "Just a second!" I scrambled out of bed, getting tangled in the sheets in the process. I fell to the floor with a loud thud.

Alex burst through the door. "Is everything—" When he saw me on the floor in a jumbled mess, he bit his lip. No doubt to keep from laughing. "I wanted to let you know, lunch is ready in the dining room."

"Lunch?" I untangled myself and stood up, tossing the sheets back on the bed. "What time is it?"

"12:30. I take it you slept well."

"Yeah, thanks."

"Told you my t-shirt would keep you warm." He winked at me, and I felt my cheeks blush. "Looks good on you, too." He started to leave, but hesitated in the doorway. "The dining room is downstairs. Take the hallway on your left all the way to the end."

I nodded, feeling rather naked in nothing but a long t-shirt and underwear. "Got it."

"Oh, and don't worry about making your bed. We have servants for that. So, hurry up and get dressed and head on down for lunch." He closed the door, leaving me to wallow in my embarrassment.

Lunch turned out to be an elaborate affair. The dining room was the size of the school cafeteria. There were side tables filled with lavish displays of just about every kind of food. In the middle of the room was a long table. A table filled with people I didn't know. I did a quick head count and realized there were twelve other people living here. I was lucky number thirteen.

Alex nodded to me with a mouthful of mac and cheese. I glanced around the table. Everyone else was eating big meals—rack of lamb, lobster, filet mignon. All but Alex. Victoria rose from the table and came to greet me. "Good morning, Jodi."

"Morning? It's afternoon. Sleeping Beauty slept through an entire morning of training." I didn't need to ask who the girl was who'd said that. Alex rolled his eyes, confirming that she was the infamous Abigail. She had short black hair, cropped at her chin, and, even though she was sitting down, I could tell she had the perfect figure.

"Come," Victoria said, ignoring Abby's comment. "There's an empty seat next to Alex." Before I could sit, Victoria said, "Everyone, this is Jodi, the newest member of our family." I nodded and gave everyone a small smile before sitting and trying to avoid their stares. A waiter appeared behind me and asked me what I'd like to eat. I turned slightly to answer him and shuddered. His face had a bluish tint, and his eyes were sunken. He held a pitcher of water in his hand and poured a glass for me. The skin on his hand was sagging and blackened in a few places. After he poured my water, he stared at me, waiting for an answer. But I couldn't talk. There was no doubt about it. This man was dead.

"She'll have the mac and cheese. Same as me," Alex said.

I turned to him and whispered, "Thank you."

"No problem. They take some getting used to."

"They?"

Alex used his fork to point at the other servants in the room. Their backs had been to me when I came in, but now I could see their faces. Each one of them was in a different stage of decay. Some were missing patches of skin, while others looked waxy and pale. My stomach lurched.

"Excuse me." I bolted out of my chair and rushed for the door. I bumped into the guy carrying my plate of mac and cheese, smashing the contents of the plate all over the front of my outfit. He apologized, which only made me feel sicker. He was the one who had been—from the looks of him—ripped from his grave, and yet he was apologizing to me. I ran, heading back down the hall and out the front door. I kept going down the steps and across the lawn, stopping at a weeping willow and losing myself under its hanging branches. I sat down and cried.

"Jodi." Alex rushed over and sat next to me.

"I guess there's no such thing as alone time around here. At least not when the people you're running from are so fast."

"You're running from me?" By the tone of his voice, I could tell he was hurt.

I raised my head, meeting his eyes. "You were totally okay with what was going on in there. Those people were dead, and you guys were making them wait on you. I mean, how can you enjoy a meal with decaying people serving you? My God! They prepared the food, too, didn't they?" My stomach churned again. "And the comment you made about having people to make the beds, those are the people, aren't they?"

Alex nodded. "But it's not as bad as you think."

I stood up. "Not as bad—please, tell me that's a sick joke. They're walking dead. Dead that you and your family brought back to life so you wouldn't have to do chores."

"You think they'd be better off in the ground, being eaten by maggots?"

This time I couldn't stop it. The visual was too much on top of what I'd already seen. I leaned forward and spilled my guts on the lawn. Alex jumped up. At first, I'd thought he was afraid of getting puked on, but he pulled my hair back, keeping it out of my face.

"I'm sorry. I shouldn't have said that."

I wiped my mouth on the bottom of my already filthy shirt, and Alex let my hair fall down my back. "It was the truth, right?" I shook my head. "I know I have to get used to this new life, but isn't what your family's doing the kind of thing that gets Hades' boxers in a bunch? If things are getting bad for the Ophi, so bad that you need me," I choked on the words, "to save you all, why would you risk making Hades angry with you? It doesn't make sense."

"Mom and Dad have never played by the rules. They run this place, and since they're doing a service to the Ophi, they feel that gives them certain privileges."

I squinted at him. "Raising the dead isn't a privilege."

"Listen, I'm not doing a very good job explaining all this to you. Why don't you come back inside? Change into some clean clothes, and I'll have some food brought—no, I'll bring food up to your room. I even promise to make it myself."

"Why?" It was blunt, but I had to know. "Why would you go out of your way for me? You don't even know me."

"But I'd like to get to know you." He smirked. "Once you've showered and brushed your teeth."

I playfully smacked his arm. I couldn't help thinking this would all be easier if it were just Alex and me, but I'd made a complete fool of myself in front of eleven other people, who I had a feeling weren't going to be anywhere near as understanding or patient with me as Alex was.

"How bad is it?"

"Well, let's just say you've looked better and leave it at that."

"No, I mean how bad have I made things with the other Ophi?"

"Oh." He sighed. "There were a few comments after you ran out. Mostly Abby laughing at you getting covered in mac and cheese. Though she did suggest we offer you up to Hades in exchange for our protection."

My eyes widened. "Can you do that?"

Alex shook his head. "No one's handing you over to Hades. You're our savior, remember?"

"Yeah, a savior with a weak stomach."

"We'll fix that. And we'll start by getting you cleaned up and fed."

We walked back to the house and parted ways at the staircase. I went up to my room and grabbed my towel and some more clothes. I took a chance that the door across the hall from mine was the bathroom. Last night I'd used one downstairs. Now, I needed a bathroom with a shower. I turned the knob and was greeted by a loud shrieking voice. "We knock in this house!"

"Oh, sorry," I said.

The door swung open, nearly yanking my arm out of the socket. Abby stood in front of me, glaring at me under her thick black bangs. "Look who it is. The dead-loving mac and cheese girl." Oh good, not even here a day and I'd already gotten myself a nickname.

"Sorry. I was looking for the bathroom."

"I should hope so. You reek!" She twitched her nose at me. "What did you do, throw up on yourself, too?"

"Can you tell me where the bathroom is?" I asked.

She pointed to the door right next to mine. "And do us all a favor, wash twice!" she yelled after me.

I ducked into the bathroom and locked the door behind me. Like the rest of the house, it was huge. I noticed there was another door on the side wall. I went over to it and knocked lightly, calling, "Hello?" I didn't want to make the same mistake twice. No one answered, so I turned the knob. I nearly fell over when I saw where the door led. My room. I'd assumed the door was another closet. "Wow, Abby must really think I'm an idiot," I muttered.

"You could say that again."

I whipped around to see Abby standing in the other doorway. "I thought I locked that."

"You did. I have a key." She held up the silver key for a second before putting it in her pocket. "I thought we should have a little chat, and seeing as how you're alone, this is the perfect time."

"What is it with Ophi and cornering people in the bathroom?"

"What are you babbling about?"

"Nothing." I put my hands on my hips, trying to make it look like I wasn't totally scared of her. "Talk."

"I've noticed you and Alex seem to be… close."

What was she getting at? "He's the only one I even remotely know around here. I wouldn't say that makes us close."

She stepped toward me. "Good. Because Alex is unavailable to you."

I knew Alex and Abby weren't a thing. Alex definitely wasn't into her. Of course, that didn't mean they had never been together. Being her ex would account for his dislike for her now. "Were you two together at one point?"

"Not were, honey. We *are* together."

I raised my eyebrows. "Huh, I guess I was mistaken when I saw him roll his eyes at you earlier in the dining room."

She shot me a look that made me wonder why I was taunting her when she had me trapped. "Was that before or after you became the Mac and Cheese Queen?"

My eyes dropped to my shirt, splattered with orange sauce and bits of macaroni.

"You may think you're someone special around here because you're supposedly the girl in the prophecy, but as far as I'm concerned, you're nothing more than a half-blood. And sooner or later, the weaker human blood that's diluting the Gorgon blood in you will show everyone just how unworthy you really are of being called Ophi." She flicked my shirt with her fingers. "On second thought, you better wash three times." She turned and walked out, leaving me completely speechless.

When I'd recovered enough to start a hot shower and get undressed, I realized I had another problem. The locket. I still wasn't sure if it opened somehow, so I didn't want to wear it in the shower. But I felt funny taking it off. Like part of me was missing, which was totally bizarre considering I'd only found the locket last night. I decided to take it off and keep it on the edge of the tub. That way it was still close, but the curtain would protect it from getting wet.

I stepped in and turned the dial to the hottest setting. Nothing calmed me down faster than a steaming hot shower. I could hear Abby's voice in my head as I washed. And I did wash three times to be sure I'd gotten rid of the vomit and mac and cheese combo scent I had going on. I had to prove to Abby that I wasn't the cowardly half-blood she thought I was. I might not know how to control my powers now, but I would learn. I'd already done something no other Ophi had done. I'd held both Medusa's hands and let her full powers flow through me. If that didn't prove I was strong or that I was in the right place, then I didn't know what would.

Even if I didn't like it and Abby didn't like it, this was my home now. The thought made me miss Mom. What kind of daughter was I that I'd slept so soundly in my new bed while Mom was probably at home crying her eyes out, not getting a minute of sleep? I allowed myself to cry, to let my feelings pour down the shower drain. Then, I made myself a promise that I'd call Mom the second I was back in my room. I'd tell her I was okay. That she didn't need to worry about me because I was safe. I'd leave out any mention of Abby and the walking dead servants. I'd just say I… I couldn't come up with a single thing to say. She hadn't believed me when I tried to tell her the truth. If I tried again, she'd only get angry. I made up my mind to call her and hang up immediately after I told her I was safe. It would break her heart, but at least she'd know I was alive.

I turned the water off, realizing I'd been in there too long and that Alex was probably waiting in my room with some food. My stomach rumbled at the thought. I dried and got dressed as quickly as I could. Gathering my hair in a ponytail, I went back to the shower for my locket. I reached between the curtain and the shower liner. Not finding it, I pulled the curtain all the way open. The ledge was empty. I looked into the tub, thinking it had fallen when I'd gotten out of the shower. It wasn't there either.

"Where is it?" I panicked. My eyes scanned the bathroom and stopped at the door leading to the hall. "Abby and her stupid key," I said through gritted teeth.

Chapter 18

Part of me wanted to storm into Abby's room and demand she give my locket back. But another part of me knew that wasn't a good idea. For one, the locket might actually belong to Abby. She could've dropped it, and one of the servants—the thought of them still made me shiver— could've picked it up and put it in my dresser drawer by mistake. Still, I had this feeling that the locket was supposed to be mine. But how could I prove it? I had to find a way. And then, I had to steal it back.

I regrouped in front of the bathroom mirror, not wanting Alex to know something was wrong. He'd thought I put the locket back where I found it, and I was hoping he'd forgotten all about it by now. I put on my best fake smile and went into my room. Just as I'd thought, Alex was sitting at the desk with a plate of food in front of him.

"I see you like it hot," he said.

"What?" I nearly jumped backward. He pointed to the steam pouring out of the open bathroom door. "Oh, yeah. It's good for relaxing your muscles." I carried my dirty clothes to a wicker hamper in the corner.

"I decided you'd probably had enough mac and cheese for one day, so I got you filet mignon. I hope that's okay."

"That's great. One of my favorites, actually." I didn't mention the reason it was one of my favorite foods was that we rarely ever had it at home. It was way too expensive.

"Good." He stood up. "Here. Sit. Eat."

"What am I, a dog? Here. Sit. Eat. I may be a little shaken up, but I can still handle full sentences."

"Technically, sit and eat are full sentences." I gave him a look, and he let it go. "Well, anyway, I convinced Victoria and Troy to give you some time to adjust. They said you could hang out here and relax until dinner. But after dinner, Victoria wants to introduce you to one of your instructors. I should warn you 'introduce you' probably means you're going to be hearing a lecture on Ophi history."

"Sounds fun. Exactly how I like to spend my evenings."

"You know, you've become even more sarcastic since you've come into your power."

"Maybe the power of sarcasm is part of the Ophi package. Abby sure seems good at it." I took the plate of food to my bed and started eating. I couldn't remember the last meal I'd had.

Alex sighed. "What did Abigail do now? Turn off the hot water in your shower? No, wait, I saw the amount of steam coming from in there."

"Do you know she has a key to my bathroom? How weird is that?" I chewed another bite, giving Alex a chance to respond, but he didn't. "I can't imagine why she'd need a key to my bathroom."

"She shares a bathroom with another girl, Bristol. Not everyone here has their own bathroom like you do. But Abby found a key a while ago and since this room was unoccupied, she decided to make your bathroom her bathroom."

"Well, I think she should hand over the key since I'm here now."

"Why? Do you have something to hide? A reason you don't want to share a bathroom with Abby?" He narrowed his eyes at me.

"Isn't her charming demeanor enough reason?"

"There's that sarcasm again. Watch it, Jodi, or people might start mistaking you for Abby."

That stung. I dropped my fork on the plate, suddenly not very hungry. Of course, I'd almost devoured the entire filet already. "I'm sorry. It's just that she got under my skin today. I know I shouldn't stoop to her level."

"Did she do something to you?"

"Like what?" He was starting to make me wonder if Abby really was a threat to me.

"Never mind. Forget I asked. Try not to let her get to you. She's mad at the world because her family sent her here. Apparently she wasn't living up to their standards, and they shipped her off. They don't even write or call."

I couldn't help feeling a little sorry for her, but I wasn't about to let her get away with stealing my locket when I hadn't done anything to deserve it.

"You want me to show you around? I think I could skip out on training this afternoon to play tour guide to the new girl."

I did want to look around, but I wasn't sure having Alex with me was a good idea. "Does everyone train in the afternoon? And what exactly is training?"

"Yes, we all train. All the kids anyway. Most of the adults are here to help us learn to control our powers better. It's kind of hard to explain what the training actually is without showing you, though. You'll see tomorrow at your first lesson."

"Okay. Well, I think I'll skip the tour for now. Rain check, though. I want to finish unpacking and check in with my mom."

"Whoa, what are you going to say to your mom? You already—"

"Yeah, I know the truth isn't a good idea. Don't worry. I've decided to tell her I'm okay. That's all. Not where I am or who I'm with. Only that I'm okay."

"And what about when she starts throwing questions at you?"

I exhaled long and hard. "I'm going to hang up."

"I don't know, Jodi. I think you should talk to Victoria first. She can help you figure out something to say so you don't have to slam the phone down on your mom. I mean, do you really think you'll be able to hang up on her if she's crying and begging you to come home?"

This was so not what I wanted to hear. I twisted the bedspread in my fingers, and then I remembered how I'd left my bed before going to lunch. "Ugh, those servants made my bed." I was definitely going to have nightmares. That is, if I could even sleep knowing there were a bunch of dead people wandering around the house.

"If you don't mind cleaning up after yourself, I'll tell them they can skip your room from now on."

"Thanks, I'd appreciate that."

"It's really not that bad though. They're great at their jobs."

"Believe me, it's nothing personal against them. I just don't think it's right. They shouldn't be here anymore. After you die, your soul's supposed to rest in peace."

"Not all souls." He walked toward the door. "Don't try to figure everything out all at once. There's a learning curve here."

"Hey." There was something I needed to know before he left. "How are you able to control the servants?"

"Eventually I'll be able to control any soul. It's an adult Ophi power. But the servants are under Victoria and Troy's control, and they make them obey us, too." He gave a small wave before leaving and shutting the door behind him.

I waited about thirty seconds before going to the door and peeking into the hallway. It was quiet. I tiptoed to Abby's door and pressed my ear against it. Nothing. I tried the knob, but of course it was locked. She was key girl—I should've assumed she'd use a key on her own door. I went back to my room and grabbed my plate off the bed. Returning my dishes to the kitchen would give me a little bit of a cover if anyone caught me sneaking around downstairs. If Abby's room was off-limits right now, then I wanted to find out more about the "dead today, alive tomorrow" servants. I wondered if there was a way to do it without actually having to see them.

At the bottom of the stairs, I got this weird feeling. Something was pulling me, like my blood was flowing against the right side of my body. I turned to see what it was that my body was trying to tell me. The statue of Medusa stood in the foyer, its back to me. I put my plate down on the stairs and walked over to Medusa. I faced her, taking in her form. In books, Medusa always looked hideous, scary. But other than the wriggly snakes on her head, this Medusa was beautiful.

I smiled at her. If I'd ever doubted that I was Ophi, the connection I felt to Medusa erased that doubt completely. I was drawn to her. The urge to touch her took over again. I reached both my hands out to hers. A surge of power bubbled through my blood. I inhaled, welcoming the boost of energy Medusa was giving me. I closed my eyes, allowing myself to be consumed by the experience. Like last time, Medusa entered my mind. I saw her standing before me. This time she didn't look like my mom. She was beautiful, more beautiful than anyone I'd ever seen. I remembered the myth about Medusa being so beautiful that Athena cursed her.

"Welcome back, my child. I was hoping I'd see you again soon." I tried to respond to her but my mouth wouldn't form the words. "Speak with your mind alone, Jodi. We are connected. I will hear your thoughts."

"What is this?" I asked. "What is this connection doing to me?"

"I am allowing you to feel the full extent of your power. You are chosen, and you must learn to use all of your power if you are to fulfill your duty to the Ophi."

"How do I fulfill my duty? What do I have to do?"

"In time, that will become clear to you. For now, follow your instincts. They brought you to me twice now. They will serve you well as long as you don't allow them to be overshadowed by what others tell you."

"What others tell me? I don't understand."

"Not everyone here is your friend, Jodi. Some will try to steer you wrong." Medusa stepped closer and looked down at her neck. The locket—my locket—hung there.

"The locket belongs to you!"

"At one time it did, but now it is yours. I left it for you, but you are not wearing it."

"I was. Until someone stole it."

"You must get it back, Jodi. It's not an ordinary locket. Inside is a vial of my blood, taken directly from the center of my body. It contains the poison *and* the power to heal all in one. That is a dangerous thing to let slip into the wrong hands."

The red veil over the green, I *had* seen it swirling. It was Medusa's blood. "I tried to open the locket. It's sealed shut."

"For good reason. Opening the locket at the wrong time would have disastrous effects. Should you ever need to use the blood inside, you will know how. But it is meant for you alone. Do you know who has the locket now?"

"Abby."

"Get it back. Soon." I felt Medusa slipping away and became aware of fingers wrapped around my forearm. I let go of Medusa and opened my eyes to see Alex.

"I'm not so sure you should be doing that. We still don't know what it will do to you."

"Medusa claimed me as one of her bloodline, remember? She's not going to do anything bad to me. Besides, I thought you'd be happy I was trying to learn more about who I am."

Alex sighed. "Speaking of bloodlines, did you call your mom?"

"No. You were right. I wouldn't be able to hang up on her. She'd cry and then I'd cry and who knows what I'd say."

"We'll figure something out."

I nodded. "Hopefully soon. I don't want to keep her wondering. It's probably killing her." Really bad choice of words. "Why aren't you in training?" I asked, needing to change the subject.

"I was, but it's over." He looked at me like I had three heads. "How long have you been down here?"

"I don't know. I was bringing my food to the kitchen, but I felt—" I wasn't sure if I should tell him about the strange pull of the statue when I'd gotten to the bottom of the stairs.

"You're hiding something from me." His face fell. "You don't trust me. I get it."

"No, that's not it." I put my hand on his arm.

He jerked his arm away. "Whoa, your fingers are burning hot."

I raised my fingers to my face, but I lowered them instantly. Alex was right. They felt as hot as burning coal. "What's that about?"

Alex touched my arm again. "The rest of you feels fine. It's just your hands." Alex and I both looked at the Medusa statue. "How long did you say you were down here?"

"Only a couple of minutes."

Alex walked over to the stairs and picked up my plate. He walked it over to me and held it up. The tiny piece of meat was scaly and dry, like it had been sitting out for hours.

"What time is it?" I asked.

"Six o'clock."

I shook my head. "No way. That's impossible. I came downstairs about a minute after you left my room."

"That was three and a half hours ago, Jodi."

My legs went limp, and I slumped forward. Alex dropped the plate in time to catch me. He dragged me over to the stairs and sat me down on the bottom step. Everything went black. I heard a shuffling of footsteps and Victoria's voice. "Alex, what happened?"

"I found her touching the statue again. Like last night. She'd been there for hours. I think the rush of energy completely wiped her out."

"My, how the mighty have fallen," Abby scoffed.

"Go to your room, Abigail," Victoria said.

My eyes fluttered open, and I was relieved that I could see again. Alex sat me up more but didn't say a word. All eyes were on me, waiting to see if I was all right. Alex took one of my hands in his. I thought he was being sweet until he said, "She feels normal now. When I found her, her hands were too hot to touch."

"Help her to her room. She needs rest."

"No," I said. "I feel okay now."

"I'd still like you to lie down for a while," Victoria said. "You were connected to the statue for way too long. We can't be sure what effect that's had on you."

I nodded. I couldn't deny that my body wanted rest, even if I didn't. I wanted to search Abby's room for my locket—Medusa's locket.

"Wait," I said, "before I go upstairs, there's something I need to ask you."

Victoria folded her hands in front of her. "Go ahead."

"When can I see the prophecy about me?"

"Why do you ask? Did you see something when you were connected with the statue?"

"Yes. Medusa's spirit appeared to me again. She said she had a gift for me. Something that had belonged to her."

Victoria stiffened. "Has she told you what the gift will be?"

"She showed it to me."

"And? What is it?" Victoria was speaking slowly, like she was trying hard to remain calm.

I looked at Alex next to me on the stairs. His face was pinched and frightened. I'd made a mistake even mentioning the gift to Victoria. I didn't know what I'd been thinking. But Medusa had said so little about it, and Victoria was supposed to help me, right? I had to test her, see if she really knew anything about it.

"It's a ring with a red stone. She didn't say when I would get it."

"Well, then no sense worrying about it this evening," Victoria said with a smile. But I could see the wheels turning in her head. The Ophi may know a lot about themselves and their own powers, but I was still somewhat of a mystery. Because once again, I was different from everyone else.

Chapter 19

After Alex brought me upstairs and made me get into bed, he sent a servant to get me some food. When I protested, he said I needed to get my strength back up. I really wasn't feeling all that bad. Confused mostly. How had I been connected to the statue for three and a half hours? It had felt like only minutes.

"Still trying to work things out in there?" Alex tapped his finger on my head.

"You could say that. I did lose a few hours of my life."

"You're probably pretty freaked out right now, huh?"

"A little, but not in the way you're thinking." It wasn't Medusa who was scaring me. Sure, she'd put me in some sort of mind trance that made time sort of stand still, but I had this feeling she was trying to help me. "I think the statue is helping me tap into my powers. When I'm connected to Medusa, I can feel every ounce of power in my body. And it's like both sides of my blood, the poison part and the part that restores life, are working together. Is that even possible?"

"Not that I know of." He looked down at the blanket on my bed, studying it like it was the most interesting thing in the world. "I was worried about you. You were feverish, and not a small fever either. I've never felt anything that hot that wasn't on fire."

"I don't understand it either, but maybe it has to do with how my blood feels when I touch Medusa. It bubbles, like boiling water, only I don't feel hot. Not inside anyway."

"You should tell all this to Mr. Quimby in the morning."

"Mr. Quimby? He's here? I haven't seen him."

"He's not here yet, but he will be in the morning. He stayed behind to tie up a few loose ends after you left."

Alex still wouldn't look at me, so I leaned forward and grabbed his hand. "What loose ends?"

He looked at me and frowned. "Little things that could've been traced back to you."

"Like what?" We'd taken care of Mom, and Matt was not a threat to the Ophi anymore.

"The deer you brought back, for one. It was doing a number on the farm animals." I'd forgotten about the deer. "The squirrel from the construction site—the vet thought he euthanized it, but really the thing was just knocked out. It's dead now, though. And then, of course, he had to say something to your mom."

"My mom? Mr. Quimby talked to my mom about me, and you chose to lead with the deer?" There had to be a reason Alex didn't tell me that right away. What was he trying to bury? Ugh! My brain was wired with words straight out of the dictionary for the dead. "What did he say to my mom, Alex?"

"I don't know for sure, but he had to cover up anything that could lead people to finding out about us."

"But I told my mom about my blood. She thought it was a joke. Crazy talk. She didn't believe a word of it."

"Yes, but you still told her things. Things a human shouldn't know."

Now I was shaking. The Ophi were very secretive. What would they do to Mom to keep her from telling our secret? "What did Mr. Quimby do?" My voice cracked.

"He wouldn't hurt her, Jodi. I promise. He had to convince her that you really were talking crazy."

"Crazy as in, 'Gee, that Jodi has a really weird sense of humor,' or crazy as in 'Jodi needs to be locked up in a padded cell'?"

He didn't answer, but he didn't need to. Things were getting frighteningly clear.

"That's the real reason why you didn't want me calling my mom. You knew Mr. Quimby was going to talk to her. To tell her that her only daughter was crazy. Now, not only does she think I ran away, she thinks I did it because I'm a complete mental case!" A knock at the door interrupted me. "What?" I yelled, not wanting to deal with anyone else right now.

The door opened, and one of the servants came into the room with a covered dish. "Your food." He brought the dish to me, and our hands touched for a second. I jerked my hand away from his, spilling the contents of the dish all over my blanket. The servant immediately began wiping the spaghetti and meatballs off the blanket with his hand. Bits of flesh peeled off his palm and stuck to the blanket.

"Stop!" I shrieked. "Just stop!"

"Only trying to help," he said.

"Yeah, everyone here is trying to help. Only I don't want help. Besides, you're the one who needs the help." My heart raced, and I could feel the blood in my veins. It simmered as I stared at the servant. "You're not supposed to be here. This is all wrong. You're supposed to be in your grave. That's where you belong."

Alex grabbed my shoulder, but he pulled away and winced. "Jodi, you're on fire. You need to calm down. Our power is rooted in our emotions. If you don't get a hold of yourself—"

"Don't tell me what to do." I shot a look at Alex before turning back to the servant. "I'm sorry you were brought back and forced to wait on people. I really am. I'm sorry you're decaying and dropping pieces of flesh on my bed. I'm sorry you're forced to stay here when you should be six feet under the ground." I wasn't trying to be mean. I really hated seeing the servants forced to exist like this. My blood boiled under my skin, making me shake. "You need to go back to your grave because that's where you belong."

"Jodi, no!" Alex yelled. I turned to him, not sure why he was so upset.

The servant nodded to me. "As you wish." He turned and left the room.

"We have to stop him," Alex said, throwing the pasta-covered blanket off me.

"What? Why?"

Alex was breathing heavily and shaking his head. "You used your power on him."

"No, I didn't. I didn't bleed on him or cry on him. I just told him where he belonged."

"He isn't human anymore. He's a spirit that's been shoved back into a decaying body. A body controlled by—"

"Your family. You did this to them."

"The servants are controlled by the adults. I told you, they only listen to the rest of us as far as giving us what we want to eat and other little things Victoria and Troy told them to do for us. But underage Ophi don't know how to control a soul raised by someone else." He glared at me. "Except you." I didn't know how to control any of my powers. He was talking crazy. "Something happened to you just now. You changed. You got scalding hot to the touch, and you commanded that servant to go back to his grave."

"No. I didn't command him to do anything. I told him where he was supposed to be."

"Which is as good as a command if you're tapping into that power. And you definitely were."

I was speechless. Once again, I'd used my powers without meaning to. "What do we do?"

"We have to go after him. You have to tell him to stop."

"But if he goes back to his grave, he'll be at rest. He should be at rest, not working here."

"Think, Jodi. He's going to dig up the ground and crawl back into his grave. Get the mental image because you need to be prepared for what you're going to see out there. And once he digs his way to his grave and crawls inside, he'll stay there. But not at peace. He's not dead, Jodi. He's a soul stuck in a dead body. And you sentenced him to stay that way for all eternity."

Oh, God! I had no idea. If that poor soul got stuck in a grave—well, that would be worse than what Alex's family had done to him in the first place. "What do we do?"

He tugged on my arm, and we ran from the room. I wasn't quite at full strength yet, but that wasn't going to stop me. I had created this problem, and now I had to fix it. I stumbled a few times, but Alex stopped me from completely wiping out. I could tell he was holding back, not running at full speed so he could keep an eye on me. After how quickly he had gotten to me after lunch, I knew the guy had some major leg turnover. Luckily, dead people don't. Even with the head start, the servant had only made it to the cemetery when we caught up with him.

Without thinking, I reached for the guy's arm. "No, don't!" Alex said, yanking me back. "He's dead, and his body is barely holding itself together. If you pull on his arm, it'll come right off."

I gagged. "Oh, this keeps getting better and better." Alex flicked on a flashlight that he must have grabbed on the way out of the house. He really was like a Boy Scout—always prepared. He shone the light on the servant, who was completely ignoring us and zigzagging through the headstones. "What do we do then? How do we stop him?"

"You have to control him. Like you did in your room."

"Why me?" My voice was high and squeaky. "I haven't even had any training yet."

"Because I don't have enough power to do it. Only the adults can control the dead once they're brought back to life. I started to learn how to do it, but my powers aren't strong enough yet." He took my shoulders and turned me so I was forced to look at him and nothing else. "Somehow, you have enough power for this. You're not like the rest of us. You're stronger. You need to concentrate. Do whatever you did upstairs."

"But I don't know what I did." For the past week, things had just been happening to me. I didn't understand any of it, and I didn't have control over it.

Alex lowered his hands and turned to see how far the servant had gotten. I followed his gaze. The guy was at his grave, shoveling dirt aside with his hands. Even from a distance, I could see his flesh falling off his hands in the process. There was going to be nothing left of him by the time he dug his own grave. I couldn't let this happen. "Tell me what to do."

"Okay, you have to concentrate and draw from your emotions."

"What does that mean?" This wasn't the time to be cryptic.

"You were angry in your room. It was that anger that fueled your power. You need a strong emotion."

My emotions were definitely running on high. "All right, what else?"

"Let the emotion wash over you. It has to take over your body. When it does, you'll feel your blood. Literally feel it from head to toe. That's when you'll know you're ready."

I put my hand up to stop him. "Let me work on that part before you tell me anymore. I don't want to get confused by too many details at once. I'm new at this."

He nodded. "We should move closer. It will help you focus on him." We ran over to the grave and stopped just far enough away that we weren't going to get pelted with dirt and bits of flesh. "You can do this," Alex said, giving my arm a quick squeeze.

I inhaled deeply, which was a mistake since the air smelled like a combination of rotting flesh and dirt. I let images of all the awful things that had happened to me fill my mind. I started small. The deer. The deer terrorizing the farm and killing the sheep. The squirrel biting into Jake's neck. Nurse Steingall and Dr. Alvarez. Matt. Matt ripping into the bunny. My blood started rippling in my veins. By the time I got to Mom, I was ready. "What's next?"

"Think about what you want this guy to do. Get firm instructions in your head, and then tell him. You need to be forceful. He has to know you are in charge."

I thought about what I wanted him to do. I wanted him to stop digging his grave. I wanted him to forget the command I'd given him before. No. That wasn't what I wanted. I wanted him to find peace. I wanted his soul to return to wherever it had been before Alex's family forced it into its decaying body. I wanted him to be free.

"Jodi, come on," Alex urged.

I opened my eyes, locking them on the servant. "Stop!" I wasn't sure if yelling was necessary, but Alex had said I needed to be forceful. The servant hesitated for a moment but then started digging again. "I command you to stop!" This time he listened. He stayed kneeling, but he stopped digging. I knew Alex wasn't going to be happy about what I was going to do next, but I'd made up my mind. "I command your soul to return to the place it was before it was put back in this body. Go now! I command you to leave your body and return to where you belong!" I was concentrating so hard, my body shook. My blood boiled under my skin. Sweat dripped down my forehead.

The servant looked at me briefly before his body crumbled on the ground. I couldn't be sure, but I thought he'd looked thankful, relieved to be free. I smiled, and my legs gave out from beneath me. Alex rushed over to me, helping me stand. He draped my arm over his shoulders to steady me. "Why did you do that?" he asked.

"Because he didn't deserve to live like that. He was being tortured. Releasing his soul was the only way I could make up for what I'd almost made him do."

Alex sighed. "You definitely aren't like the rest of the Ophi."

"Don't say that. You make them sound like awful people."

"No, I didn't mean it like that. I meant, you can do things the rest of us can't."

"You said you haven't been taught how to do that yet, but that doesn't mean you can't."

"I wish I could've done that for—"

"Matt."

"I had to use my blood on him. Kill him for the second time." Alex closed his eyes and ran a hand through his hair. "If I had your powers, I could've released his soul without having to put him through dying all over again.

"I don't blame you for what happened. And neither would Matt. You did what you could to fix the situation. A situation I created. Any suffering Matt went through was my fault. Not yours."

"Thanks, but sometimes I think it would be a lot easier if I were like you."

"Hey, you want to be the Chosen One with a prophecy written about you? Please, be my guest. Then maybe for once in my life, I could be the normal one."

"No, Jodi." He smiled and shook his head. "You could never be normal."

Somehow when Alex said it, it didn't seem so bad.

He nodded at the body on the ground. "How are we going to explain to Victoria why she's down a servant?"

Ugh, I hadn't thought of that. Victoria wasn't going to be happy about this.

Chapter 20

Alex said someone would bury the body in the morning. It felt wrong to leave the guy lying on top of the grave, but Alex had a point. We could barely see a thing in the darkness, even with the cemetery lights. We headed inside to find Victoria waiting for us at the door. "There you are. We've been looking everywhere for you. I held dinner." She must not have known Alex had food sent to my room, not that I'd gotten to eat it.

"Sorry. You didn't have to do that."

"Nonsense. It's your first real meal with us. I wouldn't think of starting without you." I guessed my little outburst at lunch didn't qualify as eating with the group. "Besides, we can't find one of the servers. Alex, have you seen him? He's the one with—"

"You don't even call them by name?"

Victoria glared at me. "They are no longer alive, Jodi. It's not as though we revived them immediately after they died. We brought back bodies that had been gone for a while."

I remembered what Alex had said about how scary it was to bring back bodies that had been dead for a long time. He'd known because his parents had done it. But these bodies didn't look like they'd decayed completely. "They couldn't have been gone for that long or they'd be nothing more than bones."

She smiled at me and put her hand on my shoulder. "I have to remember that you are new to all of this. If we use enough power while restoring a soul to its body, some or even all of the flesh returns along with it. You have many abilities, Jodi, and in time you will to learn to use them."

"Um, speaking of Jodi's abilities." Alex looked back and forth between Victoria and me. "We know what happened to your server."

Victoria cocked her head to the side. "Go on."

"I used my powers on him," I blurted out. I couldn't help it. Victoria wasn't like my mom. She looked for any reason to be disappointed in Alex. I had to let her know this had been my fault. "I didn't mean to, but I commanded him to go back to his grave."

"You controlled him?" Victoria raised her hand to her mouth in shock. I thought she was going to be upset, but instead, she smiled. "Jodi, that's wonderful. Most Ophi don't learn to do that until they reach eighteen. You're even more advanced than I thought you'd be."

"That's not all she can do," Alex interrupted. Victoria's eyes widened. "She released his soul. He was digging his way back to his grave when Jodi released him. His body is still there. Someone will need to take care of it in the morning."

"Yes, yes, of course." Victoria put her arm around me. "You can release souls. That is amazing!" Her voice was a bit awestruck as she stepped back and clapped her hands together. "We must celebrate. Come, come." She took me by the arm and led me to the dining room.

Like last time, the table was set and everyone was already seated. I wondered how long Victoria had been making them sit there staring at empty plates. Abby narrowed her eyes at me, and I got a little satisfaction out of making her wait for me. My eyes immediately lowered to Abby's neck. She wasn't wearing the locket. Maybe she wasn't quite gutsy enough to steal it and then wear it in front of me. It had to be hidden in her room, which meant I had to find a way to get in there.

Victoria whispered something to one of the servers before taking her seat at one end of the table. "Everyone, I have very exciting news." The servants brought out glasses of wine for everyone. "It seems dinner was held up for very good reasons." She paused and looked at me. "Jodi's powers are progressing better than we could have hoped. This evening, she not only took control of one of our servers, but she also released his soul." There were murmurs and gasps all around the table. Once again, all eyes were on me. "This is more proof that Jodi *is* the one we've been waiting for. And with her powers coming on so strongly—well, let's say we will all benefit from her being with us." She raised her glass, and everyone else followed. I hesitated for a second but Victoria nodded to me, so I picked up my glass as well. "Welcome to our family, Jodi."

While everyone else joined in with the welcome, Abby downed her wine in one gulp. "Yeah, welcome, Sis." She leaned her shoulder against Alex's. "Welcome your new sister, Alex."

He moved his chair away from her and closer to me. "We aren't all blood relatives, Abby."

"Sure we are. We've all got Gorgon blood, don't we?" She reached for his glass of wine and drank that, too.

Alex rolled his eyes. "You know what I mean. Jodi isn't my biological sister." I was trying to pretend I wasn't listening, nodding along to a conversation at my end of the table, but I saw Abby lean over and run her finger down Alex's arm.

"And neither am I, Alex."

Alex pushed her hand away and motioned for one of the servers. He placed his meal request and ignored Abby. Dinner was pretty normal after that. Except Alex wouldn't look at me. I wasn't sure what I'd done wrong. Abby was the one making all the comments about blood relatives and blatantly coming on to Alex. I kept stealing glances at him, which wasn't easy since we were sitting right next to each other. I sipped my wine, more for something to do than for the taste, which was strangely metallic to me.

As soon as Alex finished eating, he took his plate and went into the kitchen. I wasn't sure what he was doing since the servants cleaned up after dinner, but I grabbed my plate and followed him.

"Hey." I put my plate on the counter next to his. "Something wrong?"

"Just Abigail being Abigail."

"You don't like her much, do you?"

He raised an eyebrow. "How can you tell?"

I leaned against the counter while he fidgeted with the plates. "Well, she certainly likes you."

"Abby likes everyone."

"Not me."

"That's because—" He shook his head. "Never mind. She's not even worth thinking about." He stopped playing with the plates and turned to me. "You want to take a walk? I'll show you around."

"Yeah. Okay."

We went upstairs, but instead of stopping on the second floor where our rooms were, we went up to the third floor. It was pretty awesome. We passed a library that stretched the length of one entire wing of the mansion, a sunroom, some rec rooms with movie theater screens, and a few classrooms. Alex brought me into a classroom and sat down.

"How long have your parents been in charge here?"

"My grandparents were the ones who found this place. They wanted a safe place for Ophi to meet and teach the younger generations. Somewhere other than Serpentarius. The Ophi there don't really believe in using all their powers. My parents came here after…"

"Your grandparents died? Is that possible? I mean, can't you use your powers to bring them back?"

"That's the ironic thing about Ophi. We can't use our blood on each other. When we die, we die."

"That doesn't seem fair."

"It's another way Hades makes sure there aren't too many Ophi running around. We don't get to live forever. We're not immortal."

"Wow. So, that's why the Ophi take the whole having babies at twenty-five thing so seriously." Something in my head clicked. "But wait. How did my dad end up having me at sixteen?"

Alex stood up. "We should probably head back downstairs. My parents must be wondering where we are."

"Hang on." I grabbed his arm. "You know something. Spill."

"Look, I'm not supposed to be telling you so much. My parents and the other adults should be the ones explaining this to you."

"Yeah, well, they aren't here right now. You are."

He sighed and sat back down. "There's a reason I was sent to find you. You aren't just another Ophi. You're different."

"Yeah, yeah. We've been through all that."

"Not all of it. Your dad did something that other Ophi can't. He had you at sixteen. And he had you with a non-Ophi girl."

"So?"

"So, it's never happened before, and it won't ever happen again. At least that's what the prophecy says."

"What exactly are you saying?"

"I'm saying you're…"

"Seriously, spit it out already."

"You're descended from Medusa. The one whose blood started the Ophi line."

I slammed my hand on the desk. "Alex, I know all this already. I'm supposed to save our kind from becoming extinct. But how?"

"Your blood is different than ours. If you learn to control your power, you'll be able to raise Ophi as well as humans."

"Raise Ophi? Won't that anger the gods or something? I don't exactly want Hades coming after me."

"You don't have to worry about that." He didn't sound convincing. "We aren't talking about raising all the Ophi and taking control of the world or anything."

"Then what are we talking about?" I needed a straight answer. No more talk about prophecy and saving the Ophi race. I wanted specifics. "Am I supposed to make it so Ophi can be immortal?"

"I don't really know."

"Don't know, or don't want to tell me?" I got the feeling he was worried about getting in trouble for telling me too much.

"I don't know." He looked down at his desk like there was something really interesting written across it. "The adults pretty much keep us on a need-to-know basis. I can't wait until my birthday. Then I'll be eighteen, and they'll finally let me in on their meetings. I'll be an adult."

Somehow, I thought it bothered him more that his parents were keeping information from him than that he wasn't old enough to be in the Ophi meetings yet. I couldn't imagine not being close to my mom. Then again, I was going to have to start imagining it. I wasn't going to be allowed to be close to her anymore. I couldn't even call her. But maybe… "What do you know about my dad?"

"Not much. He was Ophi."

"Was?" He did know something. He was talking in the past tense. "Do you mean he's dead?" There was way too much death in my life.

Alex stopped staring at his desk. "I think so. I overheard my parents talking before I was sent to get you. They said your dad was important.

He had more power than the others, but he had refused to help the Ophi."
He paused and stared into my eyes. I couldn't help thinking about how
Victoria told me she thought my dad was a normal Ophi. That was a
lie, but why did she lie to me? "The way they were talking about him—
well, I could only assume it meant he was dead."

"Maybe not." I shrugged. "Maybe he left, and your parents were
using the past tense because he was gone. He could be out there looking
for me. He had no idea where Mom and I lived."

Alex didn't say a word, but I could tell he didn't agree. He thought
my dad was dead, and he didn't want to upset me by saying so. I wasn't
sure why I was holding on to the idea of Dad. I'd never met him. He
never attempted to find me. I shouldn't care if he was dead, but now that
I couldn't be with Mom, I wanted to know about Dad. I had to find him,
if he was alive.

Alex squinted at me, like he knew I was trying to come up with a
plan. "You going to let me in on what you're thinking?"

"I was wondering when my dad was here. Was it recently?"

"No, I don't think so. I'd remember him."

"Do you think he was ever here? I mean, if he didn't want to help the
Ophi, then maybe he didn't even come here."

"Jodi, I'm sorry, but I don't think I can help you."

"But you must know how I can find this stuff out."

"If you really want to know, talk to Victoria." I'd just figured out she
had lied to me about my dad. What would make her tell the truth now?

"What about your dad? You call your mom by her first name and
you barely ever mention your father."

"My parents decided that since they're in charge, they don't want
the other Ophi to think they're playing favorites with me. They told me
to call them by their first names, like everyone else does." He shrugged
one shoulder. "It makes sense. I don't want the others to not like me
because I'm the son of the two people in charge here. We don't even use
last names in this place. Other than you, no one knows Victoria and Troy
are my parents."

Well, that explained why Abby had no problem coming on to Alex
right in front of his parents. She had no clue they were related. "Family's
not all that important around here, is it?"

"We're all family, sort of. Abby wasn't wrong about that. Ophi do share the same Gorgon blood."

"Yeah, but it's not the same."

"Maybe not." He stood up. "Let's get out of here. You'll be spending enough time in these classrooms tomorrow, learning all you can about Ophi history."

"Oh, goody." I knew I needed to start training and figuring out my power. I had gotten lucky in the cemetery with that servant. I'd had Alex there to coach me; I think I'd only succeeded out of necessity. I'd been too horrified to fail. But the thought of sitting through hours of Mr. Quimby talking about blood and death wasn't exactly my idea of a fun time.

"Hey, if we don't use last names here, then what will I call Mr. Quimby tomorrow?"

"Tony. His name's Tony."

"Tony Quimby. Sounds weird. This is definitely going to be strange for me. I've never called a teacher by his first name."

"Jodi, you were homeschooled for most of your life. You called your teacher Mom until you were almost seventeen. If you could get used to the whole Mr. and Mrs. thing, you can get used to this." He had a point. "You want me to show you around some more, or do you want to go back to your room?"

"My room?" My heart skipped. He wanted to go back to my room?

"Yeah, I'll walk you back. It's on the way to my room."

"Oh."

He smiled at me. "What? Did you think I meant—"

"No!" I answered way too quickly. "I knew what you meant." I could tell by the look on his face that he wasn't buying it. "I thought maybe we'd have a meeting or some kind of lesson before bed. That's all."

"Right." He nodded. "Victoria and Troy actually cancelled tonight's lesson. They said it was a special treat so the rest of us could get to know you better." We started back toward our rooms on the second floor.

"Am I supposed to get in my PJs and go knock on Abby's door?"

"Please, don't. I'm thinking you two might want to keep your distance."

Only I couldn't do that. She had my locket. I was sure of it. We reached my door, and Alex gently squeezed my arm. "Sleep well. You've got a big day ahead of you tomorrow."

I said goodnight and went into my room, locking the door behind me. Alex was right. Tomorrow *was* going to be a big day. I had two things to find: my locket and my dad.

Chapter 21

I woke up with a plan in my head. After breakfast, I was going to do something I wasn't very proud of: I was going to use my power to get one of the servants to let me into Abby's room. I'd wait until I knew Abby was at her first lesson. Then, I'd get one of the servants alone and command him to open Abby's room for me. I'd find my locket and head to my own lesson. Being new gave me the "I got a little lost" excuse. As long as I didn't take too long to find the locket, I'd be okay.

I tried to act normally through breakfast. Mr. Quim—Tony—was there. He said it was nice to see me again, and he was looking forward to teaching me about Ophi history. I smiled and shoved some scrambled eggs in my mouth. Alex stifled a laugh. He must have known I was trying to avoid having to lie about my own enthusiasm for learning Ophi history. I shot him a look, nothing short of "shut up," but that only made him laugh more. As soon as he finished eating, Alex whispered, "Have fun!" and gave me a double eyebrow raise. I rolled my eyes and carried my plate to the kitchen. Alex was the only one I'd seen clear his plate since I got here, and he had only done it that once. But I needed to get into the kitchen and get one of the servants alone.

I put my plate on the counter next to the sink. One of the servants was busy washing a sink full of pots. I scanned the room. There was a guy shelving cans in the pantry closet. Perfect. I walked over to him and stood by his side. Luckily, the servants didn't question the Ophi because I had to stand there for a few minutes, trying to tap into my emotions. I did it the same way as last time, recalling painful images from the past week. As soon as I felt my blood bubbling in my veins, I put my hand on the servant's arm. It felt waxy and cold. Ew! It took all my concentration not to freak out and run to the sink to scrub my hand, but I stayed focused.

"Come with me," I told him. He nodded and followed me out of the kitchen. I headed upstairs, moving quickly and hoping no one stopped me. It would be difficult to explain why I had a servant tailing me. Everyone was still eating breakfast when we passed the dining room. I picked up the pace when I reached the stairs. I brought the guy to Abby's door and turned to face him again. "Open the door." He stared at me without moving. I realized my fear of being caught had taken over my anger, making me lose my control over the servant. "Damn it!" Well, that was one way to get mad. My blood boiled. "Open the door," I said again.

He took a ring of keys from his pocket and unlocked the door. "Now, wait here, and do not let anyone into this room." He nodded, and I stepped into Abby's room, closing the door behind me.

The room was painted teal green. Not exactly what I would've guessed for someone like Abby. I figured she'd want her room the color of fire or even ash. The room looked a lot like mine. Not much furniture. That was good because I didn't have much time to find the locket. I was due in my first lesson in ten minutes. I started with the dresser, since that's where I'd found the locket in my room. I searched every drawer. Abby had enough clothes to start her own store. One drawer was filled with jeans. Just jeans. Light blue, dark blue, black, gray, and even silver. I had to admit the gray ones caught my eye. The bottom drawer was filled with letters. Unopened and marked return to sender. My stomach sank as I realized she must have sent these to her family. The address didn't have a name other than Serpentarius. Alex was right. They had abandoned her here. They weren't even accepting her letters.

I couldn't let me feelings get in the way of finding the necklace, so I shut the drawer and moved on to the nightstand. An alarm clock and lamp rested on it. I turned on the lamp to give me some more light. Abby still had her curtains drawn, and her room was pretty dark. I reached around inside the lampshade, making sure she hadn't hidden it there. I even picked up the alarm clock and looked in the battery compartment. I was desperate.

I tried the bed next, patting down the sheets and checking inside the pillowcases. Nothing. I looked under the mattress and the box spring. Nothing. I only had two minutes left or I was going to be late. I checked shoeboxes and the duffel bag on the floor of the closet. Nothing and nothing. I shut the closet and was going back to the nightstand to turn off the lamp when I heard Abby's voice outside the door.

"What do you mean you can't let me go into my room? It's my room!"

"I have instructions not to let you inside this room," the servant said. Ugh! Why hadn't I been more specific when I gave him the order? I should've told him not to tell anyone I had commanded him to stand guard. I stepped closer to the door so I could hear better. Although, I was pretty sure the entire house could hear Abby yelling.

"Listen, you maggot-ridden corpse, that is my room, and I'll go in it whenever I—"

"Abigail!" Victoria's voice boomed. "What is going on here?"

"This thing won't let me in my room. I came upstairs to get something before my lesson, and he was standing here like a guard dog or something. When I told him to move, he said he couldn't allow me to go inside."

No one said anything for a moment, but I knew it wouldn't take long for Victoria to figure things out. I had to hide. There wasn't enough room under the bed, so I was going to have to be cliché and hide in the closet. I turned toward the nightstand to turn off the lamp, when I saw something peeking out from underneath. I ran over, feeling under the surface. My locket! Abby had it taped to the underside of her nightstand, but the chain was dangling down just enough to see. I yanked it free as Victoria said, "Someone's controlling him."

"They're all under someone's control," Abby said.

"No!" Victoria snapped. "Someone else is controlling him. Someone who isn't me or Troy."

I ran for the closet and ducked inside. I squeezed into the corner behind some dresses and dragged the duffel bag on top of my feet. Then I shut the door. Victoria and Abby's voices were muffled now, but I heard Victoria command the servant to step aside. She said something about him not following orders from anyone but her. Great! I made a mental note that this particular servant wasn't going to do me any good from here on out. I hoped Victoria wasn't planning on going back to the other servants and telling them the same thing. If she was smart, she would've, but I was hoping against it.

I heard a key in the lock and then Abby's voice. "It's about time. I'm going to be late for my lesson now thanks to that—" She stopped talking, and I realized why. I'd been so excited to find my locket that I'd forgotten to turn off the lamp.

"Is something wrong, Abby?" Victoria asked.

"N-no, nothing. I guess I left this light on." The lamp clicked off. Through the slatted groves in the closet door, I could see Abby reach a hand under the nightstand. She was making sure to block Victoria's view. Her nostrils flared, and she gritted her teeth when her hand came back up empty.

"Get whatever it is you need, Abigail. You're late enough as it is."

"Yes, Victoria." Abby went over to her desk and grabbed a book. Victoria motioned for Abby to follow her, but Abby stopped and stared right at the closet. She knew, but there was nothing she could do about it with Victoria ushering her out of her own room. After she left, I waited ten seconds before coming out of my hiding place. I had to make sure they would be down the hall, but if I waited too long, Abby might lose Victoria and double back, trying to trap me. I put the locket around my neck, shoving it beneath my shirt, and rushed out of there.

I headed straight upstairs and to the last classroom on the left. I spotted Abby in the room right before mine. I paused. She was telling a woman that she got held up by one of the servants. "Victoria can vouch for me," she said, as if she and Victoria were close. She turned on her heels and headed to her seat, but saw me in the process and glared. I simply smiled and waved before entering my own classroom.

"Jodi," Mr. Quim—Tony—said, "always late."

"Sorry." I took an empty seat. There were only two other people in the class, a boy and a girl. "I haven't been here long, and I keep getting confused. All the hallways look the same to me."

"Perhaps when you get to training today, you can ask Troy to teach you how to command the servants to draw you a map."

"Troy?" I was more than a little surprised to hear his name. "Troy teaches?"

"Of course. He's very powerful. What better Ophi to teach you to use your powers?"

I smiled, trying to act like Troy didn't scare me. There was something eerie about him. He didn't say much. In fact, he sort of watched while Victoria took the reins. Then, I remembered the story Alex had told me about his field trip to the park. Somehow, I knew Troy had been the instructor who'd gone with Alex.

"Now," Mr. Quim—Tony—said, "let's get moving with today's lesson." He went to the laptop at the back of the room, and in seconds an image was projected onto the screen in front of me. I gasped. Really loudly. It was an image of my locket.

"Jodi, are you okay?" Tony asked.

"Um, yeah. I think a bug flew in my mouth." The girl sitting next to me scrunched up her face in disgust. "I know, right?" I said, trying to act normal.

"All right then," Tony continued. "Does anyone know what this is?"

There was a knock on the door, and I looked up to see Abby. "Selena told me to join your class today since I was late to my own lesson." She turned and glared at me. "Apparently, I missed important instructions that she couldn't be bothered to repeat. So, here I am."

"Take a seat, Abby. We were just getting started."

Abby walked past me, knocking her book into the side of my head. "Oh, Jodi!" She put her hand to her mouth in mock horror. "I'm so sorry. I hope that didn't hurt too much."

I gritted my teeth against the pain. "Not at all." I could deal with Abby's little stunt because the second she saw the image on the screen, she'd be the one in pain. She smirked and sat down. I continued to watch her. Her eyes flickered toward the screen, and her hands clenched the edges of her desk.

"That's—"

"Yes, Abby?" Tony said. "Do you know what this is?"

She looked at me, and I smiled. "Please, tell us, Abby."

"I-I don't know." She shook her hair behind her shoulders, and I could actually see her confidence returning. "I was just surprised at how hideous it is. I mean who would wear something so ugly? Only a complete loser." Her eyes burned into me.

Tony cleared his throat. "Actually, Abby, what you're seeing is the bloodstone locket worn by Medusa herself."

I was glad Abby and I were still locked in a stare-down because I got to see the look of horror on her face.

"Medusa?" she croaked.

"That's right," Tony said. "Um, Jodi, eyes on the screen, please." I nodded and turned my attention back to the front of the room. "The bloodstone locket is the only one of its kind. It's rumored to hold a concentrated combination of Medusa's blood. Both the poison and the blood used for restoration of the dead are blended inside this locket. As you are all aware, Ophi must shed their blood, tears, saliva, or sweat to tap into these powers that Medusa bestowed upon us. But Medusa herself did not need to do any of these things. She could simply call upon both sides of her blood to become one and perform any number of miraculous feats."

"You mean she could mix her blood right inside her body?" I turned in my seat so I could see Tony.

"Yes. She described it once as feeling like her blood bubbled throughout her body, combining the powers of both sides." My jaw nearly hit the floor. Bubbling throughout her body? That was exactly how I'd felt ever since I joined my hands with the Medusa statue.

"Is this what we'll learn to do?" I didn't want to mention that I'd already dabbled in this.

Tony laughed. "No, no, no. Ophi can't perform this feat. It was reserved for Medusa alone." More like Medusa and her bloodline. She'd passed this gift on to me.

"What else could she do?" I needed to know more.

"She could release souls from their bodies, which you all will learn to do when you come of age. Most of you know that skill doesn't set in until you turn eighteen."

"But Jodi can already do that," the girl next to me said.

I whipped my head in her direction. I'd almost forgotten Victoria's little speech at dinner. She'd told everyone about what I did in the cemetery.

"Yeah," the guy behind her said. "Leticia and I heard Troy command the servants to bury the body lying in the graveyard before lessons this morning."

Tony stared at me. "Jodi, is this true?"

I nodded. "But Alex told me how to do it."

"Still, you shouldn't have that kind of power at your age."

"She has something else she shouldn't have," Abby said. "She has Medusa's locket."

I nearly fell out of my chair. Why would Abby out me like that? I knew she hated me, but why would she draw attention to the fact that I had Medusa's locket? Unless she knew they'd take it away from me. That couldn't happen.

I shook my head. "I don't know what you're talking about." Instinctively, I lowered my chin, hoping no one could see the gold chain around my neck. My shirt came up pretty high, and I hoped it was enough to conceal the locket.

"Really?" Abby said. "It wasn't you who snuck into my room and stole the locket from under my nightstand? It wasn't you who commanded that disgusting servant to keep me from going into my own room and made me late for class? Cause I could've sworn that was you hiding in my closet to avoid getting caught by Victoria."

I stood up, not sure what I was going to do. I never expected Abby to blurt everything out like that, and she'd done it in a way that made me look like the bad guy.

"Why don't you show us what you have stuffed under your shirt, Jodi?" Abby continued. "Oh, and I don't mean the toilet paper you use to stuff your bra."

"I don't stuff my—oh, forget it! This is ridiculous!"

"Jodi," Tony said, "that locket disappeared when Medusa died. According to prophecy, it would reappear to one in Medusa's bloodline. One who would have the power to mix their blood like Medusa did. One who would be more powerful than all the Ophi." He stepped forward, stopping only feet in front of me. "Did the locket appear to you?"

Abby jumped to her feet. "No, it appeared to me, and she stole it!"

"Whatever, Abby," the guy sitting behind Leticia said. I really had to learn everyone's names. "Like anyone would believe Medusa would pass her locket down to you."

"And why not?" Abby snarled.

"Because you're no better than the rest of us," Leticia said.

"You wish, Leticia!" Abby stuck her foot out, showing off her designer boots. "Where'd you get your shoes? Wal-Mart?"

"Okay, girls, that's enough," Tony said. "Abby, there's no need to insult anyone. I'm sure Leticia didn't mean anything bad by her comment. She was simply pointing out that we are all equals here."

"Not all of us," the other guy said.

"Well, Randy, I guess you're right." Tony looked at me again. "Jodi, do you have the bloodstone locket on you right now?"

What could I do? I reached inside my shirt and pulled the locket out. "It appeared to me on my first night here. But then *someone*," I paused to glare at Abby, "stole it from my bathroom while I was showering."

"Ah," Tony said, suddenly understanding everything. "Abby, I think we need to have a little talk about personal privacy soon."

But no one was really paying much attention to Tony. They were all focused on the bloodstone locket around my neck. All including Abby, and for once, I was glad I wasn't like everyone else.

Chapter 22

Tony spent the rest of the lesson talking about how special the locket was and what this meant for Ophi everywhere. It quickly got a little overwhelming. Suddenly, Leticia and Randy were treating me like I was royalty. They offered to help me train and even write my papers. Which, hello, papers? This was a little too much like real school. After Abby got over the initial intrigue of the necklace, she sulked in her seat until Tony dismissed us for lunch. I couldn't believe I'd been there for hours. Everyone had been so focused on the locket and how special I was. They'd asked me questions about my powers and wanted to know everything about me. I'd gone from the new girl to Little Miss Popular in two seconds flat.

By the time I got downstairs for lunch, everyone was talking about me. Victoria rushed over and put her hands on my cheeks. "Oh, Jodi, darling, why didn't you tell me? This is wonderful news. Even better than we could've hoped for. I mean we all knew you were special, being the one in the prophecy and all, but this! This is simply fantastic." I didn't know what to say, so I smiled and took my seat next to Alex.

"So, busy morning, huh?" His eyes lowered. "Nice necklace. I thought you put that back in your dresser where you found it." I detected a hurt tone in his voice, like he thought I'd purposely kept this from him, which I had.

"Sorry, it was just so bizarre. I felt like the locket belonged to me, and that didn't make any sense at all. I wasn't sure you'd understand."

"Oh." He shoveled mac and cheese into his mouth.

"And then Abby stole the necklace from me while I was in the shower. She used that little key of hers and helped herself. Can you believe that?" I hoped by changing the subject to Abby, he'd forget I'd hidden this from him. I looked around for Abby. She wasn't in her usual seat next to Alex; in fact, she wasn't in the dining room at all. For a moment, I worried she was in my room stealing something as payback for taking my locket back, but I didn't have anything else worth stealing. Unless she wanted my push-up bra.

"Is that what was wrong? You seemed so riled up and angry at Abby when I brought you your food. I thought you were kind of stuck up or something. Like you thought you were better than her."

"What? No! I was upset about my locket."

"That makes a lot more sense. You didn't seem like the other girls here. You know, back-stabbing and catty."

"I'm not like that at all. I just didn't like her invading my private space. She threatened me, and then she stole my locket."

"She threatened you? About what?"

"You, actually. She thought I had a thing for you."

He put another forkful of mac and cheese in his mouth and said, "Do you?"

I couldn't help laughing. "Oh, yes. I think it's the fake cheese sauce spraying out of your mouth that I find so irresistible."

He swallowed, his cheeks turning red.

"Are we good?" I asked.

"Hold on, let me get another mouthful before I answer. I know you like that."

I smacked his shoulder. Yeah, we were good. And he was right. I did like all the weird things he did, like eating mac and cheese for every meal. With all the things going wrong in my life, Alex was the one thing that was right.

After lunch, I had to report to my first training session. I was excited, nervous, and a little terrified when I remembered Troy would be teaching.

"Hey." Alex jogged to catch up to me as I headed out to the backyard.

"Hey, what are you doing? You're going to be late for your own lesson."

"Nah, I talked to Victoria, and she said that since your powers are progressing so quickly, I should help you with your training."

"Really? But I thought Troy was the one who instructed the beginners?"

"Actually, he teaches all of us, just at different times of the day. But he decided that Leticia and Randy aren't exactly on the same level as you. He'd have to go too slow for you in order to let them keep up. It's too late to switch you to the other group today—we already met this morning. So, Victoria said I should give you kind of a private lesson." He smiled and gently elbowed my arm.

"A private lesson? Did she really say that?"

He laughed. "Okay, not really, but she did ask me to help you. We won't be far from Troy and the others, but we'll be working on different skills."

"Does Troy know about this?" I didn't want to do anything to get on his bad side. The guy was seriously scary when he was angry. I couldn't erase the look he'd given Alex when we arrived from my mind. I didn't want to be on the receiving end of it.

"I'm sure he does, but if not, Victoria will back us up." He clasped his hands together and fluttered his eyelashes. It was impossible not to laugh. "'Jodi's powers are exceeding all our expectations. It's so wonderful to have her here. She's like the daughter I never had.'"

"Please, tell me that wasn't supposed to sound like Victoria," I said, still laughing. "That was awful."

"Hey, I don't imitate girls very well. Too much of a man, I guess."

"Oh, yeah, that must be it." I shook my head.

"I know that wasn't sarcasm I heard in your voice."

"No, not at all." I continued to laugh as I turned toward the open field behind the house.

Alex grabbed my elbow. "We're heading this way."

"But Victoria said my lesson with Troy was in the field."

"You're not training with Troy, remember?"

"Right. And you're sure he knows we're doing this?"

"Relax. I can handle Troy. I've had years of experience disappointing him."

"But I haven't, and I'd kind of like to avoid it."

"Come on." He tugged my arm again, and I followed him around the house to—no, this couldn't be right. I stopped short. "Alex, this is the cemetery."

"I figured that out from all the headstones. I'm smart like that."

I gave him my "this-isn't-the-time-to-kid-around" look.

"This is the perfect location for your training."

"You've got to be kidding me. Isn't this the worst place to take a necromancer?"

He shook his head and smiled. Apparently, I was amusing him. "Relax. Unless you plan on spitting on all the graves or slicing open a vein and running through all the headstones, we'll be fine."

"You really think you're funny, don't you?"

He raised one shoulder. "Kind of."

As we walked through the cemetery, I searched for the servant's grave. It was the only one that was freshly dug, so it was easy to spot. I was happy to see the servant back where he belonged. I didn't like the idea of the Ophi using dead bodies as servants. Sure, I'd controlled one of the servants and made him let me in Abby's room, but that was different. I was desperate to get Medusa's locket back, and after the lesson with Tony this morning, I was glad I'd done what I had to do to get the locket. Abby shouldn't have anything this powerful. I raised my hand and ran my fingers over the bloodstone. Who knew what Abby would've done with the locket after she found out about its power? She had some major unresolved family issues fueling her anger.

Alex brought me to a grave. "Okay, since you've already raised dead animals and…" his voice trailed off. I'd raised more than dead animals. I'd raised Matt. Only I'd done it wrong.

"I don't want anything like that to happen again. Seeing Matt attack that bunny—he was like…" I couldn't say it.

"A zombie." Alex nodded. "There's a right way and a wrong way to raise a body." To me, it all kind of seemed wrong. I mean, it wasn't normal. When you die, you're not supposed to come back. But then I thought of Mom. Alex had saved her life. If he hadn't, she'd be dead at 33, and it would've been my fault.

"I don't ever want to get it wrong again," I said.

Alex sighed. "I know you don't. That's why we're here. I'm going to explain how it's supposed to be done, and you're going to practice on these dead bodies. You've got a cemetery full of willing participants." I didn't think "willing" was the right word. They didn't have a choice. If their bodies were in reach, Ophi could raise them, and the person whose body it was didn't have any say in the matter.

"Remind me I want to be cremated when I die. No way am I letting anyone stuff my soul back into my decaying body."

"No need to worry about that, Jodi. You're the only one who can raise Ophi, remember? Unless—"

"Unless what?" He was holding something back.

"Nothing. It's not important."

"You didn't like it when I didn't tell you I'd kept the locket, right? I apologized for keeping that from you, and I'm asking you not to keep this from me." He stayed silent. "Fine." I turned and walked away. "If I don't know everything, there's no way I'm doing this."

"Wait!" he called. "Jodi, come back." I faced him, and he sighed. "I'm not supposed to tell you this, so you have to promise you won't say a word to anyone." I crossed my heart with my index finger. A little childish, but he got the point. He waved me over. "I don't want to have to say this too loud."

I stood right next to him. He smelled great. I wondered what kind of soap he used. It had a powerful yet inviting smell, and since he'd already gone through training this morning, he had a faint musk going on, too.

He cocked an eyebrow. "What?"

Oh, God! I hoped I didn't have a stupid look on my face. If he figured out I was smelling him, I'd die. At least I was in a good place if that happened. "Nothing. Just eagerly waiting to hear what you have to say."

He smirked. Yeah, he knew. Just great. He reached up and touched my locket. "Right after lunch, Victoria and Troy were talking about this. They knew the Ophi in the prophecy—you—would have the power to raise Ophi, but they have a theory about the locket."

I raised my hand to the locket and our fingers touched. He looked into my eyes, and I knew I was done for. Immediately, I thought of Matt. Sweet, nearly perfect Matt who always knew what to say and was so patient with me. Alex was almost his opposite. He was cocky, a little dangerous, had strange habits, and raised the dead, but he was also sweet and protective of me. And he smelled really good. In some ways, Alex was perfect for me. Was I ready for what I thought I might be feeling for him?

"What's their theory?" I asked, breaking the spell between us.

He took a step back, letting go of the locket. "They think that the mixture of blood inside it would give the wearer the power to raise Ophi. Only they have no idea how to do that. How to tap into that power."

It made sense. And since I was supposed to save the Ophi race from extinction, I was going to have to find a way to tap into that power. Just this morning, I was feeling great about the locket and the look it brought to Abby's face when she realized who the locket had belonged to. I was glad I was the Chosen One. I even liked all the attention I was getting from Leticia and Randy. For once being different felt good. But now, I only felt the sinking weight of responsibility on my shoulders. It was a lot to rest on one person. Especially when that one person was me. "Great, one more thing I'll be expected to figure out in order to save the day."

"Don't think about it right now. Let's try raising the dead. The correct way," he added, as if it needed to be said. "If you do it right, you'll be able to control the bodies. They'll obey you even if they don't want to."

"So, they're like slaves to us?" I thought of how the servant had tried to claw his way back into his grave because I told him to. It was awful.

"Kind of, but they're dead. What does it matter?"

"What about my mom? She's not under your control, and you brought her back."

"That was different. The longer a soul is out of the body, the less they can fight us when we put them back into their bodies. If we bring someone back right away—like with your mom—they still have full control over themselves. Her soul never left her body. I didn't have to force it back inside."

"Force it back inside? This sounds so terrible. I'm not sure I want to be able to do this. Besides, why would we want to put someone's soul back in their body and control them?" I turned away from the grave, not wanting to have anything to do with all of this. I walked over to a mausoleum a few feet away and leaned my head against it. The coolness of the stone felt good on my forehead.

Alex's footsteps crunched on the ground behind me. "Are you scared of us?" He reached for my arm, and I let him turn me around. He looked almost sad as he took my hand in his. "Are you scared of *me*?" With his free hand, he gently pushed a stray hair off my face, but his hand lingered on my cheek. His touch was electrifying.

My heart raced. I *was* scared. Scared that I was falling for him. "I—"

He leaned forward like he was going to kiss me. Without thinking, I leaned into him, too.

"Well, what kind of training is this?" Abby asked.

I jumped back. She glared at us with her arms crossed. Alex turned away from me, running his fingers through his hair. Another almost-kiss to add to my collection. It was Matt all over again.

Chapter 23

Abby ignored me and glared at Alex. "She's supposed to be raising the dead. If you can't handle training her, someone else will." She stormed off before either one of us could respond. Not that we really had anything to say. I was completely embarrassed.

"I guess we should work on your training."

I knew there was something else I had wanted to know. Something I'd asked him. But I was so lightheaded from our almost-kiss and shaken up that Abby, of all people, had caught us that I couldn't remember what we'd been talking about. Abby clearly had a thing for Alex, and this incident would only make her hate me more.

We walked back to the grave we'd been standing by before. Alex clapped his hands together. Was that an Ophi thing? Because people here sure liked clapping their hands together. "All right. You have to concentrate. This is serious stuff you're about to get into." His face was stone cold, not at all like it had been a few minutes ago. He definitely wasn't the same guy who'd tried to kiss me. "You have to learn how to control your power. Otherwise, you'll end up raising the dead by accident again. That's not exactly working out for you, is it?"

I shivered, a combination of his mood change and the truth in his words. "Definitely not."

"Good." He walked behind the headstone and placed his hands on it. "Now, when you raise the dead from a grave like this, you don't have to dig them up. You can simply call to them by dripping a little of your blood on the ground covering their grave. Our blood is powerful. If you concentrate, it will find your target. But you have to concentrate. That's the key."

"Do I picture a dead body in my head?"

"No. Unless you know what the person looked like when they were alive, that's a very bad idea." He paused for a moment, like he was trying to figure out the best way to explain it. "Okay, try this. Close your eyes and tell your blood to find the body beneath the dirt. Your blood is part of you. You'll be able to control it. And when it finds the body, you'll know it." He paused again, but this time he was making sure I was following.

"Got it," I said. "Should we try that part first and then worry about controlling the body?"

"No. You need to have a clear reason for summoning the body. It's going to *want* an explanation. If it doesn't have a purpose when it rises, it'll go crazy. The souls know they aren't supposed to be back. They get stir crazy."

"Like Matt did. He was so confused and out of control. He was acting without knowing what he was doing."

"Exactly. You don't want to put yourself through that again, so let's come up with an easy task for the soul." He looked around, and his eyes fell on the former servant's grave. "I've got it. You can tell the body that he will be serving the Ophi who live in the house. He'll cook, clean, and answer to the Ophi who live there. That will work, and Victoria will be happy to have a replacement for the servant she lost."

I hated making another soul become a slave to the Ophi, but Alex had a point. I was the one who'd returned the soul to wherever it was before the Ophi had shoved it back into its body, and it would give this soul a purpose. "All right. But I'm not making any more servants after that. If I have to keep practicing raising the dead, I'll release the souls after I'm finished."

Alex shrugged. "Fair enough." He smiled and tapped on the headstone. "Shall we give it a try?"

I closed my eyes and took a long, deep breath. I wasn't sure I was ready, but I had to start sometime. I opened my eyes again, and Alex was at my side with his knife in his hand. "Whoa!" I jumped. "Don't do that. You scared me."

He laughed. "Sorry, but you need a drop of your blood, and remember, I'm the trusty Scout who is always prepared."

"Yeah, well, I hate to break it to you, but the last thing a girl wants to see when she opens her eyes is a knife in the hands of the guy she—" I caught myself in time.

Alex cocked his head to the side and smirked. "Go on. The guy she…"

"She's training with." I took the knife from his hand and walked to the head of the grave. I needed to get moving before he had time to say anything else. I pricked my right middle finger and held it above the grave. I wasn't sure if I was supposed to speak anything out loud or just think the words, but I figured it couldn't hurt to say them. "Find the body that rests beneath the surface of the earth," I told my blood. A few drops fell onto the ground. I closed my eyes and almost gasped when an image popped into my head. I could see the drops of blood seep below the grass and dirt. They found a casket and penetrated the wood as if it was no more solid than water. They found their target, absorbing into the body, which was little more than bones.

In my mind, I heard shrieks and screams. I saw the soul soaring through the air and into the ground where it came to rest in its body. The soul fought against my blood, not wanting to be back, but the power of my blood was too strong. With the soul in place, flesh began to re-form over the bones. My cheeks felt wet and warm against the slight breeze in the air. Tears were the only outward sign of the agony I felt inside. I was torturing this soul. It was angry and in pain. The body moved slightly, and then its fists started pounding on the coffin. I didn't want to see anymore. I couldn't take it.

"No!" I dropped to my knees and started to claw at the ground, ripping handfuls of grass and dirt.

"Jodi!" Alex wrapped his arms around my waist and lifted me up. He stepped back, away from the grave. "Stop! Calm down. Tell me what's wrong."

I doubled over, hysterical. "I saw everything. That poor soul was ripped out of the afterlife. It was crying out in pain, and it was terrified when it realized it was back in its body. Back in its grave." I squeezed his arms for comfort. "Oh, God, Alex, it's punching its way through the casket. I can see it all."

"Open your eyes, Jodi." He turned me around to face him and put both hands on the sides of my face. "Look at me. Jodi, look at me!"

I opened my eyes, but I saw double. I could see Alex in front of me, but I could also see the body. Its knuckles were cut up, skin dangling from the bones. It was halfway through the casket and starting to push through the dirt. "I still see it. Please, make it go away. Make it stop. Please!"

He pulled me into his chest and rubbed the back of my head. "Shhh, it's okay. It's okay."

"How do you deal with this? How can you all raise the dead after seeing what the soul has to go through?" I cried into his chest.

"We don't see it."

I pulled away enough to look at him. "What?"

"We don't see it. We know when our blood reaches the body. We get this feeling, but we don't see any of it happening. It must be another one of your powers we don't have." By the way his forehead wrinkled, I knew he was confused by what was happening. This was new territory for the Ophi. They'd never met anyone like me before. I was the one and only Chosen One.

"You're lucky. Believe me, you wouldn't do this if you saw what I'm seeing now." I turned around to face the grave. "He's here," I said a split second before his fingers pierced the surface. I rushed over to him and reached out my hand. I had to help him. He was suffering so much. I'd never felt such fear and anger at one time.

"Jodi, no! What are you doing?"

"I have to help him. He's in pain, Alex. This is so hard on him."

"You can actually feel what he feels?"

"Yes, and it's killing both of us. Please, help me."

Alex grabbed the other hand and helped me pull the body out of the ground. We had to be careful not to damage him. The second he was free—from the ground, anyway, because he had no will of his own anymore—his eyes found me. The hatred in his expression was more than I could take.

"You need to tell him what to do, Jodi. Quickly!"

I shook my head. "I can't."

"You'll make this harder on him if you don't. The other servants—the ones in our house—they aren't suffering. Don't let him suffer."

I pulled myself together the best I could and looked the man in the eyes. "You're going to come back to the house with us. You'll live there and help the people there." I wanted to make it sound pleasant for him. Like he'd be part of a family. Maybe if I could make him think that, this all wouldn't be so bad. "You'll cook and help with the chores. Do you understand?"

"You don't have to ask him, Jodi. He'll obey you."

Alex didn't get it. "I don't care. I want him to understand. He's a soul, not an empty body or plaything. He has a right to know what's going on and to feel like he's part of this world."

Alex put his hands up defensively. "He's your soul. You call the shots."

"Don't call him that. He's his own soul."

Alex stepped closer to me and whispered, "Watch what you say. If you go putting ideas in his head, like saying he's his own soul, he may not obey anyone. A rogue living dead person could be very dangerous for all of us."

Okay, I'd try to avoid giving him too much freedom. I'd find a happy medium. "Please, follow us into the house, and we'll introduce you to the others like you. You'll feel at home with them." He stood there, staring at me, completely expressionless. At least the hatred was gone.

"He's waiting for you," Alex said. "You told him to follow you. The living dead are very literal. Whatever you tell them to do, they will do exactly that, so choose your words carefully."

"Got it." I turned and started toward the house. Every few feet I glanced behind me to make sure he was still following.

Alex smiled and shook his head. "You don't need to do that. He has his orders."

"I don't like giving orders." I turned back to the guy again. "This way, please." The least I could do was be polite. The other Ophi tended to bark orders at the servants. I didn't want to be like that. There was no reason to be like that.

I headed for the stairs leading to the front door, but Alex pointed around back. "We should bring him in through the servants' entrance. He should get used to that."

"I don't think it will be a big deal to bring him in through the front."

"Jodi, please try to remember that as much as you want them to be human, they're not. This soul has been gone for years. If you want to make things easier on him, then help him fit in with the other servants."

I hated this. More than I could ever express to Alex. I'd hoped he'd feel the same way I did, that he'd agree with me and maybe even convince his parents to release the souls of the other servants. It was ridiculous that everyone around here couldn't pull their own weight. Hell, I'd wash the dishes and make the beds if it meant these souls didn't have to be tortured like this. But the more I thought about it, the more I realized this didn't seem abnormal to Alex because he had grown up here. Around Ophi. Around all this. Being waited on by the living dead was part of his daily routine. It was hard to see what was wrong with something if it was all you knew. I felt bad for him, so I gave in.

"We're going to take you around back where the others like you go in and out of the house." The guy continued to look at me without changing his expression. "This way, please." He followed. We took him through the entrance by the kitchen. I heard the sound of pots and various other cooking utensils. The servants must have been preparing dinner. They probably spent all their time cooking. There were always so many foods to choose from at each meal. We walked into the kitchen, but the servants kept working, not even noticing us. They were like robots, doing what they were told to do and not wavering from their instructions.

I cleared my throat, but that did nothing to get their attention. Alex whistled and yelled, "Listen up." All the servants stopped what they were doing. He leaned toward me. "Victoria told them to drop everything if one of us whistles. It lets them know they need to listen. It works well since we can't really control them until we turn eighteen." I noticed one woman by the stove put her hand on a bright-red burner. She rested it there as if it wasn't even turned on. I ran over to her in horror. I heard her skin sizzle and got the faint smell of burned flesh. Her hand was blistered and red.

"Please, come here." I brought her to the sink and turned on the cold water. "Put your hand under the water."

"She can't feel pain," Alex said. "She'll be fine. Stuff like that happens all the time."

"That doesn't make it okay." I shot him a look, and he stepped back as if I'd punched him. "Look, I know this is just another day for you. You don't know any other life. But to me this is awful. These were people. And maybe they're not really alive anymore. Maybe they can't feel pain, but that doesn't make it okay for them to burn their hands on a hot stove or have to obey every command we give them."

"Ignore what she said!" Troy's voice boomed from the doorway. "Get back to work. All of you." He looked at me and then Alex, the brunt of his disapproval falling on Alex. "Both of you, in the hall. Now!"

"Wrap your hand in a wet towel," I whispered to the woman with the burned hand. Then, I followed Alex and Troy into the hall.

"What exactly did you think you were doing?" Troy asked, looking back and forth between us.

"One of the servants burned her hand. It was pretty bad. I was trying to help her."

"Wouldn't want burned flesh in the casserole." Alex was trying to lighten the mood, but Troy wasn't amused. "Jodi raised a dead body. We brought it here to replace the servant we lost yesterday."

Troy's expression softened. "Very good, Jodi. A successful raising on your first attempt is definitely commendable."

"Thank you." I was afraid Troy was going to start yelling again.

"What's that I heard?" Victoria walked toward us. "Jodi raised and controlled a body on the first attempt?"

"Yes, she did." Alex practically beamed with pride. "She's a natural."

"Well, that's fantastic! I have a full set of servants back then." She squeezed her hands together like an overly-excited child. "I am in awe of your abilities, Jodi. You may be teaching lessons soon. You seem to pick up on everything so quickly, and now that Medusa's locket has presented itself to you, well, there's no limit to your power."

Someone scoffed behind Victoria. "Precious little Jodi and her amazing powers. Please! What has she really done?" I hadn't even noticed Abby.

"How about everything the adult Ophi can do?" Alex said. "What have you done, except create a zombie that almost ripped your head off yesterday? I heard all about that. Quinn said you lost control in seconds and ran screaming toward the house. And you tried to tell people the locket appeared to you instead of Jodi?" He shook his head. "That's nothing short of laughable."

"Now, Alex, let's not be rude," Victoria said.

Abby was clenching her fists. "So Jodi's done a few things right. You all think everything she does is amazing. Like holding both of Medusa's hands. How difficult is that?" She turned and walked off. "I'll show you how tough that is."

"Abigail!" Troy yelled, but she was a girl on a mission. We followed her to the statue in the foyer. "Abby, stop right now!"

"Don't be stupid, Abby," Alex said. "You're not Jodi. You don't have Medusa's blood in your veins. At least not in the same way Jodi does. You have no idea what will happen to you if you try this."

"I know what will happen," Abby said. "I'll prove Jodi is nothing special." She reached out and took both of Medusa's hands at once. For a second, nothing seemed to happen. Abby shrugged. "See." But then her face contorted. She screamed, and her body convulsed. Her eyes rolled back into her head, and she fell to the floor.

Chapter 24

"Abby!" I yelled.

We all ran to her, but I could tell it wasn't good. Alex was right. My blood was different from the others'. Abby couldn't handle Medusa's power. She wasn't meant to. It was for me alone. I was the Chosen One. The one in the prophecy. The one meant to save the Ophi.

Troy had his fingers pressed against Abby's throat. "She's dead."

"No!" I didn't like Abby. She'd been nothing but trouble since I'd gotten here, but that didn't mean I wanted her to die. Especially not while trying to prove she was as strong as I was. She might have said she was trying to prove I wasn't special, but really, she was trying to prove she was just as special. In her mind, I'd come here and taken over—become the center of attention. After being abandoned by her family, I couldn't help seeing her side just a little. I had to do something. My hands flew to my locket. Medusa's locket. The answer was in mixing the blood. The poison with the life-bearing side.

I went to the statue, having to straddle Abby's dead body to do it. I took both Medusa's hands in mine. My hair blew all around me, and my blood began to bubble. I closed my eyes and silently begged Medusa to appear in my mind.

"I'm here, my child."

"Please, help me. I need to know how to raise an Ophi. I know the secret is in mixing my blood, but what do I do after that?"

"You want to raise the ungrateful creature that lost her life trying to disgrace our names?"

"Disgrace our names? What do you mean?"

"She does not wish you well, Jodi. She does not believe in your abilities. Both of these things disgrace your name and, by extension, mine."

"Medusa, she was stupid. She didn't know what she was doing. Please. Let me save her. Help me save her."

"Is this truly what you wish?"

"Yes."

"Very well. Your blood is mixing at this very moment. You can tell your blood to mix. It will obey. You will need to sacrifice a drop of your blood to Abby if you wish to restore life to her. But hurry. Her soul will leave her body soon, and it will be much more difficult to bring her back. If you don't succeed, she will be nothing more than a servant like the others the Ophi have raised." I wanted to ask Medusa what she thought of the servants, but there wasn't time. Abby's soul wouldn't stick around long.

"Thank you." I released Medusa's hands and turned to Abby. I reached my hand out to Alex. "Your knife. And hurry!"

He handed it over without a word. I pricked my right index finger, making sure I could feel my blood bubbling and mixing in my veins. I tipped my finger over Abby's mouth and let it drip. Under my breath, I murmured, "Bring life back to Abby. Return her to the way she was before she joined hands with Medusa." I backed up and gave Alex his knife.

"How do you know it worked?" he asked.

"Medusa said it would."

Victoria and Troy shared a glance. I could tell they were about to ask me how, but Abby choked. We all looked down at her.

"Are you okay?" Victoria asked.

"What happened?" Abby looked confused, not at all sure why she was on the ground.

"You grabbed both of Medusa's hands to prove you're as powerful as Jodi," Alex said. "Only you're not as powerful as Jodi. The statue killed you."

"What?" Abby was horrified. "Am I... like the... servants?"

"No," Victoria said. "Relax. You are still you and very much alive. Jodi saved you."

"No!" Abby shrieked, looking at me with more hatred than I'd ever seen.

I rolled my eyes. "You're welcome. And just so you know, Medusa doesn't care much for you. She said you disgraced her name. She didn't want to help me bring you back. She only helped me because I begged her."

"Why?" Abby tried to stand up and stumbled. "Why did you bring me back? You should've left me dead. I'd rather be dead than saved by you!" She stood and ran upstairs, pushing me out of her way in the process.

"Glad I could help," I yelled after her.

"Don't worry about her," Victoria said. "She'll get over it."

Troy narrowed his eyes at me. "How did you bring her back? What did you do?"

"I mixed my blood. I've been able to do it since I first touched both sides of Medusa. My blood boils and mixes on command." I left out that it sometimes happened without me wanting it to.

"The statue must have mixed Abby's blood," Alex said.

I nodded. "And it killed her."

"Which means we won't ever be able to bring other Ophi back to life." Alex stared at me. "Only Jodi can."

"Yes, well, more reason to be happy she's here." Victoria put her arm around my shoulders. "Why don't both of you go get cleaned up before dinner?" She and Troy headed off together, no doubt to discuss what had happened.

I didn't see Abby for the rest of the day. She skipped dinner, and her bedroom door stayed shut all night. I wasn't sure why, but I hoped I'd run into her in the hallway. I wanted to make sure she was okay. That she'd come back normal. I mean, I'd brought the guy from the cemetery out of his grave, but that was different. He was under my control. What I'd done for Abby was completely different; I'd brought her back to life, not made her a living dead. It was so far beyond raising the dead servants. I felt good. Even if Abby wasn't happy to be alive, I was happy she was alive. I'd found a way to use this power for something good.

I went to sleep glad to be me for the first time since I found out I was an Ophi.

On my way to breakfast the next morning, I saw a servant bringing food up to Abby's room. She wasn't taking any chances of running into me. Who would've thought saving a person's life would make them hate you more? It was like Abby couldn't deal with the thought of me saving her. Maybe it was the fact that a drop of my blood was in her body. Maybe she didn't want to feel indebted to me. I wasn't sure I'd ever find out because she was doing a really good job of avoiding me.

Alex was different around me today. Almost shy. I wondered if our almost-kiss had left him feeling as strange as it had left me feeling. We ate in silence until Victoria walked over to us, placing one hand on each of our shoulders. "Jodi, I think that, in light of recent events, we need to increase your training."

"Increase? But why? I thought I was doing well."

"You are. That's why I want to further your training." Her face fell. "I've been hearing of attacks on Ophi. Hades isn't happy with us. We think he may want to do away with us all together. So far, we've been okay here, but we need to be prepared. You are our best weapon against him."

I didn't like the idea of being a weapon, even if I was only for self-defense. But I'd had no idea things were getting worse for the Ophi. With my new power, I could help.

"We're counting on you, Jodi."

I nodded. "I'll do my best."

"I know you will." Victoria squeezed my shoulder and went back to her seat.

"Well, it looks like we'll be heading to the cemetery after breakfast." Alex spooned more mac and cheese into his mouth. I could deal with him eating that for lunch and dinner, but it was more than a little weird at breakfast.

"What about Mr. Quim—Tony's—class?"

"Trust me, increasing your training means double duty on active use of your powers. You're getting a pass on the boring lecture portion of your day."

"Can't complain about that." I downed the rest of my orange juice. "Shall we?"

"Yeah, I'm good. Fueled with mac and cheese and ready to raise some dead."

"How can you eat that at every meal?" I asked as we headed outside.

Alex lowered his eyes. "Before we got servants, Mo—Victoria—used to attempt to cook for us. All she could make was mac and cheese." He smiled, lost in a distant memory.

"You used to call her 'Mom,' didn't you?"

"When I turned ten, they decided I needed to grow up. Act like a man. So, they told me to call them Troy and Victoria. When I complained, they said they didn't want the other kids to think they were favoring me because I was their son."

My heart broke for him. His mac and cheese obsession was a cry for help. He was trying to send a message to his mother, yet she didn't seem to get it. I could tell he didn't want to say anything more on the subject, so I switched topics. "What do you have in store for me today?"

"Raising the dead, of course."

"But I did that yesterday. I thought it went pretty well." Really, I didn't want to keep feeling the torture the souls experienced when they were forced back into their bodies.

"Well, yesterday you raised one soul. Today, we're trying for two. At the same time."

My breath caught in my throat. Two? At the same time? That was twice the torture, and it would be pulling at me from different directions. I felt dizzy, like I might faint. I stopped and grabbed on to a headstone next to me. "I don't think I can do this."

"Sure you can. You're more powerful than all of us—maybe combined. I've raised two souls at once before, and if I can do it, you definitely can."

I didn't want to point out that he couldn't feel what the souls felt. That privilege was apparently reserved for me. The others had no idea what they were putting the souls through when they raised them. It was easy to ignore the suffering if you couldn't sense it. Still, I nodded and followed him to two graves, side by side.

"This is it. Mr. and Mrs. Died-a-long-time-ago."

I squinted at the names on the headstones. I thought maybe things would be easier for the souls if I could call them by name, but that wasn't going to happen because the names had worn away.

"Okay, that's enough jokes," Alex said, reprimanding himself for the crack about the dead people. He got so serious and hardcore when we trained.

"Tell me what to do."

"Raising two souls isn't that different than raising one. You're going to drip some blood on each grave and command the drops to find the bodies. That's the easy part." He stared at me. "This will take every ounce of concentration you have. You actually have to split your attention between both bodies. Commanding them together doesn't work. And if you let your focus rest on one, the other will be free to act on its own. Believe me, the second they feel you losing control, they will take advantage of it."

This seemed impossible. "How am I supposed to split my attention? I can't give two sets of directions at the same time."

"Yes, you can. It takes some practice, but it can be done."

"Well, could you at least tell me how? Because I don't have a clue." I wasn't feeling like the Chosen One anymore. I had no idea how to do this. Yet, Alex said he'd done it before, so why couldn't I figure it out?

"It's kind of like stepping back and letting your vision pan out. You have to be able to see each body. Once you have them both in your sights, you can send out simultaneous commands. But they have to be simultaneous. No commands directed at 'You two' or anything like that. Got it?"

No. Simultaneous commands? What was that?

"Let's get started." Alex wasn't bothering to wait for me to figure things out. I was going to have to learn through trial and error. I just hoped the error part wouldn't be too devastating.

He handed me his pocketknife, and I pricked my right finger, spilling a single drop of blood on each grave. I closed my eyes and said, "Find the body that rests in this grave." Since I didn't know what simultaneous commands were, I said the same command again and hoped for the best.

I put one hand on each headstone to steady myself for what I knew was coming. In my mind's eye, I could see the drops of blood working their way through the soil, past the caskets, and into the bodies. I heard the terrible cries as the souls were pulled back into their bodies, saw the flesh re-form on the bones. Like last time, my cheeks were wet with tears. I was glad I had the headstones for support because I could barely stand.

"Push their pain from your mind," Alex said, helping me to stand up straight. "You can't feel their pain if you don't let it in." How did he know? He didn't have this ability. No one else did. But it was worth a try. I pushed the pain away, literally taking my hands off the headstones and pushing the air out in front of me. The pain subsided. I could still tell what the bodies were doing, but their rage wasn't consuming me anymore.

They broke through their coffins and crawled through the dirt until they reached the surface. I opened my eyes and reached for the first hand I saw. "No!" Alex said. "You must control them with your mind. You can't help one up and give them directions separately. That's not the lesson."

Damn. It had seemed like a good solution to the whole simultaneous issue. I held back. My eyes moved back and forth between both graves. I couldn't focus on both at the same time. The bodies were almost out of the ground. "Stand before me and stop!" I said as forcefully as I could, though the shakiness in my voice made me sound more like a frightened child than a powerful Ophi. The bodies stood and came right for us. My heart raced, but I told myself they'd stop. I'd commanded them to. Oh, crap! I'd given them both the same command at the same time.

I looked at the woman and said, "Stop!" I looked at the other, but he was gone. Gone? Alex screamed, but it was cut short as the man wrapped his hands around Alex's neck—leaning forward with his mouth open. He was trying to bite him!

"Jodi," Alex garbled under the weight of the man's hands on his throat. "Do something."

Now that my focus was off the woman in front of me, she lunged forward, knocking me to the ground. I kicked at her, but she wouldn't let up. The next thing I knew, her teeth were sinking into my shoulder.

Chapter 25

Whoever said the living dead were mindless was dead wrong. These two definitely had something on their minds. Revenge. They hated us for torturing them, and if they had it their way, they'd take us back to hell with them. And I was convinced these two souls had come from hell. I just hoped it wasn't Tartarus, or I'd have Hades visiting me soon.

I grabbed the woman by the back of her head and pulled. A clump of hair and scalp tore from her head. Ugh! I tossed it aside and pulled my knees up to my chest. Pushing them into her body as hard as I could, I rolled her off me. I jumped to my feet and concentrated on mixing my blood. As soon as I felt it bubble under my skin, I shouted, "I release your soul. Go back to the hell you were pulled out of." She lunged for me, but her body slumped to the ground as her soul sailed out of it. I heard her shrieking again.

Gurgling sounds drew my attention behind me. Alex was turning blue, and the man was inches from biting off his nose. I held up my hand. "Stop! I command you to return to where you were before I forced your soul back into your body. Leave now!" The body slumped forward onto Alex, who gasped for air. I pushed the body off and pulled Alex to a sitting position. He continued to fill his lungs with air and glare at me.

"I'm guessing I did that wrong." I sat down beside him.

He motioned to the bodies on the ground. "You think?" He sighed and shook his head, still gasping for air. "Victoria is not going to be happy about this."

"Sorry. I really did try my best, but I don't understand how to command two bodies simultaneously without giving them the same command."

"That's not exactly what I meant, but we'll work on that."

"What did you mean then?"

"You returned the souls. They're harder to raise if their souls have been released. That is why Victoria isn't going to be happy."

I narrowed my eyes at him. "What was I supposed to do with them? Make them into more servants?" He didn't answer, making me wonder if it was something worse. "Kill them?"

"Don't worry about it. It's not a problem. Let's try again. You'll get it right next time. I'm sure you will."

Try again? He was keeping something from me. I wanted to know what it was, but he gave me that look. The one where he made me feel like I was the only girl, Ophi or not, that existed. He was so complicated.

"Are you okay? That woman didn't hurt you, did she?"

I shrugged, and suddenly remembered my shoulder. "She bit me." I pulled my jacket and shirt down, exposing the red circular mark her teeth had made. Thank goodness I'd had on layers. "How about you?" I asked, suddenly remembering the guy had taken a few bites at Alex. "He was going for your neck and nose."

Alex tilted his head back. "Nothing major. His tooth only nicked me."

I touched his neck, next to the small red cut. "You're not going to turn into a zombie or anything, are you? I've seen movies where people get bitten by zombies and then become like them."

He laughed. "No. Nothing like that. The stuff you see in movies is just Hollywood garbage. Zombies can't infect people with their saliva."

No, that was only true for Ophi, and I wasn't sure that made me feel any better. "They wanted to eat us, though. Like Matt with the bunny." My stomach did flips. I was grossed out, in pain from the memory of what I'd done to Matt, and sad that I'd lost the first guy I might have actually loved.

"No way would they be able to eat us. It actually would've worked to my advantage if that guy had bitten me. My blood would've killed him again. Then, I wouldn't have had to wait so long for you to take care of him." He smirked to let me know he was only teasing me.

"Tell you what, next time I'll remember to let the dead guy bite you. How's that?"

He smiled before standing up and giving me his hand. "How about next time you control the living dead?"

I rolled my eyes as I let him pull me to my feet. "Well, sure, but that's not quite as much fun as watching you scream like a girl and get strangled by a dead guy." I started walking away from the two bodies, but Alex stopped me.

"Where do you think you're going? You're not done."

"I know. I was going to find two more graves side-by-side like these."

Alex shook his head. "Uh-uh. You're going to try again with these two. Only this time you're going to get it right."

"But you said it's harder to put souls back into their bodies after they've been released."

"That's right."

"Then why are you making me do this? After what happened, I'd think you'd try to make things a little easier for me."

He put his hands on my shoulders. "How pissed off are you at these two right now?"

I hadn't thought about it. I mean, I was the one who had forced them back into their bodies, but they had been pretty ruthless. My shoulder still ached, and Alex had a cut on his neck. Those bodies had wanted to devour us, make us suffer. "Now that you mention it, I am pretty pissed at them."

"Good. Use that. Let it fuel you. Your emotions are what will keep your power grounded."

So he kept telling me, but it seemed backward. Emotions were what caused people to fly off the handle, not control themselves. But we weren't ordinary people. We were Ophi. "Okay. These two will work fine." Now, if only I could figure out how to control them. I reached for my locket and gave it a quick squeeze. "Help me, Medusa. Please, show me how to control them at the same time."

"Are you praying?" Alex asked, but before I could answer, my eyes instinctively closed, and Medusa's image filled my head.

"See them both side by side. Speak to one aloud and the other in your mind. Your blood is in their bodies. It will carry your message without it being spoken aloud." She vanished before I could thank her. I opened my eyes and let go of the locket.

"Jodi?" Alex waved his hand in front of my face.

"I'm ready. I know how to do it." Alex handed me his knife again. Thankfully, it only took a drop of blood to raise the dead. Otherwise I would've been anemic by now. I dripped my blood onto each body. The second I heard their wails, I blocked the sound from my mind. Still, I felt their pain, their torment. The souls recognized me and fought me, but I pushed through, willing my blood to command them. I wouldn't let their pain and anger consume me. I was in charge, not them. Warm blood trickled from my nose, and I wasn't sure if it was my allergies again or if it was a side effect from using my power. I quickly wiped it away.

The bodies stood up and came right at us. I commanded my blood to mix, feeling strength and confidence as it bubbled. I stared out at them, allowing myself to see them both. Then, at the same time, I gave two commands. One aloud. "Do not move." One in my mind. "Stay still." Both bodies stopped and waited for their next command. It took all my energy to remain focused on both of them. My head felt like it was going to split open, but I held the bodies firmly in place with my mind. I commanded them to obey every word I said and not to make any moves without my approval. My body shook the longer I held on to them.

"Jodi, that's enough." Alex stepped between me and the bodies, blocking them from my view. "You're done. You did great."

I allowed my blood to stop bubbling. The power subsided, and I relaxed a little. I stumbled, but Alex steadied me. "I need a break." I squinted against the raging headache. This training was doing a number on me. All that concentrating made it feel like someone was squeezing my brain in a vice. But I'd done it. The bodies stayed frozen in place. I'd controlled two bodies at once, simultaneously.

"Headache?" Alex still held onto me.

"Yeah, a pretty bad one."

"I remember. It used to happen to me, too. But once you get better at harnessing your power, you won't need to concentrate so hard. It will come more naturally, and the headaches will go away."

"I can't wait for that."

He reached into his jacket pocket and came out with some tissues. "This is pretty normal the first couple of times, too." He dabbed at my nose. I'd forgotten about the nosebleed.

"I must look great right now. Bloody nose, tear-streaked cheeks, and a head the size of a balloon."

"It only feels like a balloon. I can assure you it's still head-sized. And as for the rest of you, you look like Jodi." I wasn't sure if I should take that as a compliment. My head wouldn't let me think too much about it. I winced against the pain.

"Here." He tilted my head back a little and gently pressed two fingers against each of my temples. He massaged them, making the pressure melt away a little. "Does that help?"

"Yeah." I closed my eyes and moaned a little. I immediately tensed up, embarrassed.

He laughed. "I have that effect on girls."

"More like you have that effect on headaches."

"Okay, I deserve that after all the training I've been putting you through."

I opened my eyes to look at him. "I don't get you. One minute you're being a total hard–ass, and the next you're being nice to me. What gives?"

"I'm trying to help you. Sometimes I need to be tough on you. Other times…" He stopped rubbing my temples and stared into my eyes. His right hand came up to my cheek and brushed away a leftover tear. He leaned forward, and I met him halfway. The moment our lips touched, something came over me. It was like I was starved for contact with another person. My arms flew around his neck, pulling him into me. We backed against the mausoleum, not even caring that the two bodies I'd raised were staring at us. I kissed him with everything I had. Since finding out I was Ophi, I'd been afraid to touch anyone. My touch meant death. With Alex, I didn't have to be afraid, and that relief took over.

I didn't know how long we stood there kissing, only that I could've continued for a lot longer if Victoria hadn't come rushing over. "Alex! Jodi!"

Embarrassed, I pulled back, smacking my head against the mausoleum. "Ouch!"

Alex removed his hands from my waist and stepped away from me. "Jodi raised and controlled two bodies." He tried to take focus off the scene Victoria had just witnessed.

She didn't look at the bodies. She looked at me. I was the girl making out with her son. Even if she didn't allow Alex to call her Mom, that didn't change the fact that he was her son. I felt my cheeks blush.

"I've called an emergency meeting. You're both to report to the conference room." She looked back and forth between us. "Immediately."

"Yes, ma'am." Alex spoke in a way that made me wonder why he hadn't saluted her, too. I nodded and watched her walk away. Alex motioned for me to go first, but I stopped at the two bodies.

"What about them? Should we release them or bring them with us?"

Alex's shoulders slouched as he stared at the ground in a daze. I'd never seen him like this. There was no sign of his cockiness. I wondered if he was going to get in trouble for kissing me. We hadn't really done anything wrong, not that I'd be looking Victoria in the eyes anytime soon. "Alex?"

"Um." He shook his head. "We don't need them right now. Go ahead and release them, I guess."

I narrowed my eyes at him, wondering if he regretted kissing me. It had seemed like he was enjoying himself... before Victoria showed up.

I stepped in front of the two bodies and allowed my blood to mix once more. I released their souls and turned toward Alex, only to find he was halfway to the house.

I didn't know what to think or feel. Before, I had been thinking about Matt, but then Alex and I kissed, and it felt right. There had always been something between us. Even before I knew his name. Yes, I'd called the cops on him, but what about all the things I'd let him get away with? Staring up at my window all night long, ransacking my room, leaving me a dead rat. He'd done all those things, and yet I'd felt attracted to him. Like my blood recognized something in his. And once I got here, I kind of got the impression he felt the same way about me. But now?

Victoria clearly wasn't happy about seeing Alex and me together. Maybe we weren't allowed to be together. Maybe he needed to kiss me to get over his crush. Maybe I wasn't anything more than the person who was supposed to save him and the other Ophi.

I walked into the house, realizing I had no clue where the conference room was. From what I did know about the layout of the mansion, I guessed it was somewhere downstairs. Since the sitting room, dining room, kitchen, and servants' quarters were all to the right of the stairs, I headed left. I passed a ballroom and kept going. I heard voices up ahead on the left. The door was closed, but not fully shut. I pushed it open, and all eyes turned on me.

"Everyone, take your seats please," Victoria said, only looking at me briefly before moving to the head of the long conference table.

I went for my usual place next to Alex—at least that was my usual place at meal times—but he was sitting between Leticia and Abby. And Abby's arm was looped through his. When Abby saw me heading toward them, she whispered something in Alex's ear. He nodded, still not pushing Abby away or taking his arm back. My eyes stung, but I forced myself to walk past them. There were no empty seats on that side of the table, which meant I had to take the long embarrassing walk around the back of the table, past Troy's glaring eyes, and to the other side. I sat down without looking at anyone, though I felt their eyes on me.

"I have bad news," Victoria began. Like I needed more bad news. "A few minutes ago, I received a phone call. It seems Hades has claimed a group of Ophi in Washington. I know this news comes as a particular shock for some of you." Her eyes moved to Leticia. "Your parents were among those who were taken. I'm terribly sorry for your loss."

Leticia started bawling. Randy stood up. "What about my father? Is he—?"

Victoria held up her hand. "We're not sure. I was informed that he is missing. I will certainly stay on top of the matter and report back to you as soon as I know anything more."

"What does this mean?" I asked.

Victoria finally looked at me. "It means we must call on your powers, Jodi. We need to go to our brothers and sisters in Washington, and you must raise them."

"Me? But I'm not ready. I raised two human bodies today, and I wasn't very good at it. It took me a couple tries. These are Ophi we're talking about. What if I mess up?"

"I'm well aware of what occurred in the cemetery today." Victoria's eyes bored into me, and I knew she was talking about the kiss. "I'm also aware of the fact that you are the Chosen One. And whether you are ready or not, we must call on you to perform your duty to us."

There was no "if" I was ready. I wasn't. But that didn't seem to matter to anyone.

Chapter 26

"So, what, you're going to ship me off to Washington? Just like that?"

"You wouldn't go alone," Victoria said.

"I'll go." Alex stood up, finally untangling his arm from Abby's. She stared at him in disbelief before she turned and gave me the evil eye.

"Alex, sit," Victoria said. "If Jodi needs an escort, either Troy or I will accompany her."

I stood up and leaned forward with my hands resting on the table for support. "It's not that I need an escort. I've never tried to bring Ophi back to life once their souls have left their bodies. I'm not even sure how to do it. I had help bringing Abby back. Medusa walked me through it. This is so much bigger than that. I just started my training a few days ago. How can you ask me to do something this huge? If it's Hades claiming these Ophi, then they must have done something to upset him and make him come after them." The words poured out of my mouth.

Alex nodded. "She's right. You can't ask her to do this. It's too dangerous. You'd be making her a target for Hades, and if he takes her next, we're all doomed."

I was so grateful for his support. I needed someone on my side.

Leticia slammed her fist down on the table and stood up. "I don't care if Hades does make her a target. My parents are dead." She turned to me. "You are the only one who has the power to bring them back. You have to do it. Why else are you here, if not to help us?"

My heart broke for her. I knew what it felt like to lose a parent, and she'd lost two. "Leticia, I get it. I do. Before I came here, I accidentally killed my mom. I cut myself making dinner, and she touched my blood. She was trying to help me, and it got her killed. If Alex hadn't been there to bring her back, I—"

"You got her back. She's alive because Alex brought her back. I'm asking you to do the same for me. Bring my parents back. Please, Jodi." Her whole body shook, and I wanted nothing more than to give in and save her parents.

"No," Alex said. "By the time we get Jodi to Washington, their souls will have moved on. We have no idea what we'd be bringing back. We might be creating more servants, only these would be Ophi." He shook his head, focusing on Leticia. "How would you handle seeing your parents like the servants? Nothing more than shells of who they were?"

Leticia turned to Randy, who had stood up at her side. She buried her face in his chest.

"I'm sorry." I didn't know what else to say. "I wish there was something I could do."

Victoria cleared her throat. "Let's take a break. We need to think of a plan. A way to save us from being attacked by Hades. And we need to learn more about Jodi's powers, how she can raise Ophi, and what the timeframe is on raising them. Leticia," she paused, waiting for Leticia to peel herself away from Randy. "Leticia, if we find a way to bring them back—as they were—Jodi will do it."

"Yes, I will." I nodded. I wanted to help. I really did. I couldn't bear to see Leticia hurting like this. And to think I was heartbroken over not being able to talk to my mom right now. At least she was alive.

Victoria clapped her hands. "Then it's settled. We'll form another plan. For right now, life continues as usual. Everyone is to report to your afternoon lessons." I looked at my watch. Ugh, Alex and I had trained right through lunch. Victoria left the room and everyone else slowly followed. Everyone but Alex.

"Thanks for sticking up for me," I said. "I kind of thought after what happened... well, I don't know what I thought."

"Listen, I can't talk long right now. Victoria said I had to report to Troy for training."

"Who's training me then?"

"Quinn. He's pretty good. You'll like him."

"But—" Alex didn't let me ask any more questions. He ran off.

Afternoon training with Quinn was rough. He wasn't exactly nice, despite what Alex had said. But I was getting better at raising multiple bodies. I was up to three when a few others joined us—Bristol, Molly, Erik, and Damon. They had all grown up in the Ophi world, and it was really obvious that they weren't happy about my decision not to try to raise the dead Ophi. As soon as dinnertime rolled around, I got out of there. I ran into the house, bumping right into Alex.

"Hey," I said, happy to see him.

He looked around like he was making sure we were the only two people in the foyer. "I want you to know that Victoria told me I was compromising things by getting too close to you. She told me to pull away. To make it seem like I was interested in Abby." He scoffed. "As if I could ever be interested in her. But, please believe me. I was only doing what Victoria told me to." He was telling the truth; I could tell by the tortured look in his eyes. "I have to go. If we walk into the dining room together, I'll get another lecture from Victoria."

I nodded and flashed him a quick smile. "Alex," I called before he disappeared down the hall. "I believe you."

He smiled and walked off, leaving me alone in the foyer.

This time I was the one who skipped dinner. After that meeting and the awkward afternoon of training, I was in no mood to chat and eat with everyone. Besides, I had better ways to occupy the next hour. With everyone in the dining room, I was free to find out more about my dad. I had to know what happened to him. Alex couldn't remember if my dad had ever been here, but that didn't necessarily mean anything. If Dad had trained here like most Ophi did, he could've left when Alex was a baby. I needed to find some sign that he'd been here. Maybe they kept records of the people who studied here.

I grabbed an apple from the fruit bowl in the living room and went up to the library, which was completely empty. No servants re-shelving books and no lights on. Perfect, and there was an entire floor between me and everyone else. I found the light switch on the wall and flicked it on. The room was huge, and there were books everywhere. Something told me they didn't follow the Dewey Decimal System either. I sat down at a computer in the center of the room and searched the system for books about Medusa's descendents, the Chosen One, and prophecies. I got a stack of books and began flipping through them, but they were all old. Too old to tell me anything about my dad.

I went back to the computer and tried something else. I clicked out of the library catalogue and searched the hard drive. I looked for files about students, teachers, anything with names of people who had been here. I didn't come up with anything. The computer was a dead end. I walked to the back of the library and found a filing cabinet. I didn't think anyone actually filed things anymore. Why would you when you could store things in a computer?

I pulled on the handle, but the drawer wouldn't budge. Locked. I had the worst luck. I looked around for something to use to pick the lock. The shelves to my right were metal, and there was a pin sticking out of the end. I pulled it out. It just might work. I had no idea how to pick a lock, so I stuck the pin in the keyhole and jiggled it around. Every so often I'd tug on the handle to see if it worked. Nothing. I wasn't any good at the stealthy stuff.

"Need a little help?"

I whipped my head around. Alex stood with his arms crossed. I let out a sigh.

"I never pegged you for the breaking and entering type."

"Well, since I'm neither breaking nor entering, I guess you were right." I stood up and slammed my hand down on the filing cabinet.

"Here, let me try." Alex reached for the metal pin in my hand, completely taking me off guard. He didn't even know what I was looking for. Why would he help me, no questions asked? He fiddled with the lock for a few seconds. "What are you looking for anyway?"

Ah, now that was more like it. "I want to know more about my dad. He must have come here. At least for a little while, to train. So, there must be something here that will tell me more about him. Anything. I don't even know his name, and with everything that's going on with the Ophi and Hades, I just need my family. I can't even call my mom. I feel so alone. Leticia and the others want me to save the Ophi, and you're the only one who even thought about what doing that might mean for me. I need this. No matter how small. I need to find something. Something I can hold on to." I was losing it. Again.

Alex wrapped his arms around me. "You have me. You're not alone. I don't care what Victoria and Troy say. I'm here for you. I won't let you go through this alone."

I raised my head, tilting it back to see him. He really was all I had now. "Alex, I—" How could I thank him for being here for me? For going against his family? I stretched up on my toes and pressed my lips to his. He kissed me back, and for a moment I forgot about everything that was going on. I let it all slip away. The only thing I allowed myself to think about was Alex.

A few minutes later, we both pulled away, completely breathless. "All right, well, this filing cabinet seems to be locked tight. How about we look somewhere else?"

"I checked everywhere else already. This is my last shot. At least in here, anyway."

He took a deep breath and squatted down in front of the filing cabinet. "Then I guess we make this thing open up, one way or another." He maneuvered the pin in the keyhole and then looked around the library. "I need something else to slip in the lock with this. Something wider."

"What about your pocketknife? Will the blade work?"

"It might." He whipped it out and slipped it into the lock with the pin. He wiggled both around, and I heard a click. Without hesitating, I grabbed the handle and tugged. The drawer slid open.

"I could kiss you right now!"

"I wouldn't object." He gave me a sly smile.

"Tell you what, let's see what's in here before everyone finishes dinner. Then we'll talk about that kiss."

I could tell he was trying not to look disappointed, but he reached into the drawer and pulled out a leather-bound book. "What is that?" I asked.

He opened it. The first few pages were lined with signatures. "These must be Ophi."

I leaned closer, checking out the names. Only they weren't just names. "Look. The names have dates next to them."

"I know what this is." He didn't sound happy at all. "This is the death register. When an Ophi dies, his or her name is recorded along with the date."

I wasn't sure this was going to be any help after all. I didn't know my dad's name. It was part of what I was searching for, and I had no idea if he was alive or dead.

"Do you know anything about your dad? Anything that might help us figure out if his name is in this book?"

I shook my head. "I've never even seen my birth certificate, but Mom told me my dad's name isn't on it. When he walked out on her, she decided to raise me on her own. As far as she was concerned, I didn't have a father."

Alex continued to flip through the names anyway. He didn't want to give up hope. "Look, this name has an asterisk next to it. Derek Colgan."

I stared at the name. Derek Colgan. I remembered finding an old yearbook in Mom's closet. It was from her sophomore year. Her last year in high school. After she had me, she got her GED. She said they'd mailed her a yearbook since she was home with me. "When I was little, Mom used to show me pictures of her classmates. She pointed out all the ones who had made comments about her pregnancy. She even let me draw funny faces on their photos, but one of them was an empty box. There was no picture. I can't be sure, but I think it could've been Derek Colgan. It was close to the beginning of the alphabet, and I remembered making the two E's in his first name into eyes and the R in between them a nose." If he was really my father, then he wasn't raised like Alex. He'd been around humans before he came into his powers.

Alex pointed to the date next to Derek's name. "January 12—"

"That was only a little over a month after I was born. He was—"

"Seventeen," Alex said. "No wonder I don't remember him. I was only a month old."

"So, my dad's dead." I shouldn't have cared. I mean, I'd never met him, and he'd run out on my mom. Left her pregnant and a single parent. A teen parent. I should've been happy he was dead. But I wasn't. He was my father. My blood.

"At least now you know. You don't have to wonder anymore."

I was sure Derek was my dad. I couldn't explain how I knew it; I just did. It was a feeling I had deep in my blood, but I still didn't know how he'd died. What if he left my mom because he came into his powers? He might have wanted me, but not have been able to do anything about it. Maybe he stayed away to protect my mom and me. I'd thought I just wanted to know where he was. For closure. But instead, finding out his name and that he'd died right after I was born left me with even more questions.

"Do you want to go for a walk? Clear your head?"

"No." I took the book from his hands and put it back in the filing cabinet. "I'm tired. It's been a long day, and I just want to go to sleep."

"Are you sure? Because if you're worried about Victoria, I can handle her."

"No. I'm not worried about her. I need to process things, and I kind of can't do that unless…" I didn't want to hurt his feelings. He'd been so helpful, and I really appreciated that, but I needed to be alone.

"Say no more. I'll walk you to your room." He nodded toward the door, but I reached up and kissed him lightly on the lips.

"That's for helping me get into that filing cabinet."

We didn't see anyone on the way to my room. I guessed dinner had run long. Everyone was probably arguing over how to handle the situation with Hades. I was glad I'd skipped it, but my stomach rumbled. Alex looked down at my stomach. "I'll send a servant up with something for you."

"Thanks, but I think I'm going to crash. If I eat now, it might wake me up, and I don't want that."

We stopped at my door. "All right then. I guess this is goodnight." We heard footsteps on the stairs.

"That's probably Abby. You better go. Oh, and, Alex, thank you." It sounded dumb and not nearly enough to express how I really felt about all he'd done, but I was short on time, so it would have to do.

He smiled and gently kissed my lips before I ducked into my room. I didn't even bother with a shower. I climbed into bed, fully dressed. A plate of wine and cheese sat on my nightstand. One of the servants must have brought it up. My grumbling stomach wouldn't let it go to waste. I polished off the cheese and wine and fell asleep wondering what Derek Colgan had been like.

I slept soundly, which was odd considering all I had going on in my head. I think my subconscious must have been trying extra hard to keep me in dreamland. I couldn't blame it. I'd dreamed that my dad was alive. He came to the mansion and demanded that Victoria and Troy let him take me home with him. He said he'd find a way we could be around Mom without hurting her, and we'd be like a real family. Finally. The only strange thing was that in the dream, I wasn't wearing Medusa's locket. I hadn't taken it off since I'd gotten it back from Abby. I even showered with it now. But in the dream, my neck was bare.

When I opened my eyes in the morning, the first thing I did was stretch and squint against the sunlight. I'd left my curtains open and sun poured into my room. My room, which was a mess. I sat up straight, jolted awake by the sight of clothing spilling out of open drawers. My closet was wide open and things were falling off hangers. I couldn't help thinking it looked a lot like my bedroom at home after Alex had ransacked it and left a dead rat in my closet.

Someone had gone through my things. At first, I couldn't figure out why. I'd barely brought anything from home, and nothing was remotely valuable. Nothing except… my hands flew to my neck. I looked down and saw nothing but my shirt.

My locket was gone.

Chapter 27

I threw the covers off me and tore the sheets apart. Tossing my pillow aside, I saw the glimmer of something gold between the bed and the headboard. My locket! I pulled it out and clutched it to my chest. Relief washed over me. I knew Medusa wasn't my immediate family or anything, but right now, she was the only family I felt close to. And the locket was a huge part of that.

I examined every inch of it, making sure it hadn't been damaged in any way. It looked fine. The clasp must have come loose in my sleep. I put it back on, double-checking the clasp. Satisfied that the locket was good as before, I got started on cleaning my room. Nothing seemed to be missing. Maybe because whoever did this—my money was on Abby—didn't find anything they thought was worth stealing. I figured it must have been payback for sneaking into her room and taking back my locket.

I lingered in the shower, not wanting to head down to breakfast. Leticia was most likely still a wreck, and I doubted the group had come up with a better plan for how to stop Hades' attacks on us. The only reason I had for going to breakfast at all was Alex. I wanted to see him. The memories of our kiss and how he'd helped me find out my dad's name were at the forefront of my brain. He was the one person I could count on right now.

I put my fears aside and went down to the dining room. As usual, I was the last one there. People here must get up with the sun or something. Alex had his usual bowl of mac and cheese, and the moment I took my seat, a servant placed a bowl in front of me, too.

"What's this?" I stared at the bowl of artificial cheese and elbow noodles.

"I figured you could use a little something extra to get you through your day."

"You've got that right. I woke up to my room completely torn apart."

Alex dropped his fork in his empty bowl. He leaned closer to me and whispered, "Was anything missing?"

"No." I glanced past him to Abby. She was facing away from us, talking to Randy. I couldn't ever remember seeing them talk before. Randy usually sat across from me, and Quinn usually sat on the other side of Abby. "It had to be Abby."

"Why would Abby go through your stuff? You don't exactly have anything that's her taste. She's—"

"Stuck up and bitchy." The words sort of came out. I hadn't meant to say them. At least not loud enough for anyone to hear.

Alex nodded. "That too. But I meant to say she's really into designer labels and things that cost more money than cars."

My eyes dropped to my plain shirt, which I'd bought off the clearance rack. "Yeah, I definitely don't own anything like that."

"I didn't mean—"

I held up a hand to stop him. "No, it's okay. I know you weren't trying to insult me." I looked around the table, noticing that everyone was engaged in private conversations. Yet every one of them glanced in my direction at some point or another. "Gee, I wonder who they're all talking about?"

"Don't worry about them. They're still freaked out about the attack in Washington, and no one has any ideas about how to fix the problem."

"Other than shipping me off and practically throwing me at Hades' feet." I took a bite of mac and cheese. I cringed at the fake cheese taste. "Ugh, really? How do you eat this stuff? I think it has an age limit of six or seven. I'm way too old to think food this gross tastes good." I pushed the bowl away from me and sat back in my seat. Alex laughed and grabbed my bowl. He dug right in, and all I could do was shake my head as I helped myself to a plate of pancakes in the center of the table.

I looked around, deciding that, if everyone was going to be sneaking glances at me, the least I could do was catch them in the act and make them feel guilty. It was fun at first, but then I got to Victoria's spot at the table. "Hey, where's Victoria?"

"She was gone when I got up," Alex said, finishing off my mac and cheese. "Troy said she was flying to Washington to check out the situation."

"Oh." I was shocked that she'd gone alone. I figured she'd try to make me change my mind or kidnap me while I was sleeping. I mean, what was she going to be able to do for a bunch of dead Ophi? But the good thing about Victoria being gone was that she wasn't here to make sure Alex and I stayed apart. Troy was too busy to notice us, so things were kind of back to normal.

After breakfast Alex and I headed to the cemetery to work some more on raising multiple bodies. In fact, that was all I worked on for the next two days. All I did was eat, sleep, and train. My headaches were starting to get a little better, but the nosebleeds were just as bad. I felt so rundown at the end of it all that when we went back into the mansion, I walked right over to Medusa and grabbed both her hands.

Her power filled my blood and restored my energy. I knew that connecting with the statue like this usually drained my energy afterward, but I was already drained, and I needed the boost if I was going to be able to climb the stairs to my room. I let her power bring my body back to some sort of normalcy. And as I was about to let go, Medusa's image rushed into my mind with such force I almost fell over.

I staggered and struggled to stay connected so she wouldn't disappear. "What is it? Something's wrong."

"Yes, my child. Something is very wrong. You are no longer safe in this house. Enemies are among you. In these very walls. You must protect yourself. Things are not as they seem." She looked down, her eyes falling on the locket. "Not at all what they seem."

"How do I protect myself? Please, tell me what to do."

"You must find the power within yourself. It is all you have left, but it is strong enough to save you. Your father was like you. He was strong. But he did not heed my warnings. He trusted those who should not have been trusted. They gave him blood to drink. Blood they said would awaken the powers in him. They claimed it was Gorgon blood, but it was not. It was human blood, and they used it to dilute his power. Stifle his abilities."

"He drank blood? Like a vampire?" I shuddered at the thought.

"They slipped it into his wine. Pretended they were toasting his arrival and then every success he found after that. When he questioned the taste and thickness of the wine, they finally told him it contained blood. But they lied to him about why they were giving it to him. He didn't discover the truth until it was too late. I could not save him, Jodi."

My mind was stuck on something she'd said. Wine. The Ophi had toasted my arrival, too. And they'd given me wine on more than one occasion. It was different than any wine I'd ever seen, but everyone drank it. That had to mean it was okay. Unless. My wine might have been the only one laced with human blood. Maybe everyone else had been drinking regular wine. I remembered the slightly metallic taste. Could that have been blood? Ugh! I was questioning everything. I didn't know who to trust anymore. Emotions had been on high lately, especially with the attacks on Ophi, but I'd thought that was all it was. People freaking out and acting funny because of all the bad stuff going on. Now? Maybe they had been trying to sabotage me.

I didn't know what to think about anything. And Medusa was only here in spirit, so she couldn't help me figure things out right now either. Still, there was one thing she could help me with.

"Can you tell me about my dad? What did he look like? What was he like?"

"He looked a lot like you. Green eyes. Dark hair. One dimple on his right cheek, just like you. He was tall, too. Almost six feet. He was seventeen when I met him."

"He was seventeen when he died," I said.

"Yes, that is true."

"He was so young." I couldn't imagine my life ending at my age. There was so much I still wanted to do. He probably had felt the same way. Or maybe he didn't know he was going to die. I couldn't bring myself to ask Medusa. I wasn't ready to hear about his death yet. "Derek Colgan." I muttered, without really meaning to.

"I see you have learned his name. And, yes, he was young. When he discovered what was really going on here, he asked me to protect you."

"Me? But he never even met me. He left my mom right after he found out she was pregnant."

"Yes, he had to leave. He was coming into his powers and did not want to hurt her or you, but he did see you. When you were born, he went to the hospital. He told me you were beautiful and so small. He asked me to protect you. I told him you were chosen. You would receive my locket, which would unlock your true powers."

My head lowered. My eyes were still closed, but in my mind I could see the locket.

"Jodi," Medusa said, "that is not my locket around your neck."

"What? But you gave it to me."

"I did give you a locket, but that is not it. That is a fake."

"No, that's impossible. The locket hasn't been out of my sight, except for when Abby stole it. Did she switch them? No, she was upset when I got it back. She wouldn't have been that upset if this wasn't the real locket." My thought and speech were mixing in my mind. A jumbled mess.

"Child, calm yourself. I can sense my blood, any Gorgon blood, and there is none inside that stone."

Had Abby lied about everything? Was this all a big charade? She could've fooled me, pretended to be upset about me getting the locket back when all along it was what she'd wanted. Fueled by anger, I released Medusa's hands and marched up the stairs. My energy level was better than normal now.

"Jodi, wait!" Alex called. I'd forgotten he'd been with me when I connected with the statue. "What's wrong? Where are you going?"

"There's something I have to do." I stormed down the hallway and pounded on Abby's door.

"She's in a lesson right now," Alex said.

"I need to get inside. She took something of mine."

"What did she take? I thought you said nothing was missing from your room."

I froze. That was it! Abby hadn't switched the lockets back when she took it from my bathroom. She switched them a few nights ago when she ransacked my room. "That witch!"

"What?" Alex was trying to keep up with me, but I wasn't exactly filling in any of the details for him.

"Do you have keys to the rooms? Your parents run this place, so even if they don't want you advertising that fact, you must have certain privileges, like a master key."

He sighed and reached in his pocket. "For the record, I never let you in here. Got it?"

I crossed my heart.

He opened the door and stepped aside so I could go in. I went straight to her dresser and began tearing it apart, not trying to be neat or cover up the fact that I'd been here. I wanted her to know I had been there. I wanted her to know this was war.

Alex stayed in the hall. "Aren't you going to help me?"

"No way. This is between you and Abby. I've got your back, Jodi, but I don't want trouble with Abby. If she admits to taking whatever it is you think she took, then I'll go to Troy and tell him. But I'm not going to rifle through her stuff."

I stopped for a second and stared at him. "You went through my stuff. You totally wrecked my room, and now that we are on the subject, what exactly were you looking for?"

He lowered his head. "Your diary."

I laughed. "My diary? Isn't that a little elementary school of you? I haven't kept a diary since I was eight, and even then, I never wrote anything good in it. I was homeschooled and grew up with practically no money. What on earth would I have to write about in a diary?"

"How about raising the dead?" He finally stepped into the doorway. "I needed confirmation that you saw the signs."

"What signs?"

"That you were changing. You wouldn't talk to me, so I had to resort to other ways of finding out what was going on with you and how much you'd figured out on your own."

That was easy. I hadn't figured out a thing. Until Alex had told me what I was, I had no idea I was the one doing all those awful things. Raising dead animals, killing people who were only trying to help me. I had been clueless.

"Don't feel bad," Alex said, as if reading my mind. "Most Ophi grow up already knowing what's going to happen to them. It's not something our parents keep from us, so unless we end up orphaned because Hades claimed our parents, we know."

I lowered my head and realized I was holding a pair of Abby's lace underwear. Ugh! I tossed them back in the drawer and moved on to the next one.

"What do you think she took, anyway?"

"My locket." I kept searching, tossing things left and right.

"Um, Jodi." Alex walked over and touched my necklace. "Your locket is around your neck."

"No, it's not." I held it up to him. "This is a fake. Medusa told me so. When I woke up a few days ago, my locket wasn't around my neck. It was missing. I tore the bed apart, looking for it. I found it between the mattress and the headboard. I assumed the clasp came loose or something, that it had simply fallen off, but I was wrong. Abby was looking for the locket, and she found it. Found it and switched it with this fake."

"Why would she do that?"

I moved on to the nightstand and continued searching. "Because she was in Tony's lesson with me when he explained how powerful it is. You saw what Abby did with the Medusa statue. She got herself killed because she was trying to prove I wasn't the only one who could make that type of connection with Medusa. I'll bet anything that she thinks she'll be as powerful as I am if she has the locket."

We were interrupted by screams downstairs. Alex and I exchanged a worried look and raced for the door. We ran down the stairs to the foyer. I stopped short and reached for Alex to steady myself.

Victoria had returned, and she'd brought an army of Ophi with her. Dead Ophi. Living dead. Leticia was still screaming at the sight of a couple, who I could only assume were her parents, now nothing more than zombies. But my eyes were locked on Victoria. My locket was around her neck.

Chapter 28

"What did you do?" Leticia shrieked, falling to her knees.

Randy rushed over to her, but his eyes searched the group of living dead Ophi. "Where's my dad? Did you find him?"

"Yes," Victoria said grimly. "I found him." She stepped aside, revealing a corpse that had been so mangled I could barely look at him.

Randy turned to the side and threw up all over the wood floor. I couldn't blame him. I was having a hard time keeping myself from being sick.

"What happened to him?" Alex asked. "All of them. How are they here?"

Victoria walked past us. "Shall we all meet in the conference room? This entryway is feeling a little cramped." As she passed by me, she smiled. My eyes never left the locket. My locket. It wasn't Abby who had raided my room. It was Victoria.

Alex leaned closer to me. "Is she wearing—?"

"My locket." Tears stung my eyes. I knew she wasn't mother of the year, and she'd done some things that I'd questioned, but this was too much. Abby sneered at me as she followed the group to the conference room. I had almost felt bad for accusing her and tearing her room apart, but after that look, I decided she deserved it anyway. She wouldn't even be alive it weren't for me. I didn't owe her anything.

Alex and I were the last ones to enter the conference room. It was standing room only. The living dead Ophi were lined up along one side of the table like they were on display. The rest of us stuck to the other side of the table, not wanting to get too close.

"What happened to my dad?" Randy asked. "Why is he like that?"

Victoria sighed. "I had a little trouble. This locket wasn't as easy to use as I thought it would be." She fingered the bloodstone on the locket. "But, I figured it out after the first few attempts."

I looked at the Ophi she'd raised. Some of them didn't look that bad. Others were downright hideous.

"Why did you do it?" I asked. "You came into my room in the middle of the night and stole my necklace. You switched it with this fake." Everyone turned, looking back and forth between Victoria and me. "You could've told me what you were going to do. Asked me for help. Something."

"I did ask you for help." Victoria stood up straighter, and I swear she grew three inches. She looked huge and powerful. "Right in this room." She stabbed her index finger at the table. "I told you we needed you to go to Washington and use your powers to raise the Ophi we lost to Hades. You said no. You said you couldn't do it. You came up with every excuse you could think of not to try to help us, after we took you in and taught you about who you really are."

I swallowed hard. "But I didn't think I could do it. I was afraid something bad would happen. That it would go wrong and they'd turn out like—"

"This!" Leticia yelled, pointing at her parents. "Look at them! They aren't themselves. They're zombies, Victoria. You made them into zombies." She slumped forward and cried.

Victoria remained calm and unfazed. "Yes, Leticia. They did come back wrong, and the reason that happened is that I didn't know how to use the locket. It wasn't meant for me. But since Jodi was unwilling to help…" She shot me a look. "I did the best I could." She walked over to the few Ophi nearest to her. "As you can see, the first few I attempted to restore didn't come back right. My blood wasn't mixing properly, and it caused complications." She reached up to touch the huge sagging piece of flesh hanging off the side of Randy's father's face. "But then, I started to feel the locket working, and the others came back more like themselves." She walked along the line of them, stopping at a man at the very end. His dark hair was peppered with gray, and he stood about 5'10". He looked normal enough, except for the slightly dazed look in his eyes. "Go ahead, speak."

The man nodded. "My name is Calvin Davies. I was in charge of the group in Washington. We were attacked by Hades after we attempted to bring back a group of people recently killed in a plane crash. Hades stopped us before we succeeded. He said that, as payment for trying to steal their souls from him, he was taking ours." He laughed. "Victoria changed all that. While it may have taken her a few tries to get it right, you can see that I am very much like my old self."

"So, it worked." A smile spread across Troy's face. "You figured it out."

"Yes." Victoria turned to me, grinning. "I figured it out."

"What do we do now?" Abby asked. "How do we stop Hades from coming after us? I mean, he isn't going to be happy about Victoria raising all these Ophi souls. And since she's back here, it will lead him right to us."

"That's probably true," Troy said. "There's really only one thing to do. We need to raise more souls and get ourselves an army."

"A zombie army to fight Hades? Are you crazy?" Why was I the only one seeing the problem here? "He's king of the underworld. A bunch of dead bodies aren't going to stop him. He'll take control of them in seconds, and we'll all be dead. Besides, when are you people going to see that raising the dead for your own selfish purposes isn't the answer?"

Alex turned to me. "Jodi, don't get upset. We knew this day was going to come eventually. This has been our plan all along. It's the only way to defend ourselves. If we have control over the souls, Hades can't use them against us. We can set them on Hades and maybe even defeat him for good. This can work. It could mean our freedom."

I stared at him, not sure who he was anymore. Our freedom in exchange for an entire army of tortured souls didn't add up. "Don't get upset? How can I not get upset? Using people like this. Forcing all those souls back into their bodies. You're monsters!" I looked around the table and finally back at Alex. "All of you."

Abby laughed. "Well it's about time."

"Shut up, Abby," Alex said.

"Oh, come on. Don't you think this has gone on long enough? It's time Jodi found out your little secret."

"I told you to shut up," he said through gritted teeth. "This doesn't concern you."

"Oh, but I think it does. It concerns all of us."

"What secret?" I stared at Abby. "Tell me what's going on."

"My pleasure." Her smile was laced with hatred and happiness for getting to be the one to make me upset. "Consider it payback for bringing me back to life." I knew this was going to hurt. She considered my saving her as the worst form of torture. "Alex has been doing a great job of getting you to trust him." She walked over to Alex, peering at him under her dark bangs. "A little too good at times." She faced me again. "But no matter. He did what he had to."

I stared at Alex. The look on his face said Abby was telling the truth. "You lied to me."

"Did you really think he cared about you?" Abby laughed. "Honey, he already has a girl." She stroked Alex's shoulder. "And I'm twice the woman you'll ever be. Chosen One or not."

Alex swatted her hand away. "Don't touch me, Abby."

"Aw, don't be that way. You were just doing as you were told. I know that. I'm not mad anymore." She turned her eyes on me. "I'm sure it wasn't easy pretending to like her."

"Is this true? Did you just pretend to care about me?" I tried to keep my voice steady, but my hands shook with anger and embarrassment. How had I fallen for this? Alex wouldn't even look at me. "You liar! You lied to me. You made me trust you." Abby laughed at my outburst, and I ran out of the room, pushing past everyone.

I wanted to stop at the statue and ask Medusa what I should do, but I didn't want to risk having anyone catch up with me. Especially Alex. So I kept going past the statue and out the front door. I smacked into one of the servants watering the potted plants. Her watering can flew through the air. I went to catch it for her, but when it dropped into my hands, I saw that the woman's hand was still attached to it. It had broken off in our collision.

"Oh, God!" I dropped it on the steps and ran away. My legs were moving so fast I was out of control. I slipped on the last step and fell forward onto the driveway. I had scrapes all over my hands, and my jeans were shredded at the knees. The cool breeze stung as I picked myself up and hobbled to the cemetery. I headed for the mausoleum and leaned against it, using it to block the wind. I didn't have a jacket on, and I was shivering in the cold, though I knew a lot of my shaking had more to do with finding out that Alex had tricked me.

I turned around, leaning my forehead against the stone. Why had I come here? This was the spot where Alex and I had had our first kiss. It was the last place I wanted to be. Despite the scrapes on my hands, I pushed off the mausoleum and kept walking through the graves.

"Jodi!"

I forced myself to run. I couldn't handle seeing Alex right now. Ugh! I was so angry with myself for running off to the one place I knew he'd look. Only, I hadn't really expected him to come after me. Why would he? He didn't care about me. It had all been a lie. He'd played me. My blood boiled, and I stopped running. I turned to face him.

"Was this the plan all along?" I threw my arms up. "Did Victoria tell you to pretend to like me so that I'd tell you how my powers worked? She stole my locket and figured out how to use it. Obviously that was her goal. To find a way to be as powerful as me. She never wanted my help. She hated that I'm the Chosen One. She was jealous. Like Abby. So, she found a way around me."

"Jodi, listen to me." Alex kept glancing behind him. "They're coming. We need to go somewhere. Anywhere but here. They can't find us."

"I'm not going anywhere with you. You tricked me. You made me feel something for you." I scoffed. "You know, you could have a real future in acting if this raising the dead thing doesn't work out for you."

Alex turned back toward the house. I could see the others coming. "Please," he said. "Trust me this once. Come with me. I'll explain everything. There are things you don't know."

"How dumb do you think I am?"

He grunted. "I need you to believe me. It's the only way I can help you. They will hurt you, Jodi. They think you're against them."

"I am against them!"

"And they'll kill you because of it."

My mind raced. Kill people who are against them. That's why they'd diluted my dad's blood. He was against them. I knew it. And when trying to inhibit his power didn't work… "They killed my dad." Tears streamed down my cheeks for the father I'd never known. The teenage boy who had come to see me after I was born, who had asked Medusa to protect me.

"Jodi," Alex pleaded, "I wasn't lying. I did care about you. I still do. Please, let me prove it."

"I'm afraid it's a little too late for that," Abby said, coming out from behind the mausoleum. She'd crept up on us. I shouldn't have been surprised. She trailed after Alex all the time. Of course she'd follow him out here.

"Jodi, run!" Alex turned and swung at Abby, knocking her out with one punch. I gawked at Abby's body on the ground. "Go!" Alex pushed me, forcing me to run before the others caught up with us.

"Why did you do that?" I asked, weaving through headstones.

"Because I'm trying to help you." He pulled me off to the side of the cemetery, behind some sort of shed. "We don't have long, so here's the plan. I'll distract them and you keep running. Follow the dirt road until you reach the street. Then head right. Keep going and flag down—"

"Hold on." I wasn't going anywhere without some answers. "Did you really try to get me to trust you? Was that why you acted like you liked me?"

He kept glancing out at the graveyard and then back at me.

"I'm not leaving until you tell me the truth. You owe me that much."

"At first, yes. Victoria told me to get close to you. But after I got to know you… that was real. When I kissed you, it was real."

My heart told me he meant it. The feelings between us were real.

"Please, I don't know how long I can hold them off. You need to get a head start."

"What will happen to you?"

He stared into my eyes, and I saw his fear. Before I could say a word, he leaned forward and kissed me. "I'm sorry. About everything. Well, not everything." He kissed me again, pulling away quickly as the sound of footsteps got closer. "Go. And whatever you do, don't turn back."

I didn't like the sound of that at all. This seemed too much like a goodbye. "Alex—"

"Please, Jodi." He kissed me one last time and ran out from behind the shed. I hesitated for a second, just long enough to see him charge at the group. He was taking them all on at once. It was suicide. I didn't want to run away, but what else could I do? Alex was Victoria and Troy's son. No matter how angry they got at him for trying to protect me, they wouldn't let the group clobber him too badly.

I took off, running for the gate at the end of the cemetery. I heard grunting and punching behind me. Victoria and Abby were screaming at me. Telling me to stop. I heard Victoria tell her army of living dead Ophi not to let me get away, but they were in no shape to catch up to me. And if I did get caught, I'd be able to fight them off. Knowing that made me ease up. I couldn't resist looking back. I had to check on Alex. See that he was okay.

I slowed to a jog and turned to see Troy holding Alex by the front of his shirt. Alex's gaze fell on me, and he yelled my name. But I barely heard it. My senses seemed to fail as I saw Troy lift Alex's own pocketknife in the air and bring it down on Alex's chest.

"No!" I stopped running and fell to my knees at the same time Alex's body slumped to the ground. He was still facing me, and I watched the life drain out of his eyes.

Chapter 29

Everything went numb. Like I was watching a dream. No, a nightmare. Alex's vacant expression was burned into my mind. Even through the curtain of tears welling up in my eyes, I could see him clearly. I was aware of the living dead Ophi coming toward me. Of Abby approaching me and standing before me while the zombies pulled me to my feet. But I stayed focused on Alex, my eyes not leaving his.

"That didn't have to happen, Jodi. If you were half as powerful as the prophecy claimed you'd be, you never would've used Alex as your shield." She pulled her hand back and smacked me across the face. "Look at me! Forget him. He was stupid."

I wouldn't give her the satisfaction of obeying her. I didn't care if they killed me. I wasn't going down as a slave to her. As the Ophi holding me pushed me toward the rest of the group, I realized that Victoria had the power to kill me and make me a zombie. I could end up a slave to them.

I wasn't going to let that happen. Not to me and definitely not to Alex. I continued to stare at Alex, pretending I was in shock, but inside I was commanding my blood to mix. It bubbled in my veins. Victoria had my locket, but I had Medusa's blood in my veins. I didn't need the locket. What I did need was to get close to Alex's body before Victoria got any ideas of raising him herself.

"Bring her here," Victoria said.

I allowed the Ophi to walk me over to Victoria, who was standing by Alex's head. She hadn't so much as glanced at his body. Poor Alex. Killed by his father, and not given a second thought by his mother. But he had me. I'd never raised an Ophi without Medusa before, but I trusted that my blood knew what to do. Alex had said my powers were connected to my emotions. My heart was breaking for Alex. I hoped that emotion would be enough fuel to restore Alex before his soul left his body.

"Well, Jodi, you keep costing me things, don't you?" Victoria asked. "First a servant, and now Alex." She nudged him with her foot. Anger bubbled up inside me, mixing with the pain of losing Alex. The two emotions swirled like my blood. It was ready. I was ready. I had to keep Victoria from discovering what I was doing. But how?

I needed to cut myself, spill my blood to bring Alex back, but I didn't have a knife or anything sharp. Calvin and his zombie buddies were holding my scraped hands where I couldn't get to them either. My only hope was to make Victoria angry enough to attack me. It was risky, but I couldn't think of any other way. "How's the locket working out for you?" I asked, still keeping my focus on Alex. "Does it make you feel powerful? Or pathetic? I mean, it must be a constant reminder that I'm stronger than you. That you're not quite good enough to be the Chosen One."

Victoria narrowed her eyes at me and swung at my face. Her nails scratched my cheek, and I felt the warm trickle of blood. The hit wasn't that bad, but I allowed myself to go down. Right next to Alex. Thankfully, Calvin and the others had let go of me when Victoria lashed out. I pulled myself to a sitting position, leaning over Alex, but there wasn't enough blood for the cut to drip. Time for plan B. I reached up and touched my face, faking shock at being cut. I wiped the cut, smearing the blood across my fingers, and immediately pressed my bloody fingers to Alex's lips.

Victoria looked down at her son and laughed. "Nice try, Jodi, but I have your magic locket. Without it, you can't raise an Ophi." She bent down toward Alex. "But I can. Let me show you what I can do."

I saw Alex's eyelids flutter. "I don't think that will be necessary." Alex thrust his fist up, connecting with Victoria's nose. She stumbled backward, and I reached for Alex's hand, yanking him to his feet. We backed away from the group.

Victoria wiped the blood from her nose. "How did you do that? I have your locket."

"Funny thing about the locket. I only needed it to tap into my powers. Really it was more a confidence thing. But Medusa—you know her, right? My ancestor—well, she told me I didn't need the locket because her blood is in my veins. That means, just like her, I can mix my blood at will. No locket required." I looked at Alex. "You okay? You feel normal?"

"Good as new." He smiled at me.

Victoria turned to her zombie crew. "Don't just stand there! Get them."

Alex and I took off running. We went straight for the mausoleum, and Alex yanked on the doors. "What are you doing? We'll be trapped."

"We have to get in there." He yanked the door open, and without knowing what we were doing, I went in. It was a huge leap of faith, but Alex knew his family better than I did. "Jodi, I know how you feel about creating zombies, but this is life or death. You have to raise the bodies in these drawers."

I looked at the drawers lining the back wall of the mausoleum. I didn't like the idea, but I knew I could release the souls after they helped us. "Okay, but I don't think I can raise all of them before the others get in here." Alex was struggling to hold the door shut as the Ophi banged on it. Calvin smashed the window with a headstone. Glass shattered, and I jumped back to avoid it. I grabbed a shard and held it up to my hand.

"No," Alex said. "Jodi, there's something my parents didn't tell you about the prophecy." He grunted as he fought to hold the door handle still. "You don't need your blood to raise humans. Only Ophi. It's easier with your blood, but it's not necessary."

"I've never raised anything without using my blood. I'm not sure I'm strong enough."

Alex was really struggling, so I ran to the door and pushed my weight against it. Decayed arms reached through the window, grabbing for us.

"You need a power boost," Alex said.

"Yeah, well, the only way I know how to do that is by connecting with Medusa, and the statue is in the mansion."

Alex eased up on the door and looked at me. "The locket isn't. I'll slip out there and get it from Victoria. When I get it to you, drink the blood inside the bloodstone."

"You want me to drink blood? You know your family made my dad drink blood. They diluted his power with human blood, and I'm convinced Victoria did the same thing to me. That's why I was out cold the night she stole my locket. I was weak from the human blood."

"I'm not my family. Besides, the blood is Medusa's. It's the ultimate power source."

He was right, but how would he fight off all the Ophi to get the locket? Before I could ask, he said, "Close this behind me," and slipped through the door. I struggled to push it shut again. Luckily, they were probably so thrown off-guard that Alex was coming out that they forgot to push their way in.

There was a huge struggle outside, and I knew Alex didn't stand a chance. I grabbed the arm that was still swinging at me through the window. I let my blood bubble while I commanded him, "Help Alex. Attack Victoria, and help Alex get the locket from her. Go!" I released his arm, and he pulled it back through the window. I peered out. The man was going straight for Victoria, but the others were still attacking Alex. It wasn't enough. Abby had Alex in a headlock from behind. I opened the door and lunged at her, yanking her head back by her hair. I turned to the living dead Ophi coming toward me and commanded him to help Alex. The corpse fought off the others, helping Alex get free. I held tight to Abby, who kicked and swatted at me.

Alex lunged for Victoria, but Troy grabbed him instead. "I killed you once, and I'll do it again, son."

All eyes fell on them. No one moved.

"He's your son?" Leticia asked. "And you killed him?"

"Yes," I blurted out. "He and Victoria are ruthless. They only care about themselves." I shoved Abby right into Victoria. They fell in a heap. "Leticia, you don't have to follow them. Think about it. If they killed their own son, what would stop them from killing you?"

Leticia looked at her parents, standing next to Troy. She burst into tears and ran for the mansion. "Go after her and bring her back," Troy instructed her parents.

Alex's knee connected with Troy's stomach. Troy doubled over, and Alex ran to me. We clutched each other's arms.

Troy stood up, holding his stomach with his hand. "That was really stupid, Alex. This time I'm going to tear you apart so your little girlfriend can't put you back together."

"No!" We were outnumbered. I couldn't find a way out. Leticia's parents were dragging her, screaming, back to the group. Victoria and Abby were back on their feet. They closed in on us. The Ophi I had been controlling stood there motionless, waiting for orders.

Victoria burst out laughing, obviously amused at my pathetic outburst. "You're as stubborn as your father was. He disapproved of our ways, too, you know. He thought he was so much better than the rest of us."

"I bet you tried to trick him like you did to me," I said. "Pretended that he was special when really you were jealous of his power. Is that why you fed him human blood? To even the playing field?"

This time Troy joined her in laughter.

"Very good, Jodi," Victoria said. "Yes, it was my idea to give him human blood. You see, Troy and I were twenty-five when your father came here. I had just given birth." She turned to Alex. "If only I had known what a disappointment you'd turn out to be." She shook her head and waved the thought away. "No matter. I wasn't going to be led by a stupid boy who had been reckless enough to get a human pregnant. It was disgusting. A disgrace to the Ophi race, even if he did father the Chosen One. He needed to be taken care of."

"So, you killed him." Without commanding it to, my blood started boiling.

"Actually, I killed him," Troy said.

I should've known. Always the quiet one. Victoria talked a big game, but Troy was the muscle behind their relationship.

"You don't seem all that upset about this news," Victoria said.

"It's old news. Well, most of it anyway." I glared at Troy. "I broke into your files in the library. I found out my dad's name and the date of his death."

"Well, well, you have been naughty, Jodi Marshall. Like I said, you're so much like your father."

"What did you do with him? After you killed him, what did you do with his body?" I was afraid she was going to tell me they made him into a zombie. I couldn't handle that.

"Let me show you." She smiled and walked to the other side of the graveyard. We all followed. She stopped at an unmarked grave. One I'd seen before. I'd walked by it every day when Alex and I trained here. Victoria raised her hand over the grave and sliced her finger with her own nail. I screamed, but it was useless. Nothing I did was going to stop her. She flicked a drop of blood onto the dirt and stood back.

I was relieved I couldn't feel a soul I, myself, hadn't summoned. Feeling the torture in my dad's soul would've done me in. I'd be lying in a grave alongside him in no time. Still, my eyes burned with hot tears, and I felt bile at the back of my throat as I saw fingers break the surface of the dirt. I went to reach for him, but Abby grabbed me from behind, holding me back.

"No, no, Jodi. We don't help zombies around here," Abby whispered in my ear.

I stared in horror as he pulled himself out of the ground. He was no older than I was. His face looked discolored, purple in some spots.

Victoria tsked. "Ah, what a shame. It looks like the human blood in him was at odds with the Gorgon blood, even in death."

Oh, God! Those were pockets of human blood pooled under his skin.

"Jodi, meet your father, Derek Colgan." Victoria turned to my dad. "Go give your loving daughter a hug, Derek."

Abby held me still while my dad walked toward me with his arms out. "Dad." I knew I could've fought Victoria's hold on him, made him obey me instead, but I didn't want to do that to him. His arms wrapped around me, and Abby released me before she came in contact with my zombie father.

"Make sure you give a nice tight squeeze," Victoria said.

His arms tightened around me until I could barely breathe.

"Jodi, stop him," Alex said. "Use your power. You're stronger than Victoria."

"Shut up!" Victoria snapped. "You want to see real power, my dear son? Watch this." She took the locket in both hands, wrapping her fingers around the bloodstone. Closing her eyes she murmured, "Reach every dead body in this cemetery, find every soul, and bring them to me." Her body shook, making her let go of the locket. Her eyes rolled back into her head, but she managed to stay standing. It was like watching a demon possession. Something was taking over her body.

"Please, let go," I said to my father, hoping a request would work as well as a command. He released me but didn't back away.

The ground began to shake, and some of the living dead Ophi stumbled, not having complete control over their bodies. Headstones fell over left and right. Alex reached for me. "We have to get that locket," he whispered. "Even you won't be able to control a cemetery full of living dead without some help."

I nodded. He was right. I couldn't do it alone. "On three?" I asked.

"One, two, three!" We dove for Victoria, easily knocking her to the ground. Everyone else scrambled to stay on their feet. I yanked the locket from her neck, snapping the chain. "Run!" Alex pulled me up. We ran through hands and heads popping up left and right. The zombies moaned in pain as they dug their way out of the earth. Several clawed at our legs in the process, but it was their tortured cries that hurt me the most. I looked back to see if they were chasing us. Victoria was still on the ground. Troy had her head in his hands and yelled for the others to stop us.

"I have to get somewhere I can drink this," I said to Alex.

"Head for the trees. Maybe we can lose them in there."

We cut to the right toward the trees. One of the corpses was out of the ground and blocking our path. I couldn't concentrate enough to control him. Not while I was busy running for my life. Alex barreled into the guy. The force knocked the zombie over, and his head split open on the headstone. "Keep going!" Alex yelled to me.

The bodies were out of the ground now, and swarming us from every side. Apparently Victoria had commanded the bloodstone to carry a message to the corpses—a message to kill Alex and me. They clawed at our clothing and threw their bodies into us. Individually, it was doing more damage to them than us, but there were so many that it was slowing us down. The group behind us had almost caught up.

When we reached the trees, Alex grabbed a branch from the ground and started swinging at the zombies. "Drink the blood! Hurry! I don't know how long I can hold them off."

I opened my fist and stared at the locket. Medusa had told me the locket opened. When I needed to use the blood inside the stone, I would know what to do. But I didn't. I thought about the way my power worked. It was all about concentration, commanding blood to do what I wanted. I held the locket and told it to reveal its power to me. As if by instinct, I turned the bloodstone in my fingers. It clicked and released from the rest of the locket. Inside, the blood bubbled at my touch, and the top of the stone disintegrated like magic. The blood was so concentrated that I was worried what it would do to me. Would I look like my dad with purple blotches under my skin? Would the Gorgon blood fight with the human blood in my veins? I couldn't fight the Ophi if my own blood was fighting itself.

"Jodi!" Alex was on the ground. The zombies had the upper hand, and the group was at the edge of the woods. There was no time to worry. Alex and I would be dead if I didn't try this. I threw back my head and tipped the contents of the stone into my mouth.

I choked and fell to my knees. My insides twisted, making me double over in pain. My fingers clawed at the dirt as I cried out in agony. I heard Alex call my name. I lifted my head and saw the zombies had him pinned to the ground. They were waiting for the kill command, only Troy and Victoria were too busy watching my suffering to give it. At least I could be thankful for that.

Another wave of pain came over me, even more intense than the first. I screamed and scratched at my skin. It was bubbling. Not just my blood, but my skin. I felt like I was on fire, burning from the inside out. Scalding, hot blood dripped from my ears, nose, and mouth. Red, blood-soaked tears poured from my eyes. The metallic scent and taste of the blood filled my senses.

Then, everything went black.

Chapter 30

Medusa's face appeared in my mind. She wiped the blood from my eyes. "My blood is truly in your veins now, my child. The transformation is complete. But I must warn you, Hades has his eye on you. He senses your power, especially now. He will come for you. If you look inside yourself, you will find there is a way to make amends with him." She kissed my forehead. "Open your eyes, and face your enemies head on."

My eyelids fluttered open. I was facing away from the group, but their cheers and celebrations at my death rang in my ears. I hesitated for a moment, gathering my strength. Medusa had said Hades would come after me. I was his next target. She also said there was a way to get him off my back. I had to figure out what that meant. Fast.

Abby's foot was in front of my face, so I lay motionless, letting her believe I was dead. "Who's the powerful one now?"

Faster than I'd thought it possible to move, I reached out and grabbed both her legs, knocking her backward. I sprang to my feet. "I am."

She scrambled away from me. "No. You were dead! We all saw you die from drinking Medusa's blood."

"Jodi, do you have the power to bring yourself back to life?" Alex had tears in his eyes as he finally got free from the zombies.

"I was never dead. I went through a transformation." Somehow, it all made sense now. "The Gorgon blood had to overtake the human blood in me."

"So, you're not human at all anymore?" Alex asked.

That hit me harder than I'd thought it would. If there was no human blood left in me, what connection did I have left with Mom? "I'm fully Gorgon now."

Victoria started to laugh. "You killed the human in you, and yet there is no soul for Hades to claim. I think we know who he'll come for next."

That was what Medusa had meant. I had angered Hades by taking my own human life without sending him my soul. I had to find a way to even things out with him before he came to claim my soul.

"I almost want to wait and see how Hades will kill you," Victoria said, "but I've kind of had my heart set on doing it myself." She held her arms out to her sides. "Zombies, kill her." She brought both hands forward, pointing at me.

The zombies started toward me, and my blood responded. It mixed, letting me know I was in control. "Stop!" They froze in their places.

"No!" Victoria screamed. "I summoned you. I am your master. Do as I say and kill her!"

The zombies wavered slightly. "Ignore her commands. Feel my power, and obey only me." I hated the way they bent to my will, but I knew I was the one who could set them free. And I would, as soon as they helped me with Hades.

Victoria cried out in frustration, but I ignored her.

"Seize them. All but Alex. Do not harm them. I only want them trapped."

Alex shook his head. "Jodi, you can't let them go. They're monsters, like you said. We have to kill them." I could see the words pained him, and I couldn't let him have a part in his parents' deaths. Sure, Troy had killed Alex, and both Troy and Victoria were evil. But Alex wasn't. I didn't know what killing his own parents would do to him. Evil apparently ran in his genes. I wasn't taking any chances by tapping into it.

"No, I can't kill them, Alex. I'm not a murderer, and I won't let you be one either. There's another way."

The Ophi huddled together, trying not to allow the zombies to touch them. "I will kill you for this, Jodi Marshall. I promise you that," Victoria yelled.

"Don't make promises you can't keep, Victoria." I walked over to her, staring through the two zombies blocking her from me. "Your problem is that you're always jealous of everyone else. Afraid someone might have more power. Might find out you are no better than any other Ophi. In fact, you're probably the weakest. You couldn't even see what a great son you have. You treat him like he means nothing to you. Like you're disappointed in his abilities. But he didn't need to steal my locket to become powerful. I've seen him raise the dead, and I'm not talking about making zombies. He brought my mom back to life before Hades could claim her soul. I bet you've never saved a person's life."

"Why would I? Humans are vile, worthless creatures. They're beneath us. I brought Ophi back to life."

I nodded. "Yes, you did. Should we ask Leticia how well you performed that task? One out of twelve isn't the best ratio, and just looking at the one you claim you brought back successfully, you can see he's not a hundred percent right." I looked back at Alex. He was definitely still himself. "I'm one for one. Well, two for two, if you count Abby."

The sky turned dark, and wind blew all around us. Alex rushed to my side. "What's happening?" I asked him.

"It's Hades. He's coming."

I'd been so busy going back and forth with Victoria that I'd forgotten about Hades. I had to do something. "Dad?" I called out, searching the zombies. "I need you. Please, come here."

He stepped out from behind the group and walked over to me. "I need you to do me a favor. I need you to go to Hades. Tell him I have an offer for him." He stared back at me, completely expressionless. All my life, I thought about meeting my dad. What he'd look like. What he'd say to me. This wasn't at all how it was supposed to be. Finding out he was dead was one thing. Seeing him like this, it was torture. "I know you came to see me in the hospital." I hoped his soul would understand, even if it couldn't respond to me on its own. "I know you left Mom and me because you were trying to protect us. I'm not mad at you. I love you, Dad." I wrapped my arms around him and cried on his shoulder. "I release your soul. Go to Hades, and ask him to come here."

His body went limp in my arms, and I crumbled under the weight of it. Alex bent down and hugged me from behind. I sobbed until the earth started shaking. The ground cracked and opened a few feet from me. Screams filled the air, as the Ophi scrambled to avoid falling into the earth. The zombies stumbled after them, trying to keep them surrounded as per my orders. Black smoke rose from the crack and settled before me, taking shape.

Hades was younger than I thought he'd be—or at least he looked younger. I figured the gods could appear in any form they wanted to.

"It was very foolish for you to send your father with such a message, Jodi Marshall. I'm sure you heard I was already looking for you, and you went ahead and made it all too easy for me to find you." His voice was low and, dare I say, kind of sexy?

"I-I have an offer for you," I stammered. It was cliché as all hell, but this guy was seriously hot. I wondered if he had chosen this form on purpose to lure me to the underworld with him. I mean, if I didn't know he was Hades—and if I wasn't already crushing on Alex—I'd have followed this guy just about anywhere.

"I do not work in offers. I get what I want and that's all."

"Hear me out," I said. "These are the Ophi who have been stealing your dead. I know you've been looking for them, too. I'm proposing that you take them to the underworld with you. Have them help you control the dead. Who better to control all those souls than necromancers?"

He raised an eyebrow, amused by my comment. "All I ask is that you leave the rest of the Ophi alone. The ones who don't use their powers for evil. The ones who release the souls they summon." I motioned to the zombies Victoria had created. "I can release all their souls back to you, and I can teach other Ophi how to do the same. Let Alex and me stay here and use this place as a real school. One that will teach Ophi how to use their powers the way they were meant to be used."

"You can't give us over to him," Leticia shrieked.

"She's right," Victoria said. "You'd be betraying Ophi everywhere. Hades has been picking us off one by one. He's the reason we had to create so many zombies. We needed protection from him. It was the only way to save ourselves—our race."

Hades glared at Victoria. "You know I only seek vengeance on those who wrong me. I'm not evil. I claim souls that are mine to claim. When you raise a soul and steal it from my underworld, you are obligated to replace it. If I choose to replace it with your soul, that is my right as a god."

I could see his point. "I promise I'll give you back all the souls that have been taken from you here. We won't have servants anymore either. We'll operate under your rules. If we take a soul from the underworld, we will return it or replace it."

Hades nodded. "Very well. I can agree to your terms, Jodi Marshall." He leaned closer to me. "I was quite fond of Medusa, and I can see much of her in you. She got a bad name over the years. People seemed to like to make up horror stories about her."

I smiled. There was a time when I had believed those stories. Now, I knew the real Medusa, and I was proud to be her family.

"Very well. I shall take these Ophi back to the underworld with me."

"Wait," I said. "Will it kill them? I mean, going to the underworld? Will they have to die in order to go there?"

"Jodi, I'm the king of the underworld. I get to make my own rules."

"Keep them alive," Alex said. He quickly added, "Please. It will torture them more to be alive and sentenced to eternity in the underworld."

It seemed fitting. They'd been so content to order the zombies around, and while they'd still be doing that in a way—ordering the dead around—they'd be taking orders from Hades. There was a certain amount of justice in it.

"Jodi," Leticia said, tears streaking her face. "Please, don't make me go. I've never summoned a soul. I only came here a few days before you did. I'm not like them. Please, believe me. I want to learn from you. Be the kind of Ophi you are."

"I'd like to, too," Randy said.

I looked at Alex. "What do you think? Can we trust them?"

He sighed. "They were only doing what Victoria and Troy told them to do. Most of them were. Even Tony and, dare I say, Abby."

"No way," Abby said. "I don't do anything because I'm told to."

Wow, she'd rather spend eternity in the underworld than be around me.

Hades raised an eyebrow. "You're not thinking of going back on our deal, are you, Jodi Marshall?"

I took a step toward him. "Just Leticia, Randy, and Mr. Quim—I mean Tony. That's all. They really didn't do anything wrong." I wanted to say the other kids hadn't done anything wrong either, but they were mini versions of Victoria and Troy.

Hades growled, and I stepped back, thinking I'd ruined everything. "I'm taking my souls now, before you try to weasel any more away from me."

"Thank you," I said.

"But I will be watching you, Jodi Marshall. If you do not keep up your end of the deal, I will come for you. I don't believe in second chances."

"I understand."

With a wave of his hand a swirl of black smoke rose from the crack in the earth. It twirled in a mini tornado and scooped up the Ophi. All but Tony, Leticia, and Randy. The tornado disappeared into the crack. Screams echoed through the air. Hades gave me one last look, a look so terrifying I shivered. He would be watching me. Closely.

He disappeared in a mist of smoke down into the earth. The ground shook as the crack closed. I turned to the living dead still standing, waiting for directions. "Return to where you were before Victoria summoned you. I release your souls."

Each body slumped to the ground, and this time, I could not only feel their souls releasing, I could see them as wisps of silver light floating through the air. I watched them go, realizing I was the only one who saw them.

I sat on the cold ground, picking up Medusa's locket and putting it in my pocket. Alex joined me. "Don't feel bad. You did the right thing."

"I sentenced them to eternity in the underworld. They were your family, Alex."

He sighed. "I lost my family a long time ago, when my parents decided that power was more important than anything else."

"And my dad. Seeing him was—"

"I'm so sorry Victoria did that to you. She never should've brought him back. That was the lowest thing she's ever done."

"I want to get his name put on his grave. It shouldn't be unmarked."

"I can do that."

"And I'm going to have to call my mom. Tell her that I'm okay and that I can't come home. I'm not human at all anymore. Seeing her is too dangerous."

Alex didn't say anything. He knew there was nothing to say. We'd both lost our parents today, in some way or another. I could at least call my mom, hear her voice, but I'd never be able to tell her the truth. At least not all of the truth. I'd tell her I found Dad, that he was gone now. I'd tell her I was going to school and that I was going to teach and help others. That would be about all the truth she'd be able to handle. I had no idea what reason I'd give for not being able to see her ever again, but I'd deal with that another day.

Leticia, Randy, and Tony were keeping to themselves, almost like they were afraid of me. I smiled at them, trying to ease the tension. Leticia smiled back. "Thank you for saving us, Jodi. I'll never forget that."

"None of us will," Randy said.

"You were worth saving." I meant it. Leticia and Randy were innocent. They'd been in my classes and were only just starting to learn about their abilities. Neither one had raised the dead yet, and that meant I could teach them to do it the right way.

"I always knew you were a smart girl," Tony said. "Even if I wasn't really a teacher."

"Sure you were, and you still are." Tony knew all about Ophi history. We needed him. "You have a lot of knowledge to pass on to us. That spells teacher to me."

"What happens now?" Leticia asked.

I stood up and brushed off my pants. "We start our own school. We'll call the Ophi at the Serpentarius nightclub. Tell them about Hades and the others. Maybe we can convince them to join us."

"I'll call them," Tony said. "I know the guy that runs the place."

I smiled and nodded. "Thank you."

Everyone started for the mansion, but Alex grabbed my arm when we came to the mausoleum. "I don't know why, but I always liked this mausoleum."

I thought about our first kiss. "You know, I can see why." I reached up on my toes, wrapping my arms around his neck, and kissed him like I'd never kissed anyone before, Ophi or human. My blood bubbled inside my veins, rushing to every part of my body. I could get used to being a full-blown Ophi. Just like I could get used to being in Alex's arms.

I wasn't sure how any of this would work out, the school or Alex. All I knew was I had to figure things out fast. By making a deal with Hades, I'd made myself responsible for all Ophi. I was in charge now. And that meant I was the one who would have to answer to Hades.

Dying sucks—and high school senior Ember McWilliams knows first-hand. After a fatal car accident, her gifted little sister brought her back. Now anything Ember touches dies. And that, well, really blows.

Ember operates on a no-touch policy with all living things—including boys. When Hayden Cromwell shows up, quoting Oscar Wilde and claiming her curse is a gift, she thinks he's a crazed cutie. But when he tells her he can help control it, she's more than interested. There's just one catch: Ember has to trust Hayden's adopted father, a man she's sure has sinister reasons for collecting children whose abilities even weird her out. However, she's willing to do anything to hold her sister's hand again. And hell, she'd also like to be able to kiss Hayden. Who wouldn't?

But when Ember learns the accident that turned her into a freak may not've been an accident at all, she's not sure who to trust. Someone wanted her dead, and the closer she gets to the truth, the closer she is to losing not only her heart, but her life.

For real this time.

Cursed

Jennifer L. Armentrout

Author of Half-Blood

978-0-9831572-7-4

PODs

A Novel

The end
of the world
is only the
beginning.

Michelle Pickett

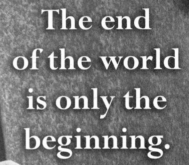

ACKNOWLEDGEMENTS

There are so many people I want to thank that it's hard to know where to begin. Since this book was largely inspired by my amazing agent, Lauren Hammond, I'll start there. Lauren, I can't thank you enough for the way you motivate me and push me to be a better writer. This story flowed out of me, and I have you to thank for that. Your excitement was the best motivation I could've asked for, and your mythology expertise was much appreciated as we got this ready to go out on submission. Thank you a million times over.

Next I have to thank Kate Kaynak and the incredible team at Spencer Hill Press for taking a chance on this book and me. You've made my dream a reality, and that's something I'll never forget. Kate, your cover design blew me away, as did all the other things you've done to promote this book. You do so much for your authors, and I'm truly grateful to work with you. To my editor, Trisha Wooldridge, thank you for finding ways to make Jodi's story really shine. Your edits and comments along the way were nothing short of phenomenal. I'm so glad you'll be with me to see this series through. Rich Storrs, Keshia Swaim, and Shira Lipkin, my copy editors, thank you for making sure this book was ready for the world. Kendra Saunders, you are a marketing genius, and I know I'm in more than capable hands with you. Thank you. The editors would love to thank Dr. Rachel Vuolo and Caroline Godin for their input on the medical scenes

I also have to thank my daughter, Ayla, who at such a young age understands why I have to stop playing and run to my computer to jot down ideas. Ayla, you are my inspiration. Thank you for celebrating with me along the way, even if you don't fully understand everything I get so excited over.

To my husband, Ryan, thank you for putting up with all the times I had to ignore you to write, revise, or talk to my agent. You've been so supportive of my writing career, and I can't thank you enough for that.

I can't forget my mom, Patricia Bradley. You've read everything I've written and given me honest feedback. You push me and aren't afraid to tell me when I can do better. Your critiques are priceless, as is your support. To my dad, Martin Bradley, thank you for all your support. You do so much to encourage me and promote me, and it means so much. Heather DeRobertis, my incredibly talented sister, who loves all things creepy, you rubbed off on me after all. Thank you for introducing me to the world of horror and paranormal. I feel at home here.

Of course, thank you to my friends and family. You're always there for me. Nicole, thank you for all the talks and for listening to me cry when I wasn't sure if I could make it in this industry. You've always supported me and told me I could get here. All the authors at Spencer Hill Press, you've welcomed me into this family, and I'm honored to me among such talented writers. To my agency sisters and writer friends, there are too many to name but you know who you are, thank you for being there for me and helping me promote this book. And finally, a huge thank you to the book bloggers who have spread the word about *Touch of Death* since the initial cover reveal. You guys are amazing and are the heart of this industry.

Kelly Hashway is a former language arts teacher who now works as a full-time writer, freelance editor, and mother to an adorable little girl. In addition to writing YA novels, Kelly writes middle grade books, picture books, and short stories. When she's not writing or digging her way out from under her enormous To Be Read pile, she's running and playing with her daughter. She resides in Pennsylvania with her husband, daughter, and two pets.

www.kellyhashway.com